Death by Association
A DIY Diva Mystery

by

Paula Darnell

For information, email Cozy Cat Press, cozycatpress@aol.com or visit our website at: www.cozycatpress.com

Cover font thanks to
https://www.facebook.com/workinsstudiodesign

COZY CAT
P R E S S

ISBN: 978-1-946063-68-7
Printed in the United States of America

10 9 8 7 6 5 4 3 2 1

To my daughters Andrea and Sara and my husband
Gary with love and appreciation for their support

Chapter 1

"Bear, no!" I warned, as my chocolate Labrador retriever lunged toward a rabbit that had suddenly popped out from under a leafy bush and landed on the sidewalk just a few feet ahead of us. "Stay here, boy."

Bear wanted to chase the bunny, but I grabbed his collar, holding him back until the little rabbit hopped away, across the street and onto the manicured, green fairway of Hawkeye Haven's golf course, which meandered through our walled, guard-gated community.

Although Bear would have liked nothing better than to follow the bunny and have a chance to explore the verdant expanse of the golf course, if I were seen walking my dog there, I'd be slapped with a huge fine by Hawkeye Haven's aggressive homeowners' association.

The golf course was reserved strictly for players, so neither residents nor their dogs were allowed to walk there. (HOA Regulation 101 states that "only golf course employees and golfers cleared through the golf course pro shop or starter station are allowed on the course, and all others are in violation and will be subject to fines and penalties or arrest for trespassing.") Although we were banned from walking on the golf course, and we always walked on the sidewalk, rather than on the neighborhood front lawns, at least Bear could enjoy the grass in our backyard, where he loved to romp and play fetch.

Bear stared longingly at the rabbit as it stopped and, teasing, looked back at him before bouncing away across the golf course.

"Come on, Bear," I urged, releasing his collar while keeping a tight grip on his leash, and we resumed our walk. When the rabbit's appearance had startled us, I'd been thinking about the do-it-yourself jewelry class that I'd be teaching later in the morning.

The rabbit forgotten, Bear trotted happily along while I mentally reviewed the project that I would present to my DIY Crystal Necklace class later at the community center. Although the project was a relatively simple one, the crystal necklaces that the students—all residents of Hawkeye Haven—would be making qualified as true dazzlers with plenty of sparkle. Each student would be stringing three strands of faceted Swarovski crystal beads to make a necklace in the color of her choice, each necklace featuring a large crystal pendant in the center. When I previewed the project, there had been plenty of oohs and aahs, and I'd been sure that the women in the class would be well pleased with their showy necklaces.

I had accidentally stumbled into my job by turning the DIY craft, fashion, and home dec projects that I loved to design into cash, first with a blog, which had attracted a book editor's attention, and then with a series of books, each with a different DIY theme. I supplemented my writing income with design jobs for crafts' manufacturers, and now that I was teaching DIY classes at Hawkeye Haven, I had the perfect way to test my projects and instructions by presenting them to my students, who just happened to fit the profile of my books' readers.

Bear's ears perked up as a dog, sensing Bear's presence in his home territory, began to bark frantically in a neighbor's backyard as we passed by on the front sidewalk. Bear acknowledged the other pet with a short courtesy "woof" and continued on his way, unperturbed.

Much as I hated to rouse the neighborhood with our early morning walks, dawn remained the best time of the day for a big furry dog like Bear to take a walk in the summer. Even though the humid heat of late August would soon fade into more tolerable autumn weather, we were experiencing record-breaking high temperatures, and the hot spell was forecast to last several more days.

Sometimes I couldn't quite believe that I had chosen to live in the central Iowa town of Center City and in a guard-gated community to boot. The summer sunshine would burn my pale skin to a lobster red if I weren't so diligent about constantly applying sunscreen before I ventured outdoors, and I never had become accustomed to the high humidity that usually accompanied the summer heat. Iowa winters, with lots of snow and frigid weather, were even worse than the summers. I had traded the mild climate of Seattle for the more extreme weather of Iowa.

My cousin Tracey, my best friend from the time we were toddlers, had moved to Hawkeye Haven on the outskirts of Center City a few years before I had because a new job opportunity had come her way. After my husband was killed in an auto accident, everything about Seattle reminded me of him and our life together. Tracey convinced me that a change of scenery would do me good. Since I could work anywhere, I had decided that she was right, so three years ago I had moved, too. Still, at times, I missed the misty rains and moderate weather of Seattle, where I had lived the first thirty-five years of my life.

By now, we'd come about a mile from home. Normally, Bear and I would have encountered at least a couple other pet parents walking their dogs, but it was unusually quiet, especially for a garbage-collection day, when a lot of residents set out their trash early in the morning. (HOA Regulation 34 states that "trash containers shall not be put out for collection more than twelve hours before scheduled collection time and shall be removed out of sight no more than twelve hours after collection time.")

As we turned right at the next intersection, Bear began pulling on his leash, and I knew the reason. On weekdays, our route took us to the back gate of Hawkeye Haven, where Bessie, the daytime security guard, worked during the week, and Bessie always had a homemade treat, shaped like a dog bone, waiting for Bear when we stopped by the guard's station, which stood on a wide median between the lanes leading in and out of Hawkeye Haven. On weekends, when Bessie didn't work, I took a different route so that Bear wouldn't anticipate receiving a treat during his walk, although I always had a snack waiting for him at home so that he wouldn't be disappointed.

As we approached the guardhouse, I saw that the side door was open, inviting us to join Bessie inside, where a large desk and control panel took up most of the front of the small room. Usually Bessie was outside or at the desk when we arrived each morning, and although I didn't see her there today, Bear and I both spotted his treat waiting for him on a paper towel at the edge of the desk. Without further ado, Bear took the snack gently, almost delicately, in his soft Lab's mouth and then chomped it with relish.

"Bear," I scolded, "you're supposed to wait for Bessie to give you your treat."

I looked toward the back of the guard house, down a short, narrow hallway that led to two smaller rooms—a restroom and a tiny kitchen that contained only a microwave, a dorm-sized refrigerator, and a coffee maker.

That's when I saw her.

Bessie, her face ashen, her curly gray hair askew, and a trickle of blood oozing from beneath her head, lay motionless on her back. I gasped and called her name, but there was no response, and I realized that Bessie, who was in her mid-seventies, must have had a heart attack or a stroke and fallen, hitting her head on the concrete floor. Was she alive?

"Bessie, Bessie!" I exclaimed. Beside me, Bear whined nervously, sensing that something was wrong.

I knelt beside Bessie, and I felt relief when I could see that she was breathing, but she lay as still and silent as before. I jumped up and punched in 9-1-1 on the desk console phone. In the few seconds it took for the emergency operator to answer, I noticed that Bessie's gun wasn't in her holster, and I didn't see it anywhere else either. Come to think of it, I'd never seen it any place other than in her holster. I pulled open the bottom desk drawer, where I knew that she stored her purse while she was working, and although her handbag was there, its contents were strewn about the drawer. I didn't see her wallet among them. I groaned. Bessie hadn't suffered a heart attack or a stroke. She'd been attacked!

"9-1-1; what is your emergency?"

My voice sounded hoarse as I hurriedly explained the reason for my call.

"Help is on the way. Is she conscious?"

"No."

"Is she breathing?"

"Yes, she's breathing, but it seems kind of shallow."

"Do you see any signs of injury at all?"

"Yes, she . . . ." Already, I could hear sirens screaming, and within seconds, a Center City Fire

Department rescue truck turned into the short stretch of street leading to the gate.

"They're here," I told the operator. With the local CCFD station less than half a mile from the back gate of Hawkeye Haven, I wasn't surprised by the speed of the firefighters' arrival.

"All right. Please wait there so that you can give a statement to the police when they arrive."

"I will." I hung up the phone and went outside to signal the firefighters, who quickly stepped into the small guardhouse to examine Bessie. Whimpering softly, Bear lay beside her.

"Come on, Bear, let's go outside and give them some room." I tugged his leash, and he jumped up. With Bear in tow, I backed out the side door and into Luke Johnson, the head of security at Hawkeye Haven, whom I often saw at the community center on the days I taught my DIY classes there. Luke was a tall man who had short, sandy hair, a freckled complexion, and the best posture I'd ever seen. Although I didn't know him well, he'd always seemed like a pleasant man who was interested in doing his job efficiently. I'd heard that he'd been in the military before he'd taken the job at Hawkeye Haven.

"Oh, Luke, I'm sorry."

"Laurel McMillan, right?"

I nodded. "That's right."

"Well, Laurel, can you fill me in on what happened here?"

"Oh, sure—uh, oh," I hesitated as a car approached the entrance and stopped behind the rescue unit. I recognized the driver as Alice Sandstrom, a ninety-year-old resident who sometimes took one of my DIY classes. I shuddered to realize that she still drove a car because I knew that her vision wasn't very good.

"Just a second—I need to get those residents to detour around to the main gate," Luke said as another car pulled up behind Mrs. Sandstrom. Luke sprinted over to divert both drivers.

Alice seemed confused, but, in a moment, I saw the passenger of the second car, a young woman wearing bright fuchsia yoga pants and a rhinestone-studded, white tank top, step out of the car she was riding in and go to Alice's car. I heard the yoga lady volunteer to drive Alice around to the main gate and then home. Nodding in agreement, Alice slid across the bench seat to the passenger side of her ancient black Cadillac. She definitely looked relieved.

In the meantime, one of the firefighters had rolled a gurney into the small room, where there was barely enough space to place it next to Bessie, but somehow he managed. Bessie was hoisted onto the gurney and wheeled to the rescue truck, just as two Center City police vehicles arrived, each manned with one officer. After a brief conversation with the policemen and Luke, the firefighters loaded Bessie into their unit and quickly departed, sirens screaming.

Suddenly I began shaking. Although I hadn't realized it earlier, the incident had unnerved me, and my legs began to feel wobbly. Just as I started to sway, Luke grabbed my shoulders and eased me to the ground. Bear sat beside me, licking my face as I lay on the sidewalk, and I could hear Luke urging me to lie still. My head was swimming, and I knew that Luke had caught me right as I had begun to faint.

"Sorry," I mumbled as I started to get up.

"Take it easy, Laurel. Don't try to get up just yet. I'll bring you some water." In a minute, Luke returned with a cold bottle of water, which he must have taken from the tiny refrigerator in the guardhouse's mini-kitchen.

Taking the bottle, I sat up. Gratefully, I took a few sips of water.

What a wimp I was! I felt extremely foolish, especially because I wasn't the person who'd been attacked. Fortunately, the back gate of Hawkeye Haven wasn't a high-traffic area, and nobody else was around to witness my humiliating fainting spell except for the two cops, who looked slightly impatient, and Luke, who seemed genuinely concerned.

"Thanks, I'm okay now."

After I reported everything I could remember about what I had witnessed to the Center City officers and Luke, I just wanted to go home. His morning routine interrupted, Bear had been panting and pacing around nervously as I talked to the police. When he began whining, I knew it was time to leave.

"Well, if there's nothing more, I should head for home."

"Thanks, Ms. McMillan," one of the policemen said. "A detective may be contacting you."

I nodded. Luke, who had been manning the gate in Bessie's absence, awaited the arrival of the substitute guard he had called to take over the day shift. "Laurel, if you can wait a few minutes until Toby takes over, I can give you and your dog a ride home," he offered.

"No, thanks, the walk will do us good. I'll check with you later to find out how Bessie's doing. Let's go, Bear."

Eager to resume his walk, Bear needed no further encouragement, and we trotted home at a record pace. I fervently hoped that Bessie would recover. She'd looked frail and helpless lying on the hard cement floor, and she hadn't regained consciousness while the firefighters were attending to her. Even though she was a woman in her mid-seventies, her gruff manner probably made her appear tougher than she was.

Although some of the residents thought it odd that an old lady packing a sidearm guarded the back gate at Hawkeye Haven, and some of them weren't shy about expressing the opinion that it was not the right job for the "old gal," I'd always thought of Bessie as a woman who could take care of herself, but she'd been no match for whoever had attacked her and stolen her gun.

At ten o'clock, my DIY Crystal Necklace class would be meeting in the classroom at the community center, and I planned to arrive early so that I could try to find out what I could about Bessie's condition. I had overheard the firefighters saying that she would be transported to Center City Regional Hospital, but I doubted that anybody at the hospital would be willing to disclose her condition to someone who wasn't a relative.

Fortunately, I had assembled my class supplies already and packed them in my DIY-collaged roller suitcase—a bag I had decorated with copies of old travel photos in sepia tones—for easy transport. I was still so shaken by the attack on Bessie that my stomach was doing flip-flops. Hoping to calm myself before class started, I sipped some weak tea, rather than my usual coffee, and nibbled some dry toast. Bear's baritone "woof" reminded me that it was time for his breakfast, too. With his tummy full, Bear would be ready for his morning nap by the time I left for class.

Although I normally dressed casually when I taught my DIY classes at the community center, especially because some of the projects could be rather messy, for this class I decided to wear a jade-colored silk jersey dress with a deep scoop neckline so that I could show off my crystal necklace. Seeing me wearing my own DIY necklace might encourage the students to complete their necklaces in the two-hour class time. I'd made my necklace with aurora borealis clear crystals. Not only did the flashy beads look really spectacular, but my necklace also complemented the scooped neckline of my green dress. Green has always been one of my favorite colors because it looks good with my shoulder-length auburn hair.

I stepped into a pair of high-heeled, strappy ivory sandals and decided that, although they weren't the most comfortable shoes I owned, I should be able to wear them for a few hours without crippling myself. Even though I could have walked the few blocks to the community center, I certainly wasn't going to do it in high heels, and, besides, I needed to take my suitcase full of class supplies with me, so I loaded it into my old silver Honda SUV, told Bear to be a good boy, and left him to his morning nap.

As I drove to the community center at the excruciatingly slow speed of fifteen miles per hour (HOA Regulation 81 states that "speeding, careless, or reckless driving are health and safety violations and will result in the maximum fines and penalties allowed by law."), I planned to find out whatever I could about Bessie's condition. Anger welled up inside me as I wondered what kind of monster would attack an innocent old lady who was just doing her job. My chest felt tight as I thought about how she had looked when I had found her unconscious, sprawled on the hard concrete floor of the guardhouse. I remembered wondering at first whether she was dead or alive. Although I had been relieved when I could see that she was breathing, I was still worried because she had been unconscious the last time I had seen her. Was Bessie recuperating from her injury now or was she struggling for her life?

Chapter 2

As I drove up the wide boulevard leading to the complex where the community buildings stood, I appreciated the recreational facilities that were available to the residents of Hawkeye Haven. At the end of a circular drive, the Olympic-sized swimming pool's water gleamed in the bright sunlight, with striped yellow and green, canvas-covered cabanas set on each side. As inviting as the pool looked, there were no swimmers or sunbathers in sight yet.

The community center building was located to the left of the pool. This building housed the HOA's administrative offices, meeting rooms, classrooms, gym, racquetball court, and an indoor swimming pool. The golf course, its pro shop, and restaurant were on the pool's right.

Outside the pro shop, a lone golfer was making chip shots on the perfectly maintained practice putting green, the only part of the golf course that could be seen from the road although it stretched in back of the facilities. The landscaping around the community center was dominated by maple trees that lined the circular drive. Purple and yellow pansies decorated a little island in the center of the drive, and neatly sculptured hedges framed the sidewalks leading to Hawkeye Haven's community center and the building that housed the golf course's pro shop and locker rooms as well as a restaurant.

Two workers were carefully trimming the hedges while another landscaper mowed the lawn that lay between the buildings in front of the swimming pool. I saw KM Landscaping trucks in Hawkeye Haven almost every day. No wonder our HOA dues were so expensive. What with all the work that went into maintaining common community property, including literally tons of snow removal in the winter, and guards at the gates, the community budget was sky-high.

After parking my Honda, I headed into the community center, rolling my suitcase full of supplies to the room that had been assigned for the day's class. I stashed my suitcase in a corner of the room and walked down the hallway to the HOA manager's office in hopes of learning about Bessie's condition. Although there probably wasn't any woman in the world whom I disliked more than Patty Morrison, I figured that she would probably know how Bessie was doing. There was nobody at the reception desk, but I could see Patty sitting in her office, so I walked around the counter that separated the administrative offices from the lobby and tapped on the door frame of her office.

"Patty?"

"I'm busy!" she snapped.

I decided to ignore that comment, and said, "I was just wondering if you had heard anything about Bessie's condition."

"That's confidential. Shouldn't you be in class?"

"I can't imagine why it should be confidential, and, by the way, class doesn't start for half an hour yet."

She sniffed. "It's really none of your business."

"Bessie's my friend. I'm concerned about her."

"Don't you think you've already caused enough trouble visiting the guardhouse with that flea-bitten dog of yours? The guards are there to work, not to pass the time of day with the residents."

"I've never interfered with any of the guards, and my dog does *not* have fleas."

She waved dismissively, and since it was obvious that I wasn't going to get any information from her, I turned and stalked out of her office. I was fuming as I walked down the hallway toward my classroom, but I couldn't say that I was surprised by Patty's attitude. She was my least favorite type of person—someone who didn't bother with being polite unless there was something in it for her, in which case she would pretend to be a best friend until she got what she wanted.

I remembered the first time I had ever met her. I had already been hired to teach some DIY classes by the director of the HOA's previous management company. According to Patty, it was a waste of the HOA's money to hire instructors for special-interest classes, even though the sales staff of Hawkeye Haven always pitched them as one of the community's amenities that prospective homeowners could take advantage of at no extra charge. One of the first things Patty tried to do after her management company took over was to fire me. Fortunately, I had signed a three-year contract for my teaching services, and my attorney had assured me that the agreement was ironclad. Evidently, he was right about the contract because Patty dropped her idea of getting rid of me. Instead, having given up on firing me directly, she didn't hesitate to let me know that she considered my services unnecessary, and she never lost an opportunity to make a snide remark whenever she saw me. Usually, I ignored her, but I had to admit that I had let her get under my skin today.

As I twisted the door handle of my classroom, the door sprang open, and I tripped, falling forward into the room, but luckily I managed to stay on my feet. Someone had opened the door from the inside at the same time I was opening it from the hallway. I looked up and saw Luke, who had a sheepish expression on his face, on the other side of the door.

"Laurel, I'm sorry. I didn't hear you coming."

"No harm done. Were you looking for me?"

Luke nodded. "I thought you might be wondering about Bessie."

"Yes, I just tried to find out how she is from Patty, but she wouldn't tell me."

"Hmmm…well," I noticed that Luke seemed to want to say something about Patty, but refrained. "I just got off the phone with Bessie's son, Tom."

"Is she okay?"

"Her vital signs are stable, but she's unconscious. She never did regain consciousness after the attack."

"Oh, no."

"Tom said she's scheduled for some tests this morning, and then maybe they'll know more about her condition."

"Poor Bessie! I still can't believe that someone would attack her like that. It's all so senseless."

Luke nodded. "I agree. It's a terrible thing. I hated to have to be the one to tell her son what happened this morning. He was beside himself."

"The poor guy. Bessie talks about him all the time. He's her only child, and Bessie says that he's always pressing her to move in with him and his family, but she doesn't want to disrupt their lives. Honestly, I don't think he'd keep asking her if he didn't really mean it."

I could hear voices in the hallway then, and I knew that my students were beginning to arrive. I needed to unload my suitcase and set out the class materials and sample necklaces I'd made to show to the class members. Luke held the door open while the first six women trooped in.

"Morning, ladies," he greeted them as they thanked him for holding the door open for them. "I'd better get going, Laurel. I'll let you know if I hear any news."

"Thanks, I appreciate that."

Luckily, I didn't need to re-arrange the tables and chairs in the room, so I hurriedly set out my supplies at the front table. According to the class roster, twenty residents had enrolled in the class, and I recognized all their names except one—Amber Johannson. By ten o'clock, seventeen women had arrived and were sitting in groups of three or four at five round tables that had been set up throughout the room. Although it wasn't unusual to have a few latecomers, I like to start my classes on time, so I began showing my samples of the necklace project in various colors. Before class started, I had received several compliments on the sparkling crystal necklace I wore, and I was happy that the students were enthusiastic about making their own crystal necklaces. Because the components of the necklace were small, and it would have been difficult for the students to see the steps in its construction, I had put together a PowerPoint slide show that I could project on a huge screen that dropped down from a recessed slot in the ceiling when I turned on the classroom computer. Tiny beads, wires, and bead tips now became magnified so that it was easy for the students to see what they would be doing in just a few minutes.

As I flipped the overhead lights off and began the presentation, the door opened and the three missing students came in. I turned the light back on so that they could see to find their way to the tables. It was slightly irritating that students showed up late for my classes, but I was glad that, this time, at least, they had arrived before I'd begun to explain the step-by-step process of the necklace's assembly. In the past, some of my students had shown up half an hour late or more, and then I'd had to repeat all the instructions for them, but I had finally become resigned to the inevitable. There would always be students who showed up late. After all, they were taking my DIY classes for fun, so I couldn't be too hard on them.

Even though I always handed out a copy of each project's instructions to the students after my slide presentation, it helped them to have some direct hands-on instruction, too, so I always circulated around the classroom, sitting with each group in turn, and helped the students with any techniques that seemed difficult for them.

I began my rounds of the groups, and as I approached the table where two of the latecomers sat, I recognized one of them as the young, blonde woman who had helped Alice Sandstrom earlier by driving her car away from the back gate. She was the only woman there who had never attended one of my classes before.

"Hi, I'm Laurel. You must be Amber," I greeted her.

"Yes, Amber Johannson. My husband and I just moved here last month. It's a big change from Phoenix. I don't know if I'll ever get used to the humidity, and I'm not looking forward to the cold winters, either."

"It's tough. I'm from Seattle myself, and I know what you mean. The weather here can be really brutal, but I love the fall season in Iowa. It's so crisp and cool."

"Laurel, could you show me how to tie the knot again?" asked my friend, Amy Scott, a petite, brown-haired woman wearing a bright orange polo shirt and jeans.

"Yes, mine keeps slipping out of the bead tip," said another woman.

"Sure, it's like this." I snipped a piece of beading wire from the spool Amy offered me and demonstrated how to make the knot and close the bead tip over it, making a neat end for a strand of beads and hiding the knot completely at the same time.

"Oh, I see," Amy said, successfully forming her own knot, "like so."

"Yes, that's it, exactly."

There were approving murmurs all around as the other students managed to tie their knots and began stringing crystal beads on their wires.

"Amber," I said, "it was nice of you to help Mrs. Sandstrom this morning. I noticed that she looked confused when Luke asked her to move her car."

"I was happy to help. She's my next-door neighbor, you know. I'm afraid that she shouldn't be driving anymore. I know that she's been having trouble with her eyes lately."

"Oh, dear. I admit I was surprised to see her driving. I wonder where she was going so early in the morning."

"She goes to the supermarket at Four Corners Mall because she can take the side road from the back gate. There's hardly any traffic on that street, especially early in the morning. I know because my husband and I like to go early to the gym at Four Corners."

"Oh, I never go to that mall," Amy chimed in. "It's so out of the way. I always use the main gate, but I heard that there was quite a commotion at the back gate this morning. Do you know what happened?"

Frankly, I was surprised that the community grapevine didn't seem to be working at its usual pace today. Normally, gossip seemed to travel at the speed of light in Hawkeye Haven. Briefly, I explained that a security guard had been attacked at the back gate. Although I mentioned Bessie's name, nobody seemed to know who she was, which didn't surprise me because she was always stationed at the back gate, and few residents ever used it. As I spoke, the low conversations that had been taking place at each table in the classroom ceased. Everybody in the room had fallen silent and was listening to me. When I finished, the conversational buzz resumed, this time with the new and startling topic of an attack on a community security guard.

As I moved from table to table around the room, helping the students with their projects, it became evident that complacency had been replaced by concern, and, in a few cases, even alarm. The high walls surrounding Hawkeye Haven, the security cameras, gates, patrols, and armed guards had all combined to make the residents feel that they were safe from violent crime. Now they knew better. If an armed guard could be attacked, so could an unarmed resident. Hawkeye Haven had suddenly become a more dangerous place to live.

As much as I hated to see my neighbors in fear, I had to admit to myself that I no longer felt quite as safe as I had before this morning. Perhaps the security measures at Hawkeye Haven had lulled us all into believing that our community was invulnerable. I shuddered with the realization that there is no absolute security in the world. Nevertheless, I had no intention of giving in to fear. I had heard one of the women who lived alone announce that she would be buying a gun to defend herself. I couldn't help thinking that Bessie's gun hadn't protected her, and maybe it was the reason she had been attacked. Only the gun and her wallet had been missing from the guardhouse. Did the attacker really believe that Bessie was carrying a lot of money in her handbag? That didn't seem likely. Had the gun been what the attacker was really after? One thing was certain: until the crime was solved, a sense of uneasiness would pervade Hawkeye Haven.

As the class meeting was coming to a close, Cynthia Bowles, a garrulous retiree, who was known for her active participation in several clubs and charitable organizations, approached me and asked if she could make an announcement. She wanted to take up a collection from the students so that the class could send Bessie flowers at the hospital. Hoping that Bessie would soon be able to see and enjoy the bouquet, I nodded. I fashioned a DIY get-well-soon card from some lavender card stock that I had stashed in my supply suitcase, and, using some hole punches of various shapes, I made a lacey border around it. Cynthia and I signed the makeshift card, and she began passing it around to the students. There couldn't have been a better person to take charge than Cynthia, who was highly organized and efficient. Within a few minutes, she had collected money from everyone in the room; retrieved the get-well card; and, I had no doubt, would deliver the flowers and card to the hospital herself within a few hours.

I wrapped up the session by asking each student to show her necklace to the other students. Most of the women had been able to complete their projects during class, and the others were far enough along that they should have no trouble completing their own necklaces at home. As the students left the room, I could hear that the main topic of conversation was still the attack on Bessie. A few of my students had been surprised to learn that the guard who had been attacked was a woman in her seventies, but Bessie had told me that she had worked as a security guard for more than twenty years, and since she had started collecting social security retirement benefits a decade earlier, she had finally been able to enjoy having some extra money, most of which she spent on her grandchildren. Bessie had never considered her job dangerous, despite the fact that she was required to carry a gun at work. Her main duties—opening the gate to admit visitors and residents and keeping track of all the people who entered Hawkeye Haven—were routine and probably more than a little boring.

Most of the students had left by the time I began replacing the samples, tools, and supplies in my suitcase. Although today I hadn't needed anything except the samples, I liked to be prepared by bringing extra tools, beads, and components, just in case one of the students forgot to bring her own. I zipped the bag closed, placed it on the floor, and pulled up the handle so that I could roll it out to my car. I said good-bye to Amy and Amber, who had been lingering in the classroom.

After they left, only one student remained in the room. Although she was sitting with her back toward me, I recognized her because Sonya Arnold was the only woman I knew who habitually wore her long black hair in a ponytail. I noticed something else, too. Sonya's shoulders were heaving, and I could hear muffled sobs. I hoped that Sonya wasn't crying about a broken project, as another student had once done several months earlier. Even though the other student's tears had been ones mainly of frustration, which I could certainly understand, having been the creator of many a DIY project that didn't quite turn out the way I had planned, the incident had been a bit embarrassing, both to the crying student and her classmates.

"Sonya, are you okay?" I inquired, realizing instantly what a stupid question I had asked.

Obviously, she wasn't okay or she wouldn't be crying. I edged up to the table where she sat. Sonya was dabbing ineffectually at her tear-streaked face with a soaked tissue.

"Just a second," I said, returning to my suitcase, unzipping the bag, and pulling out a box of tissues.

I set the box on the table in front of Sonya, and she yanked a handful of tissues from it and began mopping her eyes.

"Oh, Laurel, I've been such a fool," she sighed.

"What is it? What's wrong?"

"Everything. Tommy and I aren't getting along. He's so angry with me that he's threatening to get a divorce."

She paused, but I resisted the urge to prompt her. I figured she would go on with her story when she was ready.

"Do you know Victor Eberhart?" she asked me.

"Not really. I know who he is, though."

Victor had been the president of the Hawkeye Haven Homeowners' Association for the past six months, and he was already so unpopular with the residents that some of them were circulating a petition to have him removed from office. I hadn't had any personal dealings with him myself, but I knew that I would be seeing him at the scheduled HOA meeting tomorrow night. My friend Liz was having a conflict with Victor about a demand from the HOA that she paint her house, and she'd asked me to accompany her to the meeting to provide moral support.

"Do you know his reputation?"

"I know that he isn't too popular with some of the residents," I said. "They think he's unreasonable and unfair."

"Oh, he's that and more. He's a truly despicable man. If it weren't for him, Tommy wouldn't be so stressed out. I can't believe that something we started with the best of intentions has gone so wrong."

"What is it, Sonya?"

"All we wanted to do was to make our backyard a great place for our kids. We put in a swimming pool, a playhouse, and new landscaping. Olivia—you know, the former HOA manager—told me that our paperwork was fine when she gave me the go-ahead to start construction, and our new backyard turned out even better than I'd hoped. The kids love swimming in the pool, and they adore their cute little playhouse."

"But there was a glitch?" I guessed.

"Big time. After Victor was elected HOA president, he got rid of Olivia's property management company and hired Patty's instead."

"Let me guess. Patty said that your paperwork wasn't in order, and you'd have to re-do it."

"Worse than that. She sent us a notice by certified mail informing us that we had two weeks to remove the swimming pool and playhouse or the HOA would impose fines."

"Can they do that?"

"We found out the hard way that they can. Tommy stormed over to the HOA's office to complain. Patty wasn't around, but Victor was there, and he wouldn't back down. Tommy threatened to sue, and Victor told him to go right ahead, but, in the meantime, the fines would be accumulating. Tommy's furious with Victor, but he's furious with me, too. He says I should have gotten the HOA's approval in writing."

"Oh, no."

"I'm sorry to vent, Laurel, but I've just about reached the end of my rope. The situation keeps getting worse. Yesterday, Tommy went over to the golf course to play eighteen rounds with his buddies, and he overheard Victor in the locker room bragging about forcing Tommy to rip out his brand new swimming pool. Tommy threatened to punch his lights out, and his golf partners had to drag him out of there. Then Tommy came home in a rage and said that if it weren't for my stupidity, we wouldn't be in this mess. He hasn't said a word to me since."

"Sonya, I'm sorry," I mumbled a bit awkwardly. I wanted to comfort Sonya, but I was at a loss to know what to say. I couldn't tell her to hang on, that the situation might improve, because, from what she'd told me, her predicament seemed very likely to get worse.

Somewhat to my relief, we were interrupted by the staccato clicking of high heels on the tile floor of the hallway that led to our classroom. Someone was in a big hurry, I thought. Suddenly Patty appeared in the doorway. After hearing the clatter Patty's shoes had made, I couldn't help glancing at her feet. She was wearing six-inch black stiletto platforms, and she looked gigantic as she stood there. "Laurel, class should have been over half an hour ago. What are you still doing here?" she demanded.

Based on Patty's accusatory tone, anyone would have thought I'd committed a major crime. I wasn't too concerned that she was annoyed. In fact, I knew there were no other classes scheduled to use my classroom for the rest of the day, so my leaving a few minutes late certainly wasn't going to cause any problems. Weary of her nonsense, I wasn't in the mood to argue with her.

"We were just getting ready to leave," I told Patty.

"See that you do," she hissed. "And you too, Miss Ponytail," she added as she turned and strode away, her spike heels hitting the tile floor forcefully. It was a wonder that she didn't slip on the highly polished floor as she click-clicked her way back to her office.

Sonya didn't turn around or respond when Patty called her "Miss Ponytail," but I could tell from the look on her face that Sonya was furious. I was somewhat surprised that Patty would talk to a student so disrespectfully. Why had the Board of Directors of Hawkeye Haven ever hired Patty as our HOA's property manager? During the past six months since Patty's company had obtained the contract to manage the HOA, I'd observed Patty's rudeness to residents, employees, vendors, and even a couple of board members. If there was another side to Patty, I'd certainly never seen it.

"We better get going now, Sonya. Patty seems to be on the warpath, as usual."

"Patty and Victor both," Sonya said angrily. "Victor acts as though he's just backing Patty up, but all the problems in Hawkeye Haven started when he was elected president of our HOA. Honestly, I could just kill both of them."

Chapter 3

After hearing Sonya's harrowing tale, I felt thankful
to head for the comfort of home, where Bear greeted
me enthusiastically at the door. My big Lab was happy
to see me, but, of course, he had an ulterior motive, too.
He loved the special peanut butter treats that I had made
for him, and he was angling for one now. Popping the
lid off the Dutch lady cookie jar that my grandmother
had given me, I picked out a couple of treats and tossed
them, one at a time, to Bear.

"Yummy," I pronounced, and Bear wagged his tail
in agreement.

I'd been thinking about writing a DIY dog lovers'
book, but I wasn't sure how my agent would respond to
the idea. My previous five books had focused on either
fashion or home decorating projects, and I thought it
might be a good idea to branch out. I was sure that I
could come up with plenty of cute doggie accessory
projects, but I also wanted to include some recipes for
dog treats, and that was my only concern about writing
the book because baking certainly had never been my
forté. Despite the fact that my mom was a terrific cook
and baker who had tried her best to teach me the ropes,
I'd never had much aptitude for either cooking or
baking. I'd surprised even myself when I'd come up
with a recipe for the peanut butter treats that Bear likes
so much, but that one recipe was probably the limit of
my kitchen creativity. However, I could probably ask
some of my friends to contribute their recipes. Since her
dog-bone-shaped treats were such a hit with Bear,

Bessie was one of the people I'd been planning to ask. As I was making a list of possible contributors for *DIY for Dog Lovers,* my phone rang. Noticing that the call was coming from the community center, I hesitated for a few seconds. I certainly didn't want to talk to Patty again today, so I decided to monitor the call.

"Laurel, this is Luke."

Relieved that it was Luke calling, rather than Patty, I picked up the phone.

"Hi, Luke."

"Hi, Laurel, I have some good news."

"About Bessie?"

"Yes, her son just called me, and she's regained consciousness. She recognized him, and there doesn't seem to be any long-term memory loss. She's going to be staying in the hospital for at least a couple of days for tests, just to be on the safe side, but it sounds as though she's going to recover."

"Thank goodness! That *is* good news."

"Unfortunately, she can't remember anything that happened this morning, so we may never know exactly who attacked her."

"Nothing on the video camera?"

"I'm afraid not."

The doorbell rang, interrupting our conversation. Since I was expecting a delivery of some crucial project supplies, I thanked Luke for calling me and rushed to the door to sign for the package. I spent the rest of the day, which luckily was uneventful, writing project instructions. I considered going to the hospital to visit Bessie, but I decided that it would be better to wait a day or two so that she would have some time to rest and recuperate.

***

The next morning, Bear woke earlier than usual, so early that not even a hint of light filtered through the slats of my bedroom shutters. Bear stirred, shook his massive head, and padded over the thick beige carpet to nuzzle me as he panted in anticipation of his early morning walk. I leaned over and ran my hands through his dense, silky fur as he wagged his tail in anticipation.

"Who's a good boy?" I asked him. He panted more rapidly and danced around in a circle, whipping his head back and forth and sneezing twice, an odd routine in his morning ritual because he seldom sneezed any other time. Full of energy, my furry canine companion bounced around the bedroom with so much enthusiasm that I didn't have the heart to delay our walk.

"Okay, Mommy's getting up. Mommy's getting up." I used to think it was ridiculous when I heard people refer to themselves as their pets' parents, but I had fallen into the same habit with Bear. My silliness over my dog extended to my talking baby talk to him, which he seemed to enjoy, and signing greeting cards to family members and friends with "Laurel and Bear," accompanied by a drawing of Bear's paw print.

I slipped out of bed, and Bear led the way to the bathroom and then the closet beyond, where I quickly dressed in jeans, an aqua blue t-shirt, and sneakers. Grabbing my smartphone and some plastic bags, I dutifully tied one of the bags around Bear's leash. (HOA Regulation 92a states that "all pet owners will carry in plain sight a bag or other device to pick up after their pets and must do so immediately.") I quickly snapped the leash onto his collar, and we were off.

The sky showed only the faintest hint of the approaching dawn, so it was still quite dark outside, but the streetlights were on, and it wasn't too difficult to see. Knowing that Bear would have to forego his customary treat because Bessie wouldn't be at her post, we turned left at the corner where we usually would have gone right to avoid the back gate. After we trotted briskly for a couple of blocks, we slowed to a more sedate pace. We hadn't seen or heard any signs of activity since we'd left the house—no cars, walkers, or barking dogs.

"Not so early tomorrow, Bear," I cautioned, resolving to resist the urge to jump up as soon as Bear did.

Suddenly, Bear came to a dead stop and started barking furiously.

"Come on, Bear," I urged him, afraid that he'd wake the neighbors, but his barking became frenzied, and he refused to budge.

Then I saw a shadow in the bushes ahead. A dark shape with a long tail emerged from the bushes and strolled into the street ahead of us. Startled, I realized that the shape was a mountain lion, and my heart began pounding. I couldn't believe what I was seeing—a mountain lion in Iowa? The tall corn state was hardly the usual habitat of such large felines.

The big cat turned towards us and snarled, and Bear continued his frantic barking while I started to shake. Should we run? I knew that a mountain lion could run faster than we could. Play dead? Bear hadn't ever learned that trick. Fight? Bear was a big dog, and I didn't doubt that he would try to defend me, but I didn't believe he'd be any match for the cougar.

Although it had probably been only a few seconds since the mountain lion appeared, it seemed as though the terrifying moment had gone on for a very long time. Any second now, the powerful animal could pounce, and I doubted that we'd survive the encounter. Abruptly, the cougar gathered its legs in a crouch to spring. I screamed.

A shot rang out, Bear yelped, and the mountain lion ran off across the golf course on the left side of the street and leaped over a high wall on the other side.

Tears of relief streamed from my eyes as I turned to see a man jogging toward us, holstering a revolver as he ran.

"Ma'am, are you all right?"

"Just a little shaky. Well, more than a little," I groaned.

"Sit down over here," he said, guiding me to the curb. Sensing that the danger had passed, Bear heaved a great sigh, and plopping down beside me, he put his head in my lap.

"Good boy, Bear," I cooed, as I petted him. I turned to the man, who looked vaguely familiar. I had probably seen him around the community, I thought. "Thank you so much. I don't know what would have happened if you hadn't come along just then," I said, shaking hands with the man, who had joined me in sitting on the curb.

I approved of his grip, which was firm, but not bone-crushing. Under the street lamp, I could see that he had white hair and a lined face, but he looked fit and trim. He struck me as a man of action.

"Happy to help. Robert Forrester Gable—colonel, retired, US Army—at your service, ma'am."

"I'm Laurel McMillan."

"Nice to meet you, Miss McMillan, and who's this handsome fellow?"

"This is Bear." On hearing his name mentioned, Bear sat up and began wagging his tail. He wandered over to the colonel and offered his paw, which the colonel solemnly shook.

"It's nice to meet you too, Bear."

The retired officer seemed so serious about greeting Bear that I couldn't help giggling, releasing some of the tension I still felt. I was almost giddy with relief at being safe from the mountain lion.

"Really, Colonel, I can't thank you enough for saving us. That was the scariest thing that's ever happened to me. You're a real hero."

As the colonel began to protest, a Hawkeye Haven security car pulled alongside us, and a uniformed guard jumped out. He looked so young that I'd have assumed he was a high school student if I'd seen him in any other situation.

"What's going on here, folks? We had a report that a shot was fired."

"Mountain lion, believe it or not; he must have escaped from the local zoo," said the colonel, patting his holster. "I fired one shot to scare him, and he took off in that direction." The colonel motioned toward the golf course.

"Firing a gun within Hawkeye Haven is a violation of the community's rules." (HOA Regulation 101 states that "no firearm shall be discharged within Hawkeye Haven.")

"Well, I guess I could have just let that big cat pounce on the lady and her dog."

"There's no need to be sarcastic, sir, but I am going to have to issue you a citation."

"Issue away, young man. That makes about as much sense as regulating the height of my flagpole, which the community, in its infinite wisdom, wants to control too, but you do what you have to do," said the colonel, scowling in irritation, "and, by the way, you just might want to report that mountain lion to animal control. For all we know, it could still be prowling around the neighborhood."

"Just doing my job, sir," said the guard curtly, as he scribbled a citation and handed it to the colonel, "and I *will* alert animal control."

"Thank goodness for small favors," the colonel grumbled, crumpling the citation and stuffing it in his shirt pocket. He turned to me. "Miss McMillan, please allow me to accompany you on your walk home. I doubt that the mountain lion will be coming back this way, but just in case."

I nodded, and as we began walking, we could hear the guard on his radio telling the dispatcher to call the Center City Animal Control Department. The colonel seemed to be preoccupied, and we strolled in silence. It wasn't until we were close to my house that the colonel spoke.

"Are you going to the HOA's open board meeting this evening, Miss McMillan?"

"Yes, I've never attended one, but my friend Liz asked me to come with her for moral support. She's being harassed by the HOA to paint her house. That's it over there," I pointed, "right next to mine."

"I don't see anything wrong with the paint job."

"Bingo. There isn't anything wrong with it. It's only been two years since Liz had her house painted. She tried to explain to Patty, the HOA manager, but she wouldn't listen."

"I know who *she* is, unfortunately."

"Well, Patty wouldn't budge, so Liz took her case to Victor, the HOA president, and he just laughed in her face. I think she was so upset she didn't know how to react, but now she's decided that maybe the other board members might overrule Victor, if she can plead her case to them. So that's why we're going to the meeting tonight."

The colonel shook his head in disgust.

"Ever since Victor and Patty took over, this place has become a nightmare. They're insisting that I remove my flagpole, which I installed five years ago. Somehow they've managed to establish a new rule, regulating the height of flagpoles, and they say there's no way to have my pole grandfathered. The whole thing is totally ridiculous. I'm going to the meeting to protest, for all the good it will probably do. My lawyer advised me to skip the meeting and let her handle it, but there's nothing wrong with the public airing of a legitimate grievance."

Waving good-bye to the colonel, I thanked him again, wished him success at the meeting, and told him that I would see him there. I definitely wasn't looking forward to it, and I was afraid that neither Liz nor the colonel would get too far with Victor and Patty in firm control of Hawkeye Haven's HOA.

My stomach felt queasy after my surprise encounter with the mountain lion. The colonel hadn't seemed the least bit fazed by the incident, but I felt more than a little upset that my routine morning walk with Bear had turned into a life-threatening event. I was also slightly embarrassed that I'd almost fainted again this morning. No doubt, I was a sissy. Even though I never claimed to be brave, playing the damsel in distress on two consecutive mornings wasn't exactly my idea of a good time. I sincerely hoped that Bear and I could return to our normal morning routine tomorrow.

***

"Ready for this?" I greeted Liz, as we hopped into my car for the short drive to the community center.

"Ready as I'll ever be, I guess," she replied. "I'm so glad you're coming with me."

"No problem. I just hope the board has more sense than its president seems to have."

Liz, a dynamic senior who had her own unique fashion style, nodded. She had been a real knock-out when she was younger, and she still looked glamorous. It would be difficult for the board members to ignore someone who presented such a flamboyant appearance as Liz, who wore enormous gold chandelier earrings, several flashy diamond rings, and a stunning ruby red caftan of silk chiffon trimmed with gold embroidery. Her beautifully coiffed honey-blonde hair, long eyelashes, bright red lipstick, and matching nail polish completed the picture. Not too many women could carry off such a showy look, but dressing the way she did was second nature to Liz, and she seemed oblivious to the somewhat shocked reaction people often had to her appearance.

Much as I hated to attend this evening's meeting, I wanted to stand by my friend in her fight against the unreasonable directive to paint her house. Even though Liz could well afford to have her house painted again, it seemed absurd that she might actually be forced into an unnecessary re-do because of Patty's vindictiveness. Liz had told me that she was sure that Patty had become irritated and angry with Liz when Liz had parked her car in a covered parking space in the community center's lot, a space that Patty had evidently considered her own, although it had been unmarked at the time.

In fact, the very next day, a reserved-for-community-manager sign had appeared, marking the parking spot for Patty's exclusive use. The painting notice had arrived in Liz's mail just a few days later. Angry about the demand to paint her house, Liz had complained to Patty to no avail, then bypassed her and called Victor, who, as president of the HOA, had the authority to override the management company's actions. Unfortunately, Victor didn't want to deal with the issue and referred Liz back to Patty. As a close friend of Victor's late wife Diana, Liz had expected Victor to listen, at least, to her complaint. Liz didn't deserve such shabby treatment.

"Hawkeye Haven used to be such a pleasant place to live, but now that Victor and Patty have taken over, it's just not the same," Liz commented sadly.

"I know. Every time I teach a class, I hear stories about the HOA's unreasonable demands."

"Half the people I know here have received citations in the past few months. Have you heard from the HOA, Laurel?"

"Not yet, but I'm afraid I could become Patty's next target. She didn't like it when I asked about Bessie yesterday, and then she made a point of kicking me out of my classroom when I stayed late to talk to a student."

"Do you remember that I wondered why Victor wouldn't even talk to me the other day?"

"Yes," I nodded. "It seems very odd considering that you were such good friends with his wife."

"That's what I thought, too, but a little birdie told me something that might explain it."

I grinned. I knew that the "little birdie" must have been her bridge partner Linda, who just happened to be a part-time receptionist at the community center as well as a resident of Hawkeye Haven.

"What did Linda tell you?"

Liz put her finger to her lips in a shushing motion. "Patty used to work for Victor at IFI."

It sounded as though Liz had said, "eye, fie."

"What's that?" I asked.

"Iowa Fidelity Insurance Company. They were both executives there."

"Oh, I get it. It sounds as though they're in cahoots, all right. So you think that's the reason Victor wouldn't talk to you?"

"I sure do. From what Linda told me, those two are as thick as thieves."

"No wonder Victor wanted to get rid of the old management company and hire Patty. He wanted someone he could control to have the contract."

"Mark my words," Liz sighed. "Those two are up to no good."

We had arrived at the community center, where we joined a group of people entering the large meeting room. There were probably about sixty folding chairs arranged in rows facing a long table at the front. As we took our seats, we could see Victor sitting next to Patty in the middle, and the pair was flanked by three board members on either side, three women on Victor's side and three men on Patty's side.

There was only one board member I knew—Edna Elkins, a retired nurse, whom I'd met when she had taken several of my DIY home decorating classes. She waved at me as Liz and I took seats in the front row. Liz scowled at Patty and Victor, but they both ignored her.

I'd looked for the colonel as we entered the meeting room, but I hadn't spotted him. I knew that he wouldn't miss the meeting, though, so I set my handbag on the vacant chair next to me to save him a seat. A moment later, I saw him standing at the back of the room, and I gestured for him to join us.

"Colonel, I saved you a seat in case you'd like to join us."

"Yes, indeed," he said, taking the seat beside me.

"Liz, this is Colonel Gable. Colonel, my friend and neighbor, Liz Dawson."

"Nice to meet you, Mrs. Dawson." Although the colonel didn't attempt to shake Liz's hand, since I was sitting between them, he stood and bowed, rather formally.

"Liz, please, Colonel," Liz gushed. "I haven't been a Mrs. for years," she added, none too subtly.

"Delighted, and I'm Bobby," the colonel declared, a smile softening his usually stern expression.

Oh. My. Goodness. The air crackled with electricity. Had a romance just begun to bud? I didn't have time to consider it further because the meeting was about to begin.

My attention turned to the front of the room as Victor, in a no-nonsense voice, called the meeting to order with a sharp crack of his gavel. In an efficient manner, he began methodically leading the other board members through a discussion of the items that were listed on the agenda, most of which consisted of routine business. I stifled a yawn. This was going to be slow going, as the agenda didn't allow for residents to speak until the end of the meeting, and even then each resident was limited to a time slot of two minutes. No doubt Victor and Patty had deliberately set up the agenda to discourage residents from bringing their complaints before the board.

After an hour and a half, all the items on the agenda had been covered, and the time had come for the residents to address the board. Another surprise was in store for us, though. Referring to the HOA's rules, Victor announced that the total time period allotted for the residents to speak was half an hour (HOA Regulation 133 states that, "the president of the Hawkeye Haven HOA may limit the amount of time spent on any board meeting agenda item."). An angry murmur rippled through the crowd, most of whom had attended the meeting so that they could air a grievance in public. Victor quickly quelled the noise with another sharp rap of his gavel.

"Now to be fair, we'll simply do this by the numbers." Victor glanced at Liz and the colonel. "We'll start with residents sitting in the back row and work our way forward until we run out of time. Remember that you each have two minutes. Patty, could you please time each speaker?"

Patty reached into her black Gucci handbag and pulled out a stopwatch. Obviously, Victor and Patty meant to time each speaker to the second. The colonel's face contorted with anger, but he held himself in check, although I could only imagine that it was with great difficulty. Liz, on the other hand, had no such compunctions about controlling herself.

Shaking her fist at Victor, she stood and yelled, "Victor Eberhart, you should be ashamed of yourself. Didn't you ever hear of the First Amendment? We all have a right to speak! You were elected board president, not king."

"You're out of order, Ms. Dawson. Please be seated."

"I certainly will not. I came here to have my say, and so did all these other people. We demand to be heard." Applause rippled through the audience and came to a loud crescendo. Patty shot Liz a withering look, but Victor appeared unperturbed.

"Ms. Dawson, be seated, or I will be forced to have you removed," Victor said calmly.

"We elected you, Victor, and the rest of you board members, too. You're supposed to represent us." Liz began chanting, "Let us speak!" Soon, most of the other people attending the meeting had joined in, and the noise level in the room rose several decibels.

Victor pounded the gavel. "Quiet!" he roared. "There will be silence, or I'll adjourn this meeting right now. Luke, remove Ms. Dawson."

I turned around and saw Luke standing by the door. He hesitated momentarily.

"Now!" Victor commanded.

Luke looked uncomfortable as he made his way to Liz and said politely, "Ma'am, will you please come with me?"

Her head held high, Liz surprised me by docilely taking the arm Luke offered her and regally marching from the room. I stood to follow her, but she motioned for me to stay. I figured that she probably wanted me to keep tabs on the rest of the meeting, so I took my seat.

"Okay, let's get on with it." Victor looked at his pricey Rolex watch. "Now we only have twenty-five minutes left, and we're sticking to our schedule." Despite a disapproving murmur throughout the room, Victor pressed on. "The chair recognizes Mr. Alleman."

A man in the back row stood and came forward to the podium that had been placed in the front of the room facing the board members. He cleared his throat and announced, "I yield the floor to Colonel Gable."

"The rules don't permit that," Victor snarled. "Do you want to speak, or don't you?"

"Mr. Chairman, I yield to Colonel Gable," the man repeated.

"Sit down. You're out of order."

"Oh, no, you don't," the colonel shouted. "You can't avoid the issue forever. This is supposed to be an open meeting, and I should be able to fly the flag of my country as high as I wish without any interference from you." He looked at Victor. "Or you," he glared at Patty, "or any of you other board members. This is a free country!"

Loud applause broke out, which made Victor even angrier than he already was. He'd been banging his gavel since the colonel began shouting, and now he called Luke to come forward again, this time to remove the colonel.

Reluctantly, Luke made his way once more to the front row and politely asked the colonel to leave. He reached down as if to take the colonel by the arm, but the colonel twisted away from his grasp.

"I'm quite capable of leaving on my own, young man. I realize you have a job to do, but please stay out of my way." The colonel stormed to the back of the room so quickly that Luke trailed several feet behind him.

Standing in the doorway, the colonel yelled, "You haven't heard the last of me, Victor Eberhart. You're going to regret the day you ever tried to have me remove my flagpole." With that declaration, the colonel departed.

Rising, I slipped past Luke and left the room, too. There didn't seem to be much point in my staying for the rest of the meeting since it was clear that Victor maintained tight control over the gathering and its agenda, and he had no intention of allowing anyone who disagreed with him to speak. I was somewhat surprised that none of the other six board members had objected to Victor's high-handed tactics. Certainly Edna Elkins, the only board member I knew, had never been shy about expressing herself, yet she and the other board member had sat passively while Victor played dictator and Patty looked on with approval. What kind of strange power did Victor have over these people?

The colonel was nowhere in sight when I reached the hallway, but I caught up with him and Liz as I neared the main door of the community center. The colonel didn't look nearly as upset as he had a few minutes earlier, and it was easy to tell that he was looking at the reason for his calmer demeanor—Liz. Although they seemed an unlikely pair—the stern retired military officer and the flamboyant charmer—I hadn't been wrong about their instant attraction to each other. At least some good had come from the evening's meeting. They were so busy talking to each other that neither one of them noticed that I had joined them.

I cleared my throat and observed, "That didn't go too well, did it?"

"It certainly didn't, but after all the harassment I've endured from the HOA, I can't say that I'm too surprised. My lawyer was right; I should let her handle it, and that's exactly what I'm going to do."

"Perhaps I should do the same," Liz said. "I thought that these people would listen to reason, but they won't, and I don't really want to spend a lot of time worrying about what they're going to do next. Not when there are more important things in life." She batted her eyes at the colonel, and I knew for sure that he was a goner. No wonder she'd been married four times. Men had always found her difficult to resist.

"You're right, Liz," the colonel agreed, smiling broadly.

"Would you like to join Liz and me for a drink, colonel?" I asked.

"Certainly; lead on, ladies."

"I thought maybe we could go over to Alberto's next door, if that's okay with both of you."

"Fine," the colonel agreed, and Liz nodded her assent.

I led the way across the sidewalk that connected the two buildings, with Liz and the colonel following behind me. I glanced back and noticed that the colonel had offered Liz his arm, and Liz was holding it as they followed me to the little restaurant situated in the same building that housed the pro shop for the golf course.

When we arrived at Alberto's, there were only a few other patrons, most of whom sat at the bar, although a few were scattered throughout the large dining room.

"Table for three?" the host queried.

"Yes, please," Liz piped up. "I'd rather not sit in the bar." The young man, who sported a diamond stud earring in one ear, long hair, and tattooed forearms, led us to a table on the other side of the room, far away from the bar. Staring at the host, the colonel raised an eyebrow, but said nothing.

"How's this table, folks?"

"Great," I said, allowing him to seat me as the colonel pulled out a chair next to me for Liz. We scanned the menus the host had handed us.

"I think I'll just stick with decaf and dessert," I said, suddenly realizing how tired I was. It had been a long day, and I wanted to be able to get some sleep when I went home.

"Dessert sounds good," Liz said, "but I think I'll have a glass of wine with mine. How about you, Bobby?" It sounded strange to hear Liz call the colonel Bobby, even though it was his idea. Somehow, he seemed more dignified than the nickname implied, and I knew that I would continue to think of him as the colonel. I'd continue to call him colonel, too. Come to think of it, he'd never invited me to call him Bobby, anyway.

"I'll make dessert unanimous, and I'll join you in having a glass of wine, Liz. By the way, did either of you happen to watch the news on Channel 3 today?" Liz and I both shook our heads, and the colonel continued. "It seems that the mystery of our mountain lion has been solved. We weren't the only ones to see that big cat this morning. After it leaped over the wall at the golf course, several other people reported seeing it, and animal control finally caught up with it about two miles from here. They managed to subdue it with a tranquilizer dart. Evidently, someone had been keeping it in their backyard."

"That's an awfully big kitty cat to keep as a pet," I said with a shudder.

"It's crazy, but Center City actually allows exotic pets within the city limits as long as the owners have a permit," Liz said. "A few years ago, I read an article in the paper about a man who kept three pythons in his bedroom."

"Yes, but now city officials want to crack down on permitting exotic pets in residential neighborhoods. In any case, the mountain lion's owners didn't have a permit to keep the animal. According to the news, it's going to be transported to an animal sanctuary in Utah sometime next week."

"That's good. I'm relieved to hear that it's not still on the loose," Liz commented. I had told her all about my run-in with the mountain lion when we'd met for a late morning cup of coffee. "Laurel, what a terrible experience for you! I worry about you walking Bear all alone so early in the morning."

The colonel patted Liz's hand. "Don't worry, Liz. I doubt that we'll be seeing any more mountain lions in Hawkeye Haven."

"You're right, colonel," I agreed. "We're more likely to run into problems with the humans who are running the place, I'm afraid."

Chapter 4

With some trepidation, I set out the following morning with Bear beside me. After the events of the past two days—the attack on Bessie, the threat of the mountain lion, and the meeting of the HOA—I felt wary and on edge. Although walking Bear in the darkness had never bothered me before, I'd waited until sunrise before leaving the house. Even Bear hadn't seemed quite as eager to embark on his daily walk as he normally did.

Walking in the daylight, rather than in the dark, definitely had its benefits. I began to relax somewhat as we passed neighbors' yards, planted with flourishing flowers, shrubbery, and trees.

After strolling for a few blocks, I felt my anxiety waning a bit. I hoped things would settle back into a calmer routine soon, although with Victor and Patty in charge of the homeowners' association, it didn't seem likely that there would be much relief from the HOA's harassment and unreasonable demands. It wouldn't surprise me if I were Patty's next target. The woman certainly disliked me, and she enjoyed wielding her power far too much to suit me.

When Bear pulled at his leash and turned in the direction of the back gate, I knew he wanted to take our regular weekday route. After the mountain lion incident, I wasn't too eager to retrace yesterday's steps, so I acquiesced, and we turned right. I had slipped a snack into my jeans' pocket before we left the house because I knew that Bear would be disappointed not to find Bessie waiting at the back gate for him with his usual treat. Although the store-bought dog biscuit I toted couldn't compare to Bessie's homemade treat, at least it would mollify Bear, but I knew that he'd be looking not only for his treat, but also for Bessie, who might never return to her post.

The previous afternoon, I'd called the hospital to check on Bessie's condition, and her son had informed me that she'd had a mild stroke, which had produced some numbness in her right arm. Despite the doctor's assurance that the stroke had been minor and was easily treated, the news worried me, and I wondered whether Bessie would ever be able to return to work at Hawkeye Haven. This afternoon, I planned to visit her and see for myself how she was doing. I wished that the hospital's rules permitted pets to visit the patients because I knew Bessie would perk up if she could see Bear, but somebody on the hospital staff would be sure to notice if I tried to sneak an eighty-pound Labrador retriever into Bessie's room, so Bear would have to stay home.

We'd almost arrived at the guardhouse at the back gate, but rather than approaching it, I just waved to the on-duty guard, a middle-aged man who stood outside smoking a cigarette. Confused, Bear looked at me. I pulled the treat from my pocket. "Catch," I said, tossing it to him, and he opened his mouth just in time to snag the snack. He chomped the dog biscuit a couple of times, swallowed, and wagged his tail. We were continuing on our way when I heard a low wail of sirens.

Since the fire station was close to Hawkeye Haven, and the residents could hear the sirens every time the firefighters were called out, I didn't pay much attention, but as the sirens screamed more loudly, it became evident that they were headed for Hawkeye Haven. Turning, I saw a rescue unit and a fire engine entering the back gate, followed by a couple of police cars. What now? The Center City police wouldn't normally respond to a routine fire or a medical call. Curious, I decided to follow the emergency vehicles, which had turned left onto Lily-of-the-Valley Lane after proceeding a couple of blocks on Hawkeye Haven Drive, the main road that ran through the community, connecting the front and back gates. The moaning sirens stopped abruptly, and when I reached the intersection where the vehicles had turned, I could see them, lights flashing, parked a couple of blocks down the street. My cousin and best friend Tracey lived on Lily-of-the-Valley Lane, as did my friends Amy and Cynthia, so I was familiar with the neighborhood. I would have stopped by Tracey's house to see if she wanted to join me in finding out what was happening, but my cousin had been out of town on a vacation for several days and wasn't due back home until the next evening, so I'd have to investigate on my own.

As Bear and I moved closer to the emergency vehicles, I could see several residents looking on, while others, some dressed in robes, were coming out of their houses to see what was happening. I noticed a few other curious neighbors unabashedly peering out of their windows, not bothering to hide behind curtains. I spotted Cynthia standing next to a police cruiser and joined her.

"Hi, Cynthia. I was walking Bear and heard the sirens. Do you have any idea what's going on?"

"Oh, hi, Laurel. I have no idea. I was drinking my morning coffee when I heard the sirens. Say, there's Amy. Maybe she knows something." Threading our way through the growing crowd, we moved toward Amy, who was standing on the other side of the street.

"Amy, you look pale," I observed. "Are you feeling okay?"

"After what I saw, I feel kind of sick, actually," Amy replied. "Let's go inside, and I'll tell you all about it," she invited us. "Bring Bear along, Laurel." Reaching down, she absent-mindedly petted Bear. "You're a good boy, aren't you, Bear?"

"Are you sure it's all right to bring him into the house? I could put him in the backyard."

"Sure, no problem. He'll be fine. I love dogs, but Jim was allergic to them, so we could never have one, but now that he's gone . . . " she trailed off wistfully. Her husband Jim had passed away six months ago, and she'd spent much of that time staying with her daughter, who lived somewhere on the East Coast. During the past month, she'd been trying to adjust to life in Hawkeye Haven without her husband. I knew from painful, first-hand experience that she must be terribly lonely. She didn't work, but she was keeping herself busy with a whirlwind schedule—she took every class that I offered, and she was taking golf and tennis lessons, too.

"How about some tea, ladies?" Amy offered.

"I'll make it, Amy," the ever-efficient Cynthia volunteered, and she bustled into the kitchen while Amy and I sat down on the sofa in the living room, and Bear settled himself at my feet.

In a few minutes, Cynthia came back, carrying a tray with a flowered teapot and three matching cups and saucers.

"Sugar or lemon?" Cynthia offered as she poured the tea.

"Just plain, thanks," I said, and she handed me a cup of tea.

"Amy?"

"A slice of lemon, Cynthia, thanks,"

I knew that Cynthia was as curious as I was to learn what had happened, but we waited until Amy was ready to tell us. Despite her shaking hand, Amy managed to squeeze the lemon wedge, and its juice spurted into her tea. She stirred it slowly and took a few sips. Then, still trembling, she set her cup down on the tray. "Victor is dead," she announced.

Shocked, I sensed that there was more to the story than a natural death.

Amy's next words confirmed my suspicion. "He was shot!"

"Suicide?" Cynthia questioned.

Amy shook her head. "No, he didn't shoot himself. He was murdered."

"How do you know, Amy?" I probed.

"I was going out to pick up the paper from the driveway a few minutes ago when I heard Victor's daughter, Courtney, scream. I knew it was Courtney who was screaming because she'd just pulled up in front of the house and walked up the sidewalk a few seconds earlier. Well, Karl—you know, he lives right across the street from Victor—was out in his front yard, tending to his roses as usual, and he heard it too. We both rushed over there and saw Courtney standing at Victor's feet. He was sprawled just inside the doorway, lying on his back, and he had blood all over his chest. His eyes were open, and I'll never forget the vacant look in them."

"Could he have possibly shot himself?" I wondered.

"There was a gun lying on the sidewalk, but it was at least six feet away from Victor's body. He couldn't have been holding that gun. Someone else must have shot him. I didn't even see the gun at first, and I tripped over it when I ran up the sidewalk. Finding him there, like that, was so shocking. Poor Courtney was still screaming, and Karl grabbed her and tried to calm her down while I ran back home here and called 9-1-1. When I went outside again, Karl was leading Courtney over to his house, and Eva opened the door for them. She was already dressed for the day—even had her shiny jewelry on—unlike most of us neighbors. She must have heard the commotion, and she probably saw Karl run to Victor's place, but she couldn't have known what was happening because she never came out of the house."

"Not too surprising—I haven't seen her leave her house in over a year," Cynthia observed.

"I often notice her gazing out at the street from the front bedroom window. Sometimes she watches Karl when he's taking care of his flowers. It's kind of creepy really," Amy said.

I thought it was more sad than creepy, but Amy had had a terrible shock, so I didn't say anything. Eva was Karl's agoraphobic wife. I knew her because she had taken a few of my classes back in the days before her self-imposed confinement. As long as Eva stayed home, she seemed perfectly normal, but she refused to venture beyond the front door or go outside the screened patio in her backyard.

"Poor Courtney, finding her father like that," I said.

"Yes, she's had a rough go of it, especially since her mother died. Honestly, I don't know why Diana stayed with Victor. He really wasn't very nice to either his wife or Courtney—always criticizing and belittling everything they did. He seemed to care only about two things back then—playing golf and making money. I never did have much use for that man." Cynthia shook her head in disgust.

"You're not the only one. Since he took over as president of the HOA, he certainly hasn't been winning any friends," I said. "I wonder who could have hated him enough to kill him."

"That might be a long list. He's managed—with the help of that awful woman Patty—to alienate half the people in Hawkeye Haven, what with all the citations the HOA has been issuing. Why just yesterday, I got a notice from the HOA in the mail citing me for not maintaining my back wall that faces the golf course. (HOA Regulation 59 states that "homeowners shall properly maintain their property and not allow it to fall into disrepair.") What's so crazy about the citation is that I don't even live next to the golf course! I tried to explain the situation to Patty, but she refused to listen, so I went to the meeting last night to protest, but I never got a chance to speak."

"I was there too, Cynthia. I guess I didn't see you," I said.

"I arrived late and had to wedge myself into a back corner, so I didn't see you either until you stood up to leave. Your friend Liz was really up in arms, wasn't she, Laurel?"

"She sure was. The HOA demanded that she paint her house, but she'd had a new paint job done less than two years ago."

"That's exactly the kind of thing I'm talking about. No wonder so many people hated Victor," Cynthia declared.

Our conversation was interrupted by a knock on the door.

"That's probably the police; they told me they'd be taking my statement," Amy said.

"We'd better get going then," Cynthia suggested, and I agreed. Bear was becoming restless, and we'd only be in the way if the police wanted to talk to Amy. Waving goodbye to Amy, Cynthia and I slipped past the two officers who had arrived to take Amy's statement. Outside, several uniformed police officers were canvassing the residents who were still standing in small groups, abuzz with curiosity. One of the cops approached Cynthia and me, and although we told him that we hadn't witnessed anything, he insisted on taking our names and addresses in case the Center City detectives wanted to question us.

"I should run," Cynthia told me. "I was supposed to meet Vivian at the golf course ten minutes ago. If I hurry, I can just make our tee time. Viv's going to be shocked when I tell her that there's been a murder right here in Hawkeye Haven."

Chapter 5

Vivian wouldn't be the only resident to be shocked at the news of Victor's untimely demise. If I didn't miss my guess, the Hawkeye Haven grapevine would be working overtime today. What with Victor's murder and the attack on Bessie, the residents would definitely be feeling on edge until the mysterious crimes had been solved. I only hoped that their solutions would happen soon. Murder in a guard-gated community couldn't happen too often, I thought, and neither did attacks on armed security guards. Could the two crimes possibly be related? Although I could think of plenty of people who wouldn't be mourning Victor, I didn't believe that Bessie had any enemies.

Luckily, I'd have time today to visit Bessie. It wouldn't take me too long to prepare for tomorrow's monthly Make-Your-Own-Earrings class, one of my most popular offerings. Once a month, on a Saturday morning, the class met, and we always made at least three pairs of earrings. Because I featured new styles each month, several students came to every class. As soon as I assembled my class supplies, made my sample earrings, and put together project directions, I'd be free for the rest of the day. To avoid interruptions, I turned off both my cell phone and the house phone, and then I set to work.

It was late morning by the time I finished my preparations, and I called the hospital to ring Bessie's room. The phone had rung only once when Bessie herself answered.

"Hi, Bessie. It's Laurel. Are you feeling up to having some company?"

"I sure am. It's pretty boring lying around here."

"Is now a good time? I can be there in a few minutes."

"That would be great."

"Can I bring you anything?"

"Maybe *Celebrity Spy*. I can keep up on all the gossip." Bessie chuckled. "At least, that'll give me something to do. I guess they're going to keep me here for another day."

"Well, I'm glad you're going to be able to go home soon. I'll be sure to pick up the latest issue for you."

I was happy that Bessie seemed to be in good spirits. Leaving Bear to his afternoon nap, I drove the short distance to the hospital, stopping at a supermarket along the way to pick up the latest issue of *Celebrity Spy* and a big jar of cashews, one of Bessie's favorite snacks.

When I arrived at the hospital, I was lucky enough to snag a parking spot not too far from the main entrance. The Center City Regional Hospital, a new ten-story structure, bustled with activity. I bypassed the busy reception desk since I already knew Bessie's room number and took a crowded elevator to the fourth floor, where I followed the arrow pointing towards rooms 400 –420. As I walked down the hall to number 418, I noticed that all the rooms had just one occupant, which surprised me. It had probably been at least twenty years since I'd been inside a hospital, and I remembered that, at the time, most of the patients had had to share a room with a stranger because few rooms were private.

As I approached Bessie's room, I could see her sitting up in bed. She was wearing a pink, quilted bed jacket that reminded me of something my great-grandmother had worn when I was a child. On the shelf next to the window, three bouquets of flowers and several get-well cards were arranged neatly in a row. The lavender DIY card that my jewelry class had made was displayed prominently next to a fall bouquet that Cynthia had personally delivered to the hospital.

"Bessie!" I exclaimed, carefully giving her a gentle hug, "I brought you some cashews, and here's the latest issue of *Celebrity Spy*."

"Great! Thanks, Laurel. The hospital food is okay, but cashews sure aren't on the menu, and you know they're my favorite snack."

"You look like you're feeling better," I said, remembering how pale she'd been when I'd found her lying on the floor in the guardhouse. Her color had returned to normal, and someone had styled her hair, although the hair-do couldn't hide the bandage on the back of her head.

She patted her head and nodded. "I feel better. Debby was here early this morning, before she went to work, and she fixed my hair."

"Tom's wife?" I couldn't remember the name of Bessie's daughter-in-law.

"Uh, huh. She works at Le Style Salon. Fridays are her busiest days, but she took the time to come over here before work." A tear trickled down Bessie's face.

"I'm sure she was happy to do it."

"We haven't always gotten along, but she's been a real rock these past few days. Poor Tom has been so upset, and he's been begging me to move in with them, but I don't want to rock the boat with Debby, and I don't want to live with them, anyway. Doc says I can go home tomorrow morning, and I told Tom that's exactly what I'm going to do—go home, to my own apartment. I'm champing at the bit to get out of this place."

"In that case, I *know* you're feeling better. When do you think you'll come back to work?"

"Well, that's another story. I may not be coming back."

"Oh, Bessie," I murmured. I would miss Bessie if she didn't go back to work, but I couldn't really blame her for not wanting to return to the place she'd been attacked.

"I've been thinking about it a lot—not much else to do here anyway. To be honest, I'm really feeling my age. You know I'll be eighty next month."

"No!" I really was surprised at this revelation. I'd thought that Bessie was in her mid-seventies at most.

"Yup, it may be time to retire. For the first time in my life, I really feel old. I'm still sore from the mugging, and now I can't move my arm too well—I had a little stroke, you know—but the real kicker is that I'm kind of scared to go back. Hawkeye Haven used to be such a nice place to work, but now..." she trailed off.

"I can understand your concern. Everyone was shocked by what happened to you."

"It's not just the possible danger, Laurel. It's the management, too. Luke's a great guy, but he has his hands full trying to deal with those two idiots who are running the place now."

"You mean Victor and Patty?"

"Yup, those two. What a pair! If I decide not to come back to work, I sure won't miss them," she said vehemently.

I realized that Bessie probably hadn't heard about Victor's murder, so I filled her in on all the details I knew.

"Can't say I'm surprised. It couldn't have happened to a nicer person."

"Bessie!" Although she was expressing the same sentiment that I was sure a lot of people were feeling, it was a bit shocking to hear it out loud. Victor had not been a popular man. I wondered how he'd managed to get himself elected as president of the Hawkeye Haven HOA.

"I know that sounds cruel, Laurel, but he wasn't a good man. It was terrible the way he treated his poor wife, even before she got sick. He was nasty to his own daughter, too. Courtney was their only child, so any normal guy would have doted on her, but he was always yelling at her and putting her down, like it made him a big man or something."

"I understand that Courtney was still living at home with him. I wonder why she'd do that when he was so mean to her."

"She was about to move out. She told me last week that she'd lined up a roommate and an apartment. I think she only stayed with Victor so that she could save enough money to go out on her own. She just turned twenty-one a few months ago, and she's been trying to save money since her high school graduation, but it's been tough. Until a few months ago, she'd only worked at minimum-wage jobs, but when the new canning factory opened, she was able to get a job there on the night shift."

"How awful for her to be the one to find him dead."

"Terrible," Bessie agreed. "Now she's an orphan. He wasn't much of a father, but he's all she had after her mom died."

"No other relatives?"

"She never mentioned any."

"Here's your lunch, Mrs. Kessler." We were interrupted by a hospital aide who hurried into the room and plunked a tray down on Bessie's bedside table. "I'll leave it right here for you."

As I wheeled the arm of the bedside table over her lap, Bessie struggled to sit up straighter. I removed the covers from the food—cream of mushroom soup and a turkey sandwich with a peanut butter cookie for dessert and a carton of milk to drink.

"Not too bad," Bessie commented, taking a bite of the sandwich, "but I like my own homemade bread a whole lot better than this stuff."

"You'll be home making a loaf before long," I assured her, sounding more cheerful than I felt. I didn't want Bessie to guess that I was still worried about her. She seemed much like her old self, except for the admission that she was frightened. The old Bessie had been fearless. I couldn't really blame her for feeling scared. Who wouldn't be, after the ordeal she'd gone through?

"Bessie," I asked as she sipped her milk, "do you remember anything about what happened when you were attacked?"

"At first, I didn't, and the doctor told me that I might not ever remember, but it's starting to come back to me. I remember putting a cup of coffee in the microwave, and then I heard a noise. By the time I turned around, the attacker was only a few feet away."

"A man?"

"I think so, but I'm not really sure. Whoever it was wore a ski mask. I got the impression that he was a few inches taller than me. There was something about the way the person moved—it seemed kind of familiar, but I can't think how." Bessie seemed agitated, and I was sorry that I'd broached the subject.

I patted her hand, "That's all right, Bessie. I shouldn't have mentioned it."

"It's just that I get so frustrated when I can't remember something."

"You have a better reason for not remembering something than the rest of us, but I know what you mean. It's frustrating. Just yesterday I couldn't find my car keys. I must have looked for them for at least twenty minutes before I realized that I'd left them in my jacket pocket."

Bessie sighed. "Maybe it'll come back to me eventually."

"I'm sure it will," I assured her. "You've been through a lot, but I can tell that you're feeling better. Now, I should go and let you get some rest."

"Thanks for coming, Laurel, and thanks for the magazine and the cashews. Give my favorite dog a hug for me."

"I'll do that. Too bad they don't allow pets to visit."

We both waved as I exited Bessie's room. I felt bad that Bessie had lost her self-confidence. Although she seemed to blame it on her advancing age, a younger person might feel just as helpless after suffering such an attack. It was chilling to think that Bessie might know her attacker. She'd said that there was something familiar about the person. Could it be someone living in Hawkeye Haven? And what about Victor's murder? The shooting had happened well inside the community itself, not on the fringes where the backyards of the houses were just a wall away from city streets. I wondered again whether or not the same person was responsible for both attacks.

When I arrived home, Bear greeted me at the door, bouncing around like a little kid, and I knew he was ready for some play time. I grabbed his hard rubber ball from the toy box in the den, and we went outside. I threw the ball across the backyard, and he chased after it, bringing it back to me and tossing it to me with a whip of his head. He fetched his ball again and again. It was fun watching him joyfully running back to me every time he retrieved his ball.

Bear hadn't tired of the game yet when we heard the doorbell ring, but he followed me back inside the house and trotted to the front door with me. Cautiously, I peered through the peephole. A man and a woman, neither of whom I recognized, were standing on the sidewalk outside. The woman reached into her voluminous black bag, and opened a wallet. As she opened it, I could see the metal star inside, and I realized that the pair must be Center City detectives. Beside me, leaning against me protectively, Bear stood alert as I opened the door.

"Laurel McMillan?" the woman asked, flashing her badge.

"Yes."

"I'm Sergeant Smith, and this is Lieutenant Wesson. We're detectives from Center City's Robbery/Homicide Division. May we come in?"

"It's okay, Bear," I assured my furry companion, and we both stepped back to allow the detectives to enter the living room. "Please have a seat," I gestured toward the sofa, while I perched on a loveseat that faced them.

"Smith and Wesson, huh?" I grinned, but Detective Smith made a face, and I supposed that she'd heard that joke one time too many, although Detective Wesson smiled.

Looking for a friendly word, Bear wandered over to the sofa, and Detective Smith, a red-faced, plump woman with frizzy blonde hair, dressed in wrinkled white linen trousers and a too-tight white jacket, neither of which flattered her, shrank away in distaste.

"No, Bear," I said belatedly, as my big Lab brushed against the detective's white pants, depositing some of his brown fur in the process.

"Get away, doggie," she said, shrinking from him and making frantic shooing motions.

Detective Wesson patted his own leg and held out his hand to Bear, who promptly transferred his attention to the man. Wagging his tail, Bear flopped over on his back and held his front paws up. Wesson obliged him by rubbing his tummy.

"He's a handsome fellow," Wesson said, seeming in no hurry to conduct business.

His partner had other ideas, though. She had pulled a laptop from her bag and was poised to take notes. "Let's get on with it. Mrs. McMillan, I understand that you were on scene this morning when Victor Eberhart was shot."

"No, I only came along afterwards. I saw all the emergency vehicles, and I wondered what was happening. And it's *Miss* McMillan." I'd kept my maiden name when I married, and since my husband's death, calling myself *Mrs.* just didn't seem right somehow. Why had I felt it necessary to correct her? I didn't really know anything about the murder, and I doubted that I'd ever see these two again. I looked at both of them more closely. Beads of perspiration dotted Wesson's forehead, and Smith's face was even redder than it had been a minute earlier. Both of them looked uncomfortable. It was a hot afternoon, and suddenly I realized that I had forgotten to turn my air conditioner on after returning from the hospital.

"Please excuse me for just a moment. I'm going to crank up the air conditioner. Would either of you like an iced tea?"

"That would be great," Wesson said enthusiastically.

Smith looked irritated. "No, thanks," she growled.

I stepped into the kitchen, flipped the switch to turn on the air conditioner, and then filled two glasses with iced tea, adding a slice of lemon to each, before returning to the living room, carrying one of the glasses and a small sugar bowl. After I set the tea and sugar on the oak end table next to Wesson, I retrieved my own glass from the kitchen and rejoined the detectives. My brief absence seemed to annoy Smith even more.

"Now can we get on with it?" she asked, glaring at me. Clearly, the question was merely rhetorical. "You say that you arrived at the scene of the shooting only after seeing the emergency vehicles?"

"That's right."

"Did you happen to notice anybody fleeing the scene?"

"No, but there was already a crowd of neighbors standing around when I got there."

"So you're really not a witness to anything?"

"I never said that I was," I replied.

Smith started to stand, but Wesson restrained her with a pat on her arm, and she sat down again.

"Miss McMillan, did you know Victor Eberhart?" Wesson asked.

"No, I didn't know him personally. I knew who he was, though."

"Because he was president of the homeowners' association?"

"Yes, that and..." Uh, oh. *Maybe I was on the verge of saying more than I should*, I thought.

"Something else?"

"Well, one of my students mentioned him."

"In what context?"

"It was a personal situation."

"Go on."

"She told me something in confidence."

Smith sighed loudly. "You're not a lawyer or a priest, are you? Just what is it you do anyway?" she asked sarcastically.

Although I was taken aback by Smith's tone, I explained my career as the DIY Diva and told her about the classes I taught at the community center. Smith sneered and shook her head.

"Please tell us what your student said about Mr. Eberhart," Wesson prodded gently.

"Okay." I knew Sonya wouldn't appreciate it, but I felt obliged to pass along what she had told me. "She and her husband have been having a very serious dispute with the homeowners' association, one that's probably going to cost them a small fortune. She indicated that Victor was responsible for the problem."

"Did she indicate that she harbored any ill will towards him?" Wesson continued.

"I'm afraid so."

"What did she say, exactly?"

"She said that she could kill him. Actually, she said that she could kill him and Patty, the manager of the HOA, but, honestly, I don't think she meant it literally. She was probably just blowing off steam."

Smith tapped on the keyboard of her laptop as I related the details of Sonya's story. I was sure Sonya would never forgive me for pointing the detectives her way, but, on the other hand, I knew that I should report what she'd said and let the police sort things out. I didn't believe for a moment that Sonya had sought revenge against Victor, but, then again, I really didn't know her very well. Maybe she had been serious. She was certainly furious with both Victor and Patty, and she blamed Victor for the problems she and Tommy were having, including his threat to divorce her. Come to think of it, her husband was every bit as angry as Sonya at Victor, so angry that maybe he'd wanted to kill Victor himself.

"Are you aware of anyone else who may have had a grudge against Mr. Eberhart?" Detective Wesson continued.

"Probably everybody who'd received a citation from the association since he took over as president. He was an unreasonable man. Still, I can't imagine any of the residents here at Hawkeye Haven resorting to violence because of that."

"Have *you* received any citations?" Smith queried in an insinuating manner. The woman really went out of her way to be unpleasant, and she obviously didn't care for me. I couldn't think of any reason for her behavior other than Bear's unwanted deposit of fur on her white linen pants.

"No, I haven't. You can check the association records if you don't believe me," I snapped, out of patience with her. I'd had just about enough of this woman and her snotty attitude.

"You can be sure we'll do that, Miss McMillan," Smith said.

Wesson shot Smith a warning glance. It had occurred to me that maybe the two detectives had been playing good-cop, bad-cop all along, but when I saw the way Wesson frowned at Smith, I decided it was more of a what-you-see-is-what-you-get situation. Wesson seemed to be a genuinely nice guy, but his partner would never be a candidate for Miss Congeniality.

Gulping the rest of his iced tea, Wesson pulled a small notebook out of his pocket and flipped through its pages.

"I believe there's something else I need to check with you," he said, continuing to leaf through the notebook. "Let's see." Smith stared at him impatiently. "Oh, yes, here it is. I thought I remembered seeing your name. According to our reports, you discovered one of the community's security guards after she had been attacked a couple of days ago."

"That's right. She was unconscious when I found her, and her gun had been stolen."

"How do you know it had been stolen?" Smith asked sharply.

"I guess I made the assumption since it wasn't in her holster. She's not in the habit of leaving her weapon lying around."

"Did you notice anyone in the vicinity of the guardhouse?" Wesson queried.

"No, it was early in the morning, and it was pretty quiet. I didn't see anyone."

Wesson closed the notebook, patted Bear, and stood. Thank goodness the interview was over, I thought.

"Well, thank you for your cooperation, Miss McMillan. If you think of anything else that might be of interest to us, please give me a call." He handed me his card, and I nodded. "And thank you for the iced tea. It's always good on a hot day."

"You're welcome." With Bear trailing behind me, I followed the detectives to the front door and closed it behind them before heading down the hallway to the front bedroom, which I used as my project room.

I was startled to hear the detectives' voices, seeming to come from the bedroom, before I realized that I'd left the front windows open earlier.

"Thank you so much for the iced tea, Miss Priss. It's soooo mahhhvelous," Smith mimicked.

I shrank back behind the curtain so that the detectives couldn't see me, but I could certainly hear them.

"Knock it off, Felicia."

"I thought your eyeballs were going to pop right out of your head when you looked at that woman."

"Hey, nothing says I can't appreciate a beautiful redhead."

"Oh, come on, Wes. Beautiful? With that mop of garish red hair? Give me a break! And that dog of hers was disgusting, wiping his fur all over my new white pants."

"Get over it, Felicia."

Their voices drifted away as they walked farther down the sidewalk until I couldn't hear what they were saying any longer.

During the interview, I'd been so intent on answering the detectives' questions that I really hadn't noticed Wesson staring at me, and even though I hadn't done anything wrong, I'd almost felt like a criminal myself, being questioned by the police. It was a nerve-wracking experience for me and one that I hoped I'd never have again. That the detective thought I was beautiful was a surprise to me. My cousin Tracey always said that I was totally clueless when it came to men, and I knew that she was right. The only man I'd ever been totally comfortable with had been my husband Tim.

Since Tim's death, I'd been on only a handful of first dates, none of which had led to a second date. Tracey was constantly trying to set me up with single men she knew from work, but so far, I'd been able to resist her attempts at matchmaking. Maybe my interest should be piqued by Wesson's compliment, even though he hadn't said it to me. He seemed like a nice enough guy, and the tall detective wasn't hard on the eyes himself with his neat, black hair, which was just beginning to turn gray at the temples, and his muscular physique. Oh, well. I'd probably never see him again, anyway, and I wasn't sure that I cared.

Chapter 6

After what was beginning to seem like a very long day, I planned on a quiet evening at home. I tossed a salad together for a quick dinner, fed Bear, settled on the sofa, and picked up the novel my book club had designated as the topic of discussion at our next monthly meeting, but after reading the first few pages and not remembering a thing I'd read, I dozed. The phone was ringing when I felt the book drop onto my lap, and I awoke with a start, feeling a bit disoriented. I shook my head in an attempt to clear it and picked up my cell phone. Liz was calling to invite me to have a glass of wine with her, and she suggested that I bring Bear along so that he could swim in her backyard pool. I checked on the time and told Liz we'd be over in half an hour. I wanted to wait at least an hour after Bear ate before letting him swim. Sometimes dogs, especially big dogs like Bear, suffer from a life-threatening condition called bloat, and my vet had recommended that Bear not exercise for at least an hour both before and after eating.

At the appointed time, I called Liz so that she could unlock the gate to her backyard for us. All the backyards in Hawkeye Haven are walled, and Liz and I share a common wall between our properties. Whenever I take Bear to Liz's house, we always stay outside on the patio, never entering the house. I'd made that almost-fatal mistake the first time I'd visited Liz, and she had innocently invited both me and Bear to come into her home. Unfortunately, her fluffy Persian cat, Miss Muffet, wasn't nearly as hospitable as her mistress, and Bear was hardly the ideal house guest. Bear had taken one look at Miss Muffet before lunging forward, pulling his leash right out of my hand, and tearing down the hallway in pursuit of the terrified cat. Once cornered at the end of the hall, Miss Muffet had yowled piercingly, turned around, and raked one of her front claws across Bear's nose. Startled, he had yelped in pain and jumped back, allowing Miss Muffet to escape. Running past Bear to her kitty haven, she'd climbed out of the big dog's reach. Both Liz and I had stumbled all over ourselves, offering profuse apologies for our animals' bad behavior, but we had learned our lesson. Ever since that day, whenever I brought Bear with me to Liz's house, we stayed strictly outside. We'd often see Miss Muffet watching us warily from her side of the sliding glass patio door, but, thankfully, the glass panel effectively separated the cat from the dog.

Knocking on her backyard gate to alert Liz that we were entering her yard, I opened the gate, keeping a grip on Bear's leash until we were inside, and then I removed the leash along with his collar so that he could jump into the pool. Bear paused a moment to allow Liz to pet him and then ran to the pool, splashed into the water, and began paddling around. Bear loved to swim, and since I didn't have a pool, I appreciated Liz's generosity in allowing him to use hers often. Sometimes I played in the water with Bear, but since I'd come to chat with Liz, Bear had the pool all to himself.

Wearing full make-up as usual, Liz greeted me with air kisses before handing me a glass of Chardonnay. She wore a bright yellow crinkle cotton caftan embellished with crystal beads on its wide neckband, and I noticed that she was wearing a birthday present I had given her—crystal earrings that I had made especially to coordinate with her yellow caftan.

"Liz, you look terrific!" I pronounced, acutely aware that my own preparation for the evening had consisted of nothing more than swiping on some lip gloss and brushing my hair. "No wonder you have an admirer."

"The colonel?"

"Of course, the colonel, unless there's somebody else you've been keeping hidden away." I teased.

"I really like Bobby," she admitted. "He's taking me to Chez Alsace for dinner tomorrow evening," she confided.

"Wow. I hear it's the best French restaurant in town. I wonder how he managed to get a reservation on a Saturday night."

Liz gave me an enigmatic Mona Lisa smile and shrugged. She might have known more than she told me, but she enjoyed a little mystery.

Changing the subject, she said, "Can you believe that it was only last night when we saw Victor at the meeting, and now he's dead? And you know something, I'm ashamed to say this, but I really don't care that he's gone. He was a real jerk, and he caused a lot of problems for a lot of people, and I don't mean just since he became president of the HOA either. His wife was such a good friend to me, and it was just awful the heartless way he treated her and poor Courtney. I heard Courtney was the one who found him."

"Yes, she did. That's what Amy told me. She and Karl Meyer both heard Courtney screaming and rushed over to Victor's house to find out what was wrong."

"I hope Courtney's not a suspect."

"Why do you think she might be?"

"She's never gotten along with her father, not that anyone can blame her for that. After her mom died, she used to visit me fairly often. Sometimes she'd even stay overnight. Victor didn't seem to mind. I think it gave him more time to work and to play golf. Those are the only things he ever acted like he really cared about anyway. I'm worried, though, because Courtney's never made a secret of the way she felt about her father. She's told me on more than one occasion that she wished he were dead, and I'm not the only one she's expressed that wish to."

"Uh, oh. I see what you mean. But do you think she'd be capable of actually murdering her own father?"

"I don't think so, but Courtney's a strange girl. She's always been a little unpredictable, I think. Maybe Victor did or said something that pushed her right over the edge." Liz sighed. "I don't know. Maybe I shouldn't be speculating."

"Well, I guess anything's possible. I don't think the police have arrested anyone yet. A couple of detectives came by to ask me some questions this afternoon, but I don't really know much. I did tell them that Sonya had threatened Victor, but she's certainly not the only person in Hawkeye Haven who held a grudge against him." I paused, thinking again about how angry Sonya would be when she found out I had told the detectives what she'd said about Victor. "Did the detectives stop by your house, too?"

"If they did, I missed them. I just got home a few minutes before I called you. Friday's my day at the hairdresser, you know, and then I had lunch with some of the girls." I knew that "the girls" Liz was talking about were all old friends of hers she'd known for decades. Liz had stayed in touch with former neighbors, too, and she often visited with those who still lived in town. "After that, I shopped till I was about ready to drop."

Liz stopped to pour herself another glass of wine, which she sipped as we both watched Bear swim for several minutes. After he tired of the sport, he emerged from the pool and shook himself mightily. Luckily, we were far enough away from him on the patio that we avoided the deluge. He trotted over to me, and, taking a fluffy towel I had brought with me, I rubbed him vigorously. Thanks to his thick undercoat, he was still damp, but at least he wasn't dripping wet anymore. Bear lay down with his nose across my right foot and was soon in doggie dreamland, but his snooze was interrupted a few minutes later when we heard knocking at Liz's back gate. Bear jumped up, barking, and ran to the gate.

"Hey, there, big boy."

I didn't recognize the voice until I saw Luke standing outside the gate.

"Hi, Luke. Come in." I led him to the patio, and I noticed that Liz had a strange, almost shocked, expression on her face when she saw him. I remembered that just yesterday he had removed her from the HOA meeting on Victor's orders, so I thought maybe that was the reason for the look she was giving him although I also recalled that she hadn't displayed any animosity toward Luke when he'd escorted her out of the meeting room. Odd.

Luke nodded to Liz and said, "I was on my evening rounds in the rover, and I noticed that your garage door was open. I knocked on the front door, but then I heard voices from out here, so I figured you were in the backyard. Just thought I'd check to make sure everything's okay."

It was nice of Luke to give the reason he did for letting Liz know that her garage door was open. (HOA Regulation 86 states that "garage doors must be closed at all times except for ingress/egress or when a member of the household, contractor, or service personnel is working in the garage or on the property.") Luke didn't push the rules at people the way Patty did, and I liked him for that.

"Oh, goodness." Liz's face turned red. "I thought I had closed it. Let me go see to that right now."

"Don't worry, Liz. I'll close it." I volunteered. "Stay, Bear." I definitely didn't want Bear following me into the house. Miss Muffet certainly wouldn't have appreciated her nemesis invading her territory.

When I returned, I was surprised to see Liz chatting with Luke while he showed her some pictures in his wallet.

"You have a beautiful family, Luke," I heard Liz say.

"Thanks, Ms. Dawson. Well, I'd better get back to it." I started to follow him, but he said that he would close the gate, so I sat back down beside Liz, who now had a wistful look on her face. Something was going on, but I had no idea what it was.

I declined Liz's offer of another glass of wine, and she poured herself a third glass.

"Is something wrong, Liz?" I asked. "You seem upset."

Tears rolled down her face, dragging two short trails of black mascara and making little tracks in her perfectly applied make-up. Dabbing at her eyes and cheeks with a cocktail napkin, she sighed deeply.

"He doesn't know it, but Luke's my grandson," she whispered in a tone so low that I almost didn't hear her.

"What?" Although Liz had been married four times, she'd had only one child that I knew of, a somewhat pompous character named Leonard, after his father, Liz's second husband, and, to my knowledge, Leonard and his wife had no children, but I supposed that maybe

Leonard could have had a son with a woman he hadn't married.

"Leonard's boy?" I asked.

"No, Lenny doesn't have any children, but Lenny's not my only son. When I was sixteen, I had a baby, and I gave him up. I never saw him again."

"Oh, Liz, I'm so sorry," I murmured.

Bear had settled himself at my feet once more, the sun had set, and there was something about the warm evening, the darkness, and the wine that seemed to put Liz in the mood to tell me her secret. I had known Liz since I'd moved into the house next door to hers three years earlier, but she'd never before breathed a word about the child she'd given up. As she set down her wine glass and began to speak, we were transported sixty years back in time.

"It was long ago, yet sometimes when I think about it, it seems as though it happened only yesterday. I grew up in an orphanage in Chicago, Laurel. I never knew my parents. It was such an awful place. I was a rambunctious, boisterous kid, and I was always getting into trouble. By the time I was fifteen, I'd had enough. I ran away and never looked back. I hitched a ride with a trucker who was going to Center City, and that's how I came to live in Iowa.

"Of course, I didn't have any money, so I made the rounds of the local restaurants looking for a job, but I didn't have any luck. A service station attendant—nobody pumped their own gas back in those days—found me hiding in the restroom when he was locking up the gas station for the night. To make a long story short, I ended up marrying that boy. I say 'boy' because he wasn't that much older than I was, but we managed to sweet-talk a justice of the peace into marrying us without our having to prove our ages.

"It was great for the first few months, and we had a lot of fun together. Dennis worked at the gas station, and even though he didn't make much money, we were able to rent a tiny apartment. Everything changed when I told him we were expecting a baby. I can still remember how excited I was, and I thought he'd be happy, too, but he wasn't. He didn't say much, but a couple of days later, he disappeared. He left for work and never returned. I don't know what happened to him, but I always thought he couldn't handle the responsibility, and so he walked away. I never saw him or heard from him again."

"You must have been frantic."

"Oh, I was. Not only was I all alone, but the rent on our apartment was due, and I had only enough food to last for a few days. I didn't know anybody in town, except Dennis, and now he was gone, but that wasn't the worst of it. I had no way to support myself, let alone our baby. When I told our landlord what had happened, he wasn't unsympathetic, but he said he couldn't let me stay in the apartment indefinitely because he depended on the rent to support himself.

"He suggested that a home for unwed mothers might take me in, even though I was married, since my husband had deserted me. The landlord was a nice enough old gent, but I could see that my predicament was more than he could handle. He allowed me to stay in the apartment for a while, he bought me some groceries, and he offered to drive me to the home. I really felt that I had no other option, so when Dennis didn't come back after a couple of months, I took the landlord up on his offer.

"The worst thing I've ever done in my life was to give my baby up for adoption, but I wanted him to have what I hadn't—a solid family. The people at the home promised that my baby boy would be adopted by a good family, one that could provide for all his needs.

"Liz, how awful for you!" I exclaimed. "I know it was a horrible decision to have to make."

"Yes, but I really felt I had no choice. Things were so different back then. For one thing, adoption records were sealed. It took me several years to get on my feet, but after I married Lenny's dad, we tried to find out who had adopted my baby, but we didn't have any luck. It wasn't until just a few years ago that I finally found out who had adopted him."

"Where is he now?" I asked.

Choking back tears, Liz whispered, "He's gone. He died in Vietnam during the last year of the war."

"Oh, Liz, I'm so sorry."

"It was a long time ago. Still, I think about him every day, and every day, I regret that I didn't keep him. How could I have been so stupid?"

I patted her arm. "You were trying to do what you thought was best for him at the time."

She shook her head. "I was wrong."

We sat for a long time without speaking, Liz lost in her memories. I knew that nothing I could say would comfort her, but even though her son was lost to her forever, her grandson didn't have to be.

"What about your grandson, Liz? It's not too late to have a relationship with him and his family. I noticed that he was showing you some pictures in his wallet."

"I don't know how he'd feel about it, and I don't want to disrupt his life. He seems like such a nice young man."

"He sure does. I bet he'd welcome the news that he has a grandmother."

"I'm sure that's the last thing on his mind. I don't know what he was told about his dad or whether or not he realized that his father had been an adopted child. In fact, I didn't even know that I had a grandson until a few weeks ago when I read a story in our HOA newsletter about the new head of security for Hawkeye Haven—Luke Johnson—and as soon as I saw his picture next to the story, I knew. He's the spitting image of his grandfather. I almost fainted when I saw that picture. I thought I was looking at a picture of Dennis. Of course, Luke is quite a bit older than Dennis was when he left me, but I just knew he had to be my grandson. Just to be absolutely certain, I hired a private detective, who was more thorough than the others, and, sure enough, I was right."

"Liz, I think you should tell him. I know it's a cliché, but, in this case, it's true: nothing ventured, nothing gained. It's quite a coincidence that he's working right here in Hawkeye Haven, don't you think? Could be an omen."

"Maybe so."

"You missed so much—your son's whole life—but you don't have to miss out on your grandson's life, too."

"I've been telling myself the same thing. What if he hates me?"

"He's not going to hate you."

"Lenny might, especially since I've kept him completely in the dark about his brother. And there's something else—I'm pretty sure Lenny's not going to like sharing his inheritance with someone he never knew existed."

"Hopefully, he can come to accept his brother's son in time." From the little I already knew about Lenny, I was probably engaging in wishful thinking. I was afraid that, no matter what Liz did, somebody was going to be unhappy. Better Lenny than Liz, who had suffered too much and too long, in my opinion.

"Perhaps," she agreed, although I could hear her voice quavering, and I knew that no matter what she decided, her path would be a difficult one.

Chapter 7

Arriving at class with only a few minutes to spare the following morning, I found several women, waiting in the hallway, unable to enter the classroom because the door was locked. The door had always been unlocked each time I'd taught classes, and, since I didn't have a key, I searched the building for someone who could open the door for me. Employees of the HOA management company didn't work on weekends, so at least I didn't have to check with the obnoxious Patty, who would have been quick with a nasty comment if she'd seen me. I checked both the security office and the sales office, but they were locked, too.

Except for me and my waiting students, the building appeared to be empty. I was hoping that I wouldn't have to cancel the class. I decided to check the storage area in the back of the building where the maintenance workers kept their cleaning supplies.

A thin wisp of smoke floated into the hallway through the open door of the storage room, and when I peeked in, I saw a young man wearing jeans and a blue work shirt with his name embroidered on the pocket, sitting on a folding chair, a cigarette in one hand and a can of soda in the other. Startled, he jumped up when he saw me and quickly crushed his cigarette out on the top of the soda can.

"Uh, Kenny?" I said, reading the name embroidered on his shirt.

"Yeah?"

"I'm teaching a class this morning in Room 110, and the door's locked. I wonder if you could open it for me. Class is supposed to start in a few minutes."

"Oh, sure," he mumbled, not meeting my gaze.

He grabbed some keys that were hanging on a peg beside the door and followed me down the hallway to the classroom. Kenny looked embarrassed, probably because I'd caught him smoking in a no-smoking building or maybe because he had forgotten to open the classroom.

There was quite a crowd waiting by the time we reached the classroom, and the students stepped aside when they saw us so that Kenny could unlock the door. I noticed that Cynthia seemed to recognize Kenny, but when she greeted him, he answered her with a grunt and quickly took off down the hallway.

"Hmmm. Isn't he Rachel Casswell's boy?" she asked Amy.

"Looks like him, but I'm not sure," Amy said. "Not too friendly, is he?"

"Teenagers," Cynthia remarked, shaking her head.

As I waited for all the students to push their way through the bottleneck at the door, I scanned my class roster. Although I had glanced at the roster earlier, just to find out how many students had signed up for the class, I hadn't looked at the names. In addition to students like my friends Amy and Cynthia, who attended the DIY earrings classes on a regular basis, a few names appeared that I hadn't expected to see. Alice Sandstrom, for one; Courtney, for another. And Sonya. Each one worried me for a different reason. I was afraid that Mrs. Sandstrom would have difficulty seeing the tiny components that we would be using to make earrings. I remembered that Alice's next-door neighbor, Amber, had confided in me that she thought Alice shouldn't be driving because of her poor vision.

Hopefully, Alice would be sitting at a table with someone who could assist her because, with forty students registered, I probably wouldn't be able to spend more than a few minutes with any one of them.

After giving it some thought, I realized that Courtney had probably registered for the class several days earlier, long before her father had been murdered. I doubted that she would show up. Then there was Sonya. I could only imagine the harsh words she'd have for me if the police had already questioned her, and she'd learned that I'd betrayed her confidence. I didn't relish the idea of having a confrontation with Sonya, especially in front of the class, so, coward that I am, I hoped that the detectives hadn't talked with her yet.

As they filled the room, the students seated themselves, four to a table. I counted the chairs available, and their number exactly matched the number of students enrolled. If everyone who'd enrolled showed up, each student would have a place to sit, but if extra students came at the last minute, I'd have to scramble for more chairs. I had a feeling that Kenny hadn't unlocked any other rooms, which I would have raided for extra chairs. If too many more students showed up, I'd probably have to go find him again, a chore I didn't relish. Putting thoughts of the sulky teenager aside, I set up my samples, distributed kits of jewelry supplies packed in plastic baggies, booted up the computer, and switched on the projector. By the time I was ready to present the project instructions, everyone had found a place to sit. Just four empty chairs remained. So far, so good.

Step-by-step, I explained the simple directions for the first project, advancing my PowerPoint presentation as I showed the students how to assemble their earrings. Then I held up my samples—sterling silver chandeliers with loops of dangling, delicate chain and a drop in the center—for the class to see. I'd made three samples, each with a different drop in the middle so that the students could see how varying the center drop could change the look of the earrings. One pair of earrings featured a sterling silver drop, another featured a pearl drop, and the third featured a red crystal drop. I handed the three sample earrings sets, each to a different student, so that they could examine the project more closely and then pass it on to other students. A couple of latecomers had drifted in during my presentation, but since we still had room for two more students, I began circulating around the room to answer questions and help the students. Although the chain chandelier earring project was a simple one, first-timers needed some assistance with basic techniques. I was demonstrating the correct way to open a jump ring when the door opened, and Sonya rushed in and found a place to sit. Since she didn't have a kit yet, I couldn't ignore her, so I delivered one to her.

"Hi, Sonya. You'll need this kit for the earrings," I said nervously, handing her the packet of earring components.

"Thanks. Sorry I'm late. Can you believe that the cops showed up at my house this morning and implied that I might have had something to do with Victor's death?" she asked without waiting for my reply. "Then, even though Tommy had promised me that he'd watch the kids this morning, he took off when someone from the club called him, needing a fourth for golf. I was finally able to get my neighbor's daughter to babysit at the last minute," she finished breathlessly.

One of her tablemates raised an eyebrow, and a look passed between the other two students at Sonya's table. I wasn't sure what the look signified, but, at least, Sonya hadn't confronted me about sharing her secret with the police detectives.

"Well, I'm glad you were able to find a babysitter," I said, ignoring her remark about the detectives. Even though I thought I had done the right thing by reporting her threat to kill Victor, I still felt guilty about it. Relieved, I continued my rounds.

I was on the opposite side of the room when I learned the reason that Sonya hadn't blamed me for the detectives' visit to her home. I overheard some of her neighbors, including the mother of the high-schooler who was babysitting for Sonya's children, talking about Sonya's dispute with Victor and her husband Tommy's dust-up with Victor in the locker room at the golf course. The women were speculating about whether or not the couple's problem would lead to divorce now that Victor was dead. Evidently I hadn't been the only person Sonya had confided in.

"What difference does it make that Victor's dead?" asked Rhonda Thomkins, a thirtyish blonde who was struggling to slip a jump ring onto a link of delicate sterling silver chain. Her inch-long, fuchsia, gelled nails, each decorated with a single rhinestone, probably didn't make it any easier for her to assemble the earrings.

"Well, you know, it could make a big difference to Sonya and Tommy," Keisha Graves replied, smoothing her wrinkled pink linen blouse. "The HOA might relent now, although I hear that Patty's not too easy to deal with, either. If she'd just okay their project, rather than forcing them to demolish a perfectly good, brand-new swimming pool and playhouse, maybe things would get back to normal around here. Of course, Victor never would have backed down. I don't think anyone will miss that jerk, not even his own daughter. I was his wife's nurse in hospice right at the end, and I've never seen a man behave so callously to a dying woman. He may not have cared whether his wife lived or died, but their daughter, Courtney, was really devastated when she lost her mom, and Victor didn't give her any emotional support at all."

"Poor Courtney and poor Sonya too," commented Abby Petrowski, the mother of Sonya's babysitter. "I wouldn't blame either one of them for wanting to get rid of Victor."

Rhonda gasped. "You don't seriously think Courtney or Sonya could have murdered Victor, do you?"

"As Victor's only child, Courtney will probably inherit everything, and that would be a powerful motive for murder. Victor certainly kept tight control of the purse strings when he was alive. He retired early, so he must have had a lot of money. Until he was elected president of the HOA, he didn't do anything around here except play golf," Keisha volunteered. "As far as Sonya goes, who knows? She was really furious with Victor; that's for sure."

"Shhh," Abby cautioned as she saw Sonya approaching their table. Suddenly the three ladies became quite absorbed in their projects.

"Abby, I was wondering if it would be all right for Lisa to babysit for a couple more hours after class today," Sonya said. "I need to run some errands, and it would be so much easier without dragging the kids along."

"I don't know whether Lisa has anything else planned for this afternoon or not, Sonya. It's fine with me if she wants to stay longer. Why don't you give her a call on your cell?"

"Okay." Sonya pulled her phone from her jeans' pocket, and after a brief conversation, returned it to her pocket.

"We're all set. She said that she can stay, and I told her I'd let you know."

"All right. Thanks, Sonya."

"Crisis averted," Keisha noted in a low voice after Sonya had returned to her seat on the other side of the room. "I don't think she heard us."

"It's a good thing she didn't hear us because any mention of Victor really sets her off," Abby said. "I'm surprised she showed up here today. The way she's acting as though nothing's happened—well, it's a little weird."

"Uh, oh. Look who else just showed up," Rhonda whispered, staring at the classroom door.

A buzz rippled through the classroom as Courtney entered. Several women rushed over to her to offer condolences on her father's death. Urging Courtney to come sit at their table, Cynthia and Amy finally succeeded in shepherding her through the throng and into the classroom. Amy grabbed the only remaining chair from the table where Rhonda, Keisha, and Abby were sitting and dragged it to her table, sandwiching it between her seat and Cynthia's.

"Sit here with us, Courtney," Amy insisted. "There's plenty of room." Everyone at Amy's table shifted her chair to make room for Courtney.

I plucked another kit from my stash and took it to Courtney. The only time I'd met her before had been at a previous DIY Holiday Decorations class the previous November, but I'd certainly heard a lot about Courtney and her troubles in the past day.

"Hi, Courtney. I'm very sorry for your loss," I said awkwardly, setting the project kit on the table in front of her.

"Thank you. I wasn't going to come to class today, but Eva and Karl—I'm staying with them for now— thought maybe it would take my mind off things, so I decided I'd give it a try. I feel like I should be making the funeral arrangements instead of making earrings, but the coroner's office hasn't released my father's body," she murmured, choking back a sob.

"You've had a terrible shock, Courtney, and it's going to be rough going for a while, but I think Eva and Karl are right." Cynthia patted Courtney's arm. "Let me show you what we're working on today."

Cynthia arranged Courtney's silver findings on her grooved bead board and began to explain the first project. Courtney followed along, concentrating on Cynthia's instructions. I admired Cynthia's ability to take charge of the situation. I'd always found it difficult to know what to say to someone who'd just lost a loved one. I knew all too well how difficult it was to be on the receiving end of condolences, too. While Courtney responded well to Cynthia's practical approach, I felt a little guilty about having upset Courtney with my expression of sympathy. Courtney certainly seemed genuinely distressed over her father's death, and I found it hard to believe that she could have had anything to do with his murder. With a grateful parting glance at Cynthia, I drifted back to the other tables, continuing to circle the room.

At the last table on my rounds, I found Alice and Amber, both with several pairs of completed earrings on their bead boards in front of them.

"Hello, ladies," I said. "It looks as though you've been busy."

"Amber's doing all the work," Alice volunteered. "I'm just here to supervise." She laughed at her little joke, and everyone at her table smiled. "Honestly, I don't know how you girls can work with such tiny pieces." She held up her bead board for me to inspect. "Just look at all the earrings Amber's put together for me. I'm going to give all my granddaughters earrings this year for Christmas. Maybe there'll be a little something in Amber's Christmas stocking, too," Alice hinted.

Amber held up her hand. "That's not necessary. It's fun making jewelry, and I'm happy to help."

"We'll see, dear." Alice said, her eyes twinkling.

I was happy to see that Alice was having a good time. I'd had a few students in the past who had become frustrated and even angry when they weren't able to complete their jewelry perfectly on the first try. One woman had even thrown her project on the floor and stomped out of the room. Students' emotional outbursts could easily affect others, and since I aimed for an upbeat atmosphere in the classroom, I could do without the negativity.

Despite my concerns about Courtney, Sonya, and Alice, the class went well, and the time passed quickly. Most of the women wore earrings they had made as they left the room while others held up their earrings for my approval on their way out the door. After the students left, I quickly returned my supplies and extra jewelry kits to my suitcase, turned off the projector, and shut down the computer. Perching my handbag on top of the suitcase, I rolled it out of the room and down the hallway, stopping in the reception area to dig my car keys out of my purse.

Just then, Luke entered the building, carrying a pizza box.

"Lunch," he said, tapping the box.

"Don't let me keep you, Luke. Your pizza will get cold."

"Nope. I already ate the whole thing," he confessed sheepishly. "The box is all that's left. Say, do you have a minute? I'd like to ask you about something."

"Sure."

Luke unlocked his office, dumped the pizza box in his waste basket, pulled out a chair for me, and sat down at his desk.

"I talked to Bessie this morning at the hospital. She should be on her way home by now."

"That's good. When I visited her yesterday, she couldn't wait to get out of there."

"Bessie told me that she's decided to resign. She'll be in Monday to make it official and to drop off her equipment. I thought it might be nice to have a little retirement party for her—you know, let her leave on a positive note. What do you think?"

"That's a great idea, Luke. I know she'd appreciate it. Do you want to have the party on Monday?"

"No, I need a couple of days to plan it. Actually, I was hoping you'd help organize the party. It doesn't need to be anything too elaborate, and we could hold it right here in the meeting room."

"I'd be happy to help."

"Great!" Luke sighed with apparent relief. "If you don't mind, we could check with Bessie about it when she comes in on Monday, and then we'll take it from there."

"Sounds like a plan. By the way, I've been meaning to ask you if there's been any progress in identifying Bessie's attacker. I know she's still struggling to remember exactly what happened, but I thought maybe the cameras by the gate showed the attacker."

"No such luck. Unfortunately, whoever it was managed to get into the guardhouse without being picked up on camera. One of the cameras has a full view of the entering vehicles, and the left side of the guardhouse. Nothing unusual there. The camera on the other side is angled so that it takes pictures of the exiting vehicles' license plate numbers. The perp must have been on foot, sneaking along the right side of the guardhouse, coming from behind the camera there. Most pedestrians would take the sidewalk like you did."

"I'm on the video?"

"Yes, there's a clear picture of you and your dog after you pass the camera and walk to the door of the guardhouse."

"Hmmm. Sounds as though the attacker came from inside Hawkeye Haven, not from outside."

"It certainly looks that way to me."

"It's a scary thought that one of our own would hurt Bessie."

Luke nodded. "And Victor, too, maybe. If I don't miss my guess, Victor was murdered with Bessie's gun."

"What?" I gasped.

"I showed up at Victor's at the same time as the police, and I saw the gun lying on Victor's sidewalk, a few feet from his front door. That weapon was the same model as our guards' standard issue. I told the detectives my hunch and gave them the serial number of Bessie's gun."

"Have they been able to confirm that it was the same gun?"

"I don't know, but they probably wouldn't tell me, even if they had confirmed that it was the same gun. SOP, I imagine." Luke paused, then began waving his arms. "Hey, Kenny," he called, beckoning the teenager, who'd been passing by, pushing a wide broom.

"Yeah?"

"Could you empty the trash cans in the offices when you're done sweeping?"

Kenny grunted in assent and continued on his way.

"Don't want the office smelling like pizza," Luke explained. "The ventilation's not very good in here."

"Or in the storage room? I saw Kenny smoking in there earlier today."

"Figures. I'll be sure to tell him to take it outside. That kid's a pain in the neck. The only reason he's working here is that his mother's a board member. Kenny works hard at doing as little as possible."

"My classroom was locked when I got here this morning, and, at least, he did come to unlock it for me."

"Well, that's good, but he was supposed to have it cleaned and unlocked long before your class started. Typical Kenny." Exasperated, Luke shook his head.

"I'd better be going, but I'll be in touch with you Monday so that we can coordinate the party arrangements."

I left Luke booting up his computer, and as I walked toward the front door, I pulled out my smartphone and started to text my cousin Tracey. I was rolling my suitcase, my handbag still propped atop it, with my left hand, and holding my phone with my right hand while using my right thumb to punch in a quick message to Tracey, who would be returning home this evening. I felt eager to fill her in on all the events of the past few days, events she had missed because she had taken a short trip with her parents, Aunt Ellen and Uncle Bill. Figuring that there was no point worrying her with the crimes that had taken place in Hawkeye Haven while she was out of town, I'd kept my messages to her brief for the past few days. There'd be plenty of time to catch up tomorrow, when the four of us planned to get together.

I was looking down at my cell phone, and I'd almost finished texting when I crashed into a man who was entering the building. As I extricated myself from the man's arms, I looked up and saw Lieutenant Wesson grinning down at me. Guess I'd been wrong when I'd told Liz that I'd probably never see the detective again.

Chapter 8

"Sorry, Lieutenant, I didn't see you."

"Obviously," he chuckled.

Flustered, I could feel a flush sweep over my face.

"Here, let me help you," he offered, stooping to gather up the contents of my tote bag that had spilled when I'd run into him. We scurried around, plucking the scattered items from the floor and dumping them back into my handbag.

"Thanks, Lieutenant Wesson," I said softly, still a bit breathless from the collision.

"Wes. Everybody calls me Wes. It's so much better than Ebenezer."

"What? You're kidding. Your first name's Ebenezer?"

"No. You're right. I'm kidding. It's really Duane, which I hate about as much as I'd hate being called Ebenezer, Miss McMillan."

"Laurel."

"Laurel," he said, smiling. "Were you here to teach a class today?"

"Yes, my monthly DIY Earrings class. The students make several pairs of earrings each time." Now, why had I volunteered that bit of information? Surely the detective wasn't interested in the jewelry that my students made.

"Did you make those earrings you're wearing?"

"Yes, this style was one of today's projects," I said, cupping my hand behind my ear.

"Very pretty," he commented.

He seemed about to say something else when his partner burst through the door.

"What's taking so long, Wes?" Then Detective Smith saw me. "Oh, I see," she grunted, scowling at me. "Can we get going now, lover boy?"

"That's enough, Sergeant," Wesson said evenly. "We still need to pick up those records from the security chief here. Why don't you go get them, and I'll meet you at the car." It seemed more like an order than a request. Irritably, Smith stamped down the hallway towards Luke's office, leaving me alone with Wesson.

"I'm sorry about that, Laurel," he apologized. "Sergeant Smith can be a little abrasive at times."

"I noticed."

"She's a good detective though, very detail-oriented."

I nodded, but just to acknowledge what he'd said. I didn't care how good a detective Smith might be. I didn't like the woman.

"Since I've run into you—literally—" he said, grinning at his little joke, "I would like to double-check with you about what you saw Wednesday morning." Our conversation had turned from light-hearted to serious in a split second, and, even though I hadn't committed any crimes, the same odd, guilty feeling came over me as I'd had yesterday when the detectives had first questioned me.

"Okay," I agreed.

"It's more important than ever to find out as much as possible about the attack on the security guard."

"Because her gun was used to murder Victor?"

"I didn't say that."

"But it was the same gun, wasn't it?"

Wesson frowned. "I really can't comment on the investigation. Now, I know you told us yesterday that you didn't see anyone in the vicinity of the guardhouse before you discovered that the guard had been attacked. In retrospect, are you absolutely sure?"

"I'm sure."

"What about after you found her?"

"Well, let's see. After I called 9-1-1, an ambulance, the firefighters, and the police all showed up. So did Luke, our head of security, and then a couple of residents drove up to the gate from outside. Luke asked them to go around to the front gate, so they left. I didn't really notice whether or not any vehicles drove out of Hawkeye Haven, but wouldn't they show up on camera, anyway?"

"No pedestrians hanging around, maybe out of camera range?"

I shook my head. "No, not that I noticed, but I was too worried about Bessie to pay much attention."

"All right."

"Sorry I couldn't be more help."

"There's one more thing. Why didn't you mention that Victor Eberhart had been threatened at Thursday night's HOA meeting?" Just as my guilty feeling had begun to subside, it popped up again. Wesson seemed to be implying that I had deliberately neglected to tell the detectives about important information.

"I don't think there was any threat," I said sharply.

"Other residents told us that Colonel Gable said that Eberhart would regret his actions," Wesson persisted.

"Yes, but he didn't mean it as a physical threat. He was just venting during the meeting because he thought Victor was being unreasonable to mandate the height of the colonel's flagpole. Colonel Gable's a war veteran, and he's very patriotic. Anyway, I talked with the colonel after the meeting, and he said that he planned to let his lawyer handle the situation."

"Did anyone else hear what he said?"

"Yes, my friend Liz Dawson was there, too. She heard him."

"She'll confirm that?"

"I know she'll confirm that the colonel said he'd let his lawyer handle it because that's exactly what happened," I snapped. Wesson was beginning to irritate me as much as his partner.

"All right, Laurel. Please understand that I'm just doing my job. You may know these people or think you know them, but I need to check and confirm all the information we receive."

Now I felt as though the detective were giving me a lecture. I could feel my face turning red again, the second time in only a few minutes. The same man who'd flustered me earlier infuriated me now.

"If that's all you want, I'll be going," I announced and, fuming, I flew out the front door without waiting for his reply. I could hear him calling good-bye, but I didn't acknowledge it.

That went well, I told myself sarcastically, as I stowed my suitcase in my trunk and headed for home, still angry with Wesson for making me feel like a fool. Although I couldn't deny my growing attraction to him, the detective had implied that I'd been less than honest when he and his partner had interviewed me the first time, and I didn't appreciate it.

My anger with the detective dissipated the second Bear greeted me at the door, holding his hard rubber ball in his mouth and dancing around me excitedly. Clearly, it was doggie playtime, but I had no idea when he'd sneaked the ball out of his toy box. He knew he was supposed to play fetch outside.

"Bear, no playing ball in the house," I scolded mildly, but it was impossible to be cross with my playful Lab, especially as he raced eagerly toward the patio door. I followed him onto the patio, and he whipped his head toward me, tossing the ball at my feet. Ready for his favorite retriever game, he ran to the far side of the yard and waited for me to throw him the ball. Obliging him, I tossed it his way, and he ran to fetch it, then joyfully loped toward me. After a brief tug-of-war, he allowed me to take the ball from him, and we continued the game until I tired of it. Not surprisingly, I was always the one who tired of it first; Bear probably could have gone on chasing the ball for hours, but I hadn't eaten anything all day except a microwaved frozen waffle, and I was hungry.

Rummaging in my almost-bare refrigerator netted a couple of frozen pizzas, some deli tuna salad that was long past its prime, and the package of frozen waffles I'd opened for breakfast. Not counting numerous condiments, iced tea, and bottled water. I always had plenty of those on hand. What I frequently didn't have was much real food. Unlike my mom, my aunt, and my cousin Tracey, I hadn't inherited the family cooking gene. I tossed the past-its-prime tuna salad into the garbage disposal, threw away the container, and popped one of the frozen pizzas in the oven. Still panting from his exercise, Bear followed me hopefully around the kitchen, but I made him wait until the pizza had baked before giving him a couple of carrot sticks and a slice of an apple. After downing half the pizza in record time, I wrapped the rest in foil and stowed it in the refrigerator for dinner.

Realizing that I'd been so frazzled that I'd forgotten to text Tracey after my run-in with Wesson, I fished my cell phone out of my purse and quickly sent her a message asking when she expected to arrive home. Tracey had taken a few days off work to join her parents, Aunt Ellen and Uncle Bill, on a short trip to the Ozarks, ending in Branson, Missouri, where my uncle planned to finalize arrangements with the owner of the

Show-Me Gallery to represent his wood carvings. Like my parents, Aunt Ellen and Uncle Bill lived in Seattle and had been none too happy when their only daughter had moved to Iowa, but frequent trips back and forth had mollified them somewhat. Knowing that the trio would be sightseeing most of the time, I'd kept my texts to Tracey short and benign, mentioning only that I'd catch her up on all the community happenings when they arrived home.

An hour after I texted Tracey, my phone beeped, signaling the arrival of a text message. Texting from the art gallery, Tracey said that she and her parents planned to go to an early dinner with the gallery's owner before driving back to Center City in the evening. They wouldn't arrive at Tracey's house until after midnight, and Tracey suggested that we all go out to a Sunday champagne brunch the next day. I agreed to meet them at Tracey's around noon. I was eager to see my aunt and uncle and to find out more about Uncle Bill's burgeoning artistic endeavors.

I didn't plan to tell Aunt Ellen and Uncle Bill about the crime wave in Hawkeye Haven, especially since I knew the news would undoubtedly upset them. They had always contended that their little girl Tracey and I should never have moved away from Seattle. In fact, I planned to tell Tracey what had happened in Hawkeye Haven while she and her parents had vacationed, and, hopefully, we could keep them from listening to the local news so that they wouldn't find out. The last thing Tracey and I needed was more urging to leave Center City and move back to Seattle. I was sure that Victor's murderer had targeted him specifically, so I doubted that Tracey and I were in any real danger. I really didn't think there was a serial killer running around loose in Hawkeye Haven.

However, the attack on Bessie puzzled me, but the possibility that Bessie's gun had been the weapon used to kill Victor puzzled me even more.

If my aunt and uncle found out about the attacks, they were bound to be horrified. If possible, I wanted to make sure that didn't happen.

Chapter 9

Promptly at noon the next day, I parked in front of Tracey's house, but before I reached the front sidewalk, Aunt Ellen burst from the front door and ran to greet me. Her enthusiastic bear hug all but knocked the wind out of me. Aunt Ellen is a physically strong woman who teaches exercise classes and lifts weights for fun in her spare time.

"Great to see you, Aunt Ellen," I said when she released me from the bone-crushing greeting. "How long has it been?"

"Laurel McMillan, you know darn well it's been over a year since we've seen you."

"Yes, it's been too long," I agreed. I didn't dare tell her how much I missed being close to my parents and all my other relatives and friends who still live in Seattle. She and my mother are sisters, and when it comes to nagging their children, they're both champs. They never tire of telling Tracey and me that we should move back to Seattle. Despite how often I yearned for Seattle, I felt enough at home in Center City to want to stay, and whenever I visited Seattle, my heart broke all over again, remembering Tim and our life together there. *No*, I thought, putting distance between Seattle and me felt like the right thing to do.

I'd barely recovered from Aunt Ellen's crushing hug when Uncle Bill appeared and enveloped me in another.

"Laurel, we've missed you."

"I've missed you, too, Uncle Bill. How've you been?"

"Great!" he boomed. Uncle Bill had never been known as the shy, retiring type. "Tracey, are you ready to go yet?" he yelled.

"In a minute, Dad!" Tracey called.

"Laurel, why don't you see if you can hurry her up?" Uncle Bill suggested.

"Sure." I tapped on Tracey's bedroom door. "Trace?"

"Almost ready. I just need to find my necklace." Tracey rummaged in the carved wooden jewelry box on the top of her dresser. "Dad gets so impatient whenever we're going out to eat. You'd think he never ate anything at home." Of course, we both knew that was far from the truth.

"Here's what I've been looking for, but I can't get the chain untangled," Tracey exclaimed, holding up a delicate gold-chain necklace bearing a tiny initial *T* pendant. "Mom gave me this necklace for Christmas last year, and I'm sure she'd like to see me wear it."

"Here, let me see." I held out my hand, and Tracey gave me the necklace. I worked at untangling the chain while Tracey fluffed her long, blonde hair and tucked a curl behind her ear.

"There, got it," I said, handing her the necklace.

"Tracey!" her dad bellowed. "We're going to leave without you!" I grinned because it reminded me of when we were teenagers. Uncle Bill was the same impatient guy he had always been, but beneath the bluster, everyone in his family knew that he was just a great big softie.

I put my hand on Tracey's arm and motioned for her not to leave.

"Just one more minute, Dad; I'm almost ready," Tracey called.

"Uh, Tracey, I have an idea," I said. "You won't believe what's happened here in Hawkeye Haven since you left for your trip, but if your parents find out about it, I know it will upset them. Maybe we can keep them from hearing about it. I need to tell you what you've missed, but it might be better if you can keep them from watching the local news tonight. I know they have an early flight in the morning, so they're not likely to watch the late news before you take them to the airport."

"Good grief, Laurel! Hawkeye Haven made the news? What's going on?"

"Tracey!" Uncle Bill hollered again.

"Tell you what. Why don't I fill you in after brunch? I know Aunt Ellen and Uncle Bill want to see that new sci-fi movie that's playing at the mall, and we can talk while they're at the show."

"Okay, I can't wait to hear what's happened, but we'd better go now before Dad has a cow," Tracey said. "Coming!" she yelled, almost as loudly as her father. *The old cliché that the apple doesn't fall far from the tree might apply*, I thought.

"You look lovely, dear," Aunt Ellen told Tracey, as we stepped into the living room. "You too, Laurel. Such a pretty sundress. You girls don't look a bit older than you did in high school."

Aunt Ellen dabbed her eyes with a tissue, and realizing that twenty years had passed since our high school graduation, I felt a little bit misty myself, thinking about all that had happened in those twenty years and how Tracey and I had come to live more than a thousand miles away from the rest of our family.

Oblivious to nostalgia, Uncle Bill urged, "Let's get this show on the road, girls. Who's driving?"

"I'll drive," I volunteered. "The restaurant's not too far from here, and it's right in the mall, so you won't have far to go for your movie. We'll be there in a few minutes. You'll like the buffet, Uncle Bill. There's plenty of variety."

Although Aunt Ellen's a gourmet cook, she's also very strict about portion control, and, despite Uncle Bill's protests, she manages to keep him on a diet most of the time. Today wouldn't be one of those times, however. Luckily, we didn't have to wait in line when we arrived at the buffet, and Uncle Bill took off toward the ample food display without bothering to wait until our server took our drink orders. Aunt Ellen shook her head in mock disbelief, and we all laughed.

Between Uncle Bill's frequent trips to sample new dishes, he managed to tell me that he'd successfully placed his carved wooden sculptures with the Show-Me Gallery in Branson. Only a few months after he'd retired from the King County Assessor's Office, he had launched a second career, one that gave him the opportunity to concentrate on his artistic talent.

"Uncle Bill, we're proud of you," I observed. "I hear that the Show-Me Gallery is one of the most prestigious in the country."

"I've been lucky. Des, the owner, happened to see some of my sculptures at the Seahawk Gallery when he was visiting Seattle a couple of months ago. He actually contacted me." Modest as always, Uncle Bill sounded amazed by his good fortune. "He told me that I should have an artist's website, and I agreed with him, but, to tell you the truth, I don't have a clue how to set up a website. I guess I'll look into hiring a web designer after we get back home."

"Dad, don't pay someone to set up your site. I can do it for you," Tracey volunteered.

"Really? You can do that?" Aunt Ellen seemed surprised.

"Sure, no problem. I helped Laurel with her site, didn't I, Laurel?"

"Yes, you really did the lion's share of the work. I never could have done it without you. My agent even refers her other clients to my *DIY Diva* site as an example of the way an author's website should work."

"Great!" Uncle Bill exclaimed enthusiastically. "That's a load off my mind." He quickly changed the subject. "Time for dessert, girls." I wouldn't have been surprised to see Uncle Bill rub his hands together in glee.

"Go easy on the sweets, Bill," Aunt Ellen cautioned.

"Awww, Ellen, just this once. After all, how often do we eat at a buffet?"

Aunt Ellen sighed. "Well, maybe just this once."

Aunt Ellen sipped her coffee in resignation while Uncle Bill proceeded to devour a couple of platefuls of goodies, but her eyes lit up when he finally suggested that it was time to leave for the movie. *Perfect*, I thought. Now I'd have the chance to tell Tracey about Victor's murder and the attack on Bessie.

"How about it, girls? You like science fiction, don't you?" Aunt Ellen asked.

"Sometimes, Mom, but Laurel and I want to browse through the shops in the mall for a while. Why don't we meet you and Daddy after the movie at the south elevator to the parking garage?"

"Okay, see you later," Uncle Bill said.

Tracey and I headed for the shops while her parents hurried toward the mall's cine-plex. We found an empty bench in the middle of the mall, and I hurriedly told Tracey about what had happened in Hawkeye Haven while she and her parents had been touring the Ozarks.

"I can't believe there was a murder in Hawkeye Haven only half a block from my house! That's really scary. No wonder you didn't want to tell Mom and Dad.

They'd freak out for sure. They've always been so overprotective."

"I know. Whenever they visit, I feel as though we're kids back in Seattle again."

"They're always trying to talk us into moving back, and I might even consider that someday, but now's just not the right time for me."

"I don't think I'd ever move back—too many memories."

"Laurel, you can't let Tim's death keep you from moving on with your own life. You know Tim wouldn't have wanted that."

"I've moved on," I sighed.

"Sure you have. That's why you haven't dated since the accident."

"I have so," I protested.

"A handful of first dates doesn't count."

"I guess, but I just don't seem to meet anyone I'd want to date."

"Of course not. You hang out with women all the time. Why don't you try online dating? My friend Kara met her husband on *romance.com*. Maybe you should try it."

"I don't know," I said uncertainly. "I'll think about it," I added, mainly to keep Tracey at bay. I love her to death, but once she makes up her mind about something, she's as persistent as a bull dog. "Anyway, I met someone this week."

"Laurel McMillan," Tracey said, sounding just like her mother, "you've been holding out on me."

"No, it's just that with everything else going on, well…."

"So, give. Who is he and where did you meet him?"

"He's a police detective. He and his partner came to the house after Victor was murdered. I think they questioned everybody who showed up at the murder scene. He seemed like a nice man then, but yesterday I ran into him at the community center, and he acted as though he suspected me of something. He made me mad."

"Well, at least you had a reaction. You felt something."

"I doubt that I'll see him again."

"You like him. Don't deny it."

"Okay, so I like him." I added glumly, "I guess."

"And he likes you?"

"He said I was a beautiful woman."

"He told you that?"

"No, I overheard him tell his partner that he thought I was beautiful."

"Laurel, I have the feeling that you're going to see your cop again. I bet he asks you out."

"Maybe," I said weakly. I couldn't work up much enthusiasm over the prospect. "Let's go down to Ultimate Beauty while we're here," I said, changing the subject. I didn't want to think about Wesson and his maddening ways anymore. "I need to buy sunscreen."

"Okay, I'm about out of that lavender body scrub I like, and I know they carry it."

We vacated our seats on the bench and headed down the mall toward Ultimate Beauty. Fifteen minutes later and a hundred dollars lighter, we emerged carrying our packages. As we slowly walked back down the mall, we stopped to gaze in the windows of the high-end boutiques, jewelry stores, and gift shops. Inspired by designer creations, I frequently come up with my own DIY versions of pricey items. So far, my *DIY Diva* book series included fashion, jewelry, and home decorating topics, and although I could always add many more project books on those subjects, I thought branching out with a DIY project book for dog lovers might be a good idea. With millions of pet parents as crazy about their furry companions as I am about Bear, I hoped that *DIY for Dog Lovers* would sell well.

"Isn't that Karl over there?" Tracey asked as we brushed past a kiosk vendor offering perfume samples. "It is," she confirmed as the man turned around. Karl, trailed by Cynthia and her husband Pete, spotted us, waved, and came over to greet us.

"Fancy meeting you here," Cynthia said.

"We came to the champagne buffet with Tracey's parents. They're visiting from Seattle, and right now they're at a movie, so we decided to shop while we're waiting for them."

"We just came from the buffet ourselves," Karl said, patting his ample stomach. "As usual, I ate too much, but at least we got eighteen holes in before we came over."

Pete nodded. "Great day for it," he commented.

"Karl, Laurel told me that Courtney's staying with you and Eva," Tracey said. "It was so nice of you to offer to let her stay with you."

"Glad we could help. The poor kid's had such a shock. We invited her to come with us today, but she wanted to stay home with Eva."

"How is Eva?" Tracey asked. "I used to see her at the community center once in a while, but I haven't seen her for a long time." Obviously Tracey didn't realize that Eva's agoraphobia had worsened.

"I'm afraid she doesn't go out at all anymore. Hasn't for at least a year now."

"Such a shame," Cynthia murmured.

"Her choice. I hired a therapist to come to the house to see her once a week, but half the time, she won't even answer the door when the lady comes. It's frustrating, but I really don't know what else to do."

"That's too bad, Karl. I'm sorry. I didn't realize..." Tracey said awkwardly. There was a moment of silence all around as we reflected on Eva's plight. Pete shuffled his feet and cleared his throat.

Cynthia finally broke the silence. "I had a visit from two Center City detectives investigating Victor's murder. They wanted to know who might have had a grudge against him. Unfortunately, there are a lot of people in Hawkeye Haven who had good reason to hate Victor. Maybe even Courtney."

"You didn't tell them that Courtney hated her father, did you, Cynthia?" Karl asked, looking stricken.

"She didn't hate him, Karl, but he certainly wasn't very nice to her. That's what I told the police."

"I just don't want the police getting some harebrained idea that Courtney killed her own father. When they questioned her, I thought they were being pretty rough on her. After all, the poor kid had just come home from work when she found him. I was outside watering the roses, and I heard her scream only a few seconds after she got out of her car. Even if she'd wanted to shoot him, she couldn't possibly have had time to do it, and that's what I told the cops."

"No telling how long Victor'd been lying there. With the courtyard wall hiding the front door the way it does on Victor's house, there's no way anyone could have seen anything from the street," Pete noted.

"That's true. I didn't see a thing, and I was right across the street," Karl agreed.

"And I didn't see anything either, even though I was having my coffee in the living room, and I can see Victor's house from the front bay window. I didn't know anything was wrong until I heard sirens," Cynthia said.

"I followed the firefighters and police down your street when I heard the sirens. A crowd had gathered, and that's when I saw Cynthia and Amy," I added.

"I didn't hear a thing," Pete noted. "I slept through it all. When Cynthia got home from her golf game, she told me that Victor had been murdered. She could have knocked me over with a feather. I was that shocked. I always thought we lived in the safest place in town."

"Anybody have any idea who might have killed Victor?" Tracey asked.

"My money's on Sonya's husband," Pete said. "I was in the locker room at the golf course when Tommy overheard Victor bragging about how he was going to make Sonya and Tommy rip their pool out and start all over if they wanted to have a swimming pool. Believe me, Tommy was plenty steamed. A couple of other guys and I had to drag Tommy out of there before he clocked Victor, but Victor just laughed at him. Naturally, that made Tommy even angrier."

"I don't know who did it, but I just don't like the idea that some of our neighbors think Courtney's a killer," Karl said. "People should mind their own business, especially when they don't know what they're talking about. Courtney may act a little flaky sometimes, but she's basically a good kid."

"Karl, she may be a suspect because of the financial angle since she's Victor's only heir. That would give her a motive to kill her father, wouldn't it?" Cynthia asked.

"Cynthia, not you too," Karl protested. "You can't seriously believe that Courtney had anything to do with her father's murder. I told you she'd only just arrived home from working all night at the canning factory. Even if she'd wanted to kill him, she didn't have time."

"You're right, Karl," Cynthia agreed, "and I don't think Courtney's capable of killing anyone myself. I'm just playing devil's advocate. She does have a motive, but, as you say, she didn't have time to shoot Victor. What is it they say on those true crime shows—motive, means, and opportunity? Anyway, I hope the police can sort it out. As Pete said, we always felt so safe in Hawkeye Haven. I never used to lock our doors, but since the attack on the security guard and Victor's murder, you'd better believe that I make sure all our doors and windows are locked."

"What do you think, Laurel?" Tracey asked.

"I don't know, but I'd hate to think that one of our neighbors could actually be a murderer." I hadn't told anyone else what Luke had revealed about Bessie's gun, not even Tracey. Somehow I didn't think that Luke intended that information to become public knowledge, and perhaps he regretted confiding in me.

"We should probably get going, Tracey. Aunt Ellen and Uncle Bill should be meeting us in about five minutes."

"Yeah, Dad will be anxious to get back home in time to watch the Seahawks play a pre-season game. You know how impatient he can get sometimes."

"And how," I agreed.

Chapter 10

Aunt Ellen and Uncle Bill were waiting by the door to the parking garage when we spotted them. As it turned out, Uncle Bill didn't want to miss the kickoff of the Seahawks' game, so we wasted no time in returning home.

When we arrived back at Tracey's house, I said my good-byes to my aunt and uncle. I knew Bear would be eagerly awaiting my arrival so that he could have his dinner. Since I'd never been much of a football fan, watching the game didn't appeal to me. When Tracey accompanied me to my car, she told me that it was a good thing the game would be starting in a few minutes because, otherwise, her parents would have wanted to watch the early evening news, and there was sure to be another report about the murder in our guard-gated community.

Satisfied that there was little likelihood that Tracey's parents would find out about it, especially since they had an early flight in the morning, I headed for home, feeling a bit deceptive, but rationalizing that keeping the news of the crimes from my aunt and uncle would prevent them from worrying unnecessarily. Of course, neither Tracey nor I would ever hear the end of it if our relatives found out that there'd been a murder only half a block from Tracey's house. We'd both endured more than enough nagging about our possible return to Seattle since we'd moved to Center City, and since neither of us had any intention of returning there to live, we'd just as soon avoid listening to more pleas to come back home.

Bear was beside himself with anticipation when I arrived home. He bounced around the kitchen as I prepared his long-awaited meal, and when I set his bowl on his personalized placemat next to the refrigerator, he gulped his dinner down in less than a minute. Wagging his tail, he came over to me for his dessert—a couple of the peanut butter treats he likes so much. I tossed them to him, one at a time, and he quickly ate them.

"Let's go outside, Bear," I said, sliding the patio door open. I sat on a comfortable lawn chair on the patio, Bear lounging beside me, and thought about some of the projects that I could include in my *DIY for Dog Lovers* book.

"Stay, Bear," I commanded, as I went inside to grab my portfolio, where I kept my project notes. Returning to my chair on the patio, I noticed that Bear hadn't moved at all. In fact, he looked as though he'd be napping any second.

I made a mental note to call my agent, Jenna, in the morning to discuss the book with her. It didn't make sense to do any more work on it if she thought that there wouldn't be a market for it. From the little research I'd done so far, I thought it was a viable project, but Jenna has far more expertise than I do, so I needed to consult her. I rummaged through my notes, which I had to admit weren't very organized. If and when Jenna gave me the go-ahead on the book, I'd transfer all the bits and pieces of information I'd gathered, along with my ideas and project instructions, to my computer right away.

Leafing through the odds and ends of paper with ideas scribbled on them, I found that I didn't have nearly as much material as I had thought. That could be a good thing if my agent didn't like my *DIY for Dog Lovers* book idea, or it could be a bad thing because I'd need to gather a lot more information and come up with several more projects if Jenna thought that she could sell the book. Quickly, I numbered the lines on a sheet of paper from my notebook and began listing the projects that I was fairly confident I could put together, along with the instructions for making each project.

Each project would require a finished sample, which the publisher would arrange to have photographed by a top-notch professional. Thank goodness I didn't have to provide photographs of any of the projects for my books, or my DIY Diva career might never have gotten off the ground! In the early years when I'd first started my blog, I'd never taken my own pictures of the DIY projects I had created, but I'd been very fortunate to have a good friend in Seattle who is a wonderful photographer, and she had offered to take the pictures for me to post on my blog. In return, I had made several pieces of jewelry for her, and our barter system had enabled me to launch my career. After I moved to Center City, I learned to take my own photos, out of necessity. Although I'd never win any prizes for photography, my pictures served their purpose as illustrations for projects I posted on my blog or PowerPoint slides for my class presentations.

Writing project instructions came easily to me by this point because I'd done hundreds of them for my books and classes, so that was no problem, but glancing at my list, I saw that I had only ten projects that I definitely felt comfortable with. I'd need about fifteen more for the type of DIY book I usually write. Hmmmm. Recipes for dog treats were always good. I needed to have more of those, and I needed to remember to ask Bessie about hers. My cousin Lynn fed Barkley, her beagle, little round dog treats that she made of pumpkin, but I didn't know what any of the other ingredients were.

While I was thinking about it, I grabbed my smartphone and texted Lynn, asking for the recipe. A few seconds after I sent my text, my phone beeped, signaling an incoming message. Although she was at the park with her husband Sam, her five-month-old daughter, Emma, and Barkley, she promised to email me the recipe as soon as they returned home. I smiled. My relatives and friends were the best. They'd always supported me in my work, and they frequently contributed a few projects, gave me feedback, and even helped test some of my instructions at times.

I thought about a few ways to get some more inspiration for new projects. Tomorrow I could tour the local big-box pet stores and pet boutiques, and maybe browse through some specialty dog magazines at the library or bookstore, but before I made my rounds, I'd definitely call Jenna.

With my concentration on the new book, I'd almost forgotten that I had something else to do tomorrow. Bessie would be coming in to Luke's office to turn in her equipment, and he'd be checking with her to find out whether she'd like to have a retirement party. Maybe I should be there, too. If Bessie liked the party idea, I could get some names of people she'd like to invite, and I could also ask her about the recipe for the dog treats that she'd given Bear every morning. I hoped she would go along with the party idea. After putting in ten years at Hawkeye Haven in a job that didn't provide many kudos, she deserved some recognition.

After concentrating on my to-do list for a while, I became aware of a low murmur of conversation, occasionally punctuated by laughter, which was coming from the backyard next door. Despite the separation of all the backyards in Hawkeye Haven by walls that are six feet high, sounds carry, and although I couldn't hear what they were saying, I recognized the voices as Liz's and the colonel's. *Good*, I thought. Their romance was blossoming. I wished I'd had a chance to ask Liz about the date she'd had last night with the colonel—or Bobby, as she preferred to call him—but I never call Liz before noon because she likes to sleep late, sometimes really late, and I wouldn't want to disturb her. Tomorrow I'd satisfy my curiosity and find out all the details. That resolution was another item to add to my list of things to do tomorrow. The longer I sat outside in my lawn chair with my sleeping dog snoring softly beside me and allowed my mind to wander, the longer my list grew. I finally decided my list was long enough, and after rousing Bear, I went inside to watch an old movie on TV while Bear continued his snooze on the bed I'd made for him, which sat next to the sofa in the den. Like Scarlett O'Hara, I wouldn't bother to think about anything else until tomorrow.

The next day, right after my early morning walk with Bear, I fortified myself with a cup of coffee and phoned my agent. Although the time in Center City was only 6:30 a.m., it was an hour later in New York, where my agent lives, and since she usually arrives at work fairly early, there was a good chance I'd catch her in the office. Sure enough, Jenna answered the phone herself, and I was delighted when she approved of my *DIY for Dog Lovers* book idea. Now I'd really have to get to work on it because Jenna wanted to see an introduction and a list of the projects that I proposed to include in the book, and she wanted it in two weeks. That didn't give me much time to come up with ten or fifteen more projects, so I decided to run over to the library, a pet boutique, and one of the giant pet stores in search of inspiration. I quickly showered and dressed before grabbing my bag and keys and heading out the door.

"Stay home and be a good boy, Bear," I instructed, as my big, furry Lab looked at me with sad brown eyes. If Bear had his way, I'd never leave him alone. His cheerless look had its desired effect on me, and I promised him that Mommy would bring him a doggie treat from the Paw-tisserie, a bakery that specialized in treats for pets. What a pushover I am for my pet! *That's a plus,* I thought, because lots of other people must feel the same way, and that meant that there would be a good market for my book.

In my enthusiasm to garner inspiration, I'd forgotten that Pets-R-Us didn't open until nine o'clock, and the Paw-tisserie, as well as the local branch of the library, opened an hour later. I didn't want to go home and get Bear all stirred up, only to leave again, so I pulled into a Starbucks drive-thru line. I might as well have another cup of coffee while I waited, I reasoned, but the line was even longer than I'd realized, and it was obvious that I'd be there for a while.

With time to kill, I phoned Luke to find out whether he knew what time Bessie was planning to drop by his office. I wanted to see her, if possible, especially because I was afraid that she might tell Luke that she didn't want to have a going-away party, and maybe I could persuade her that it would be fun. I wanted her to leave with dignity, her head held high, rather than disappearing without any fanfare. I knew she felt embarrassed about having been caught by surprise when she was attacked, but it could have happened to anyone, even a much younger and stronger guard. Luke didn't answer his office phone, and I didn't have his cell number, so I left a voice mail asking him to call me.

Slowly the line of cars moved forward, and I finally picked up my caramel macchiato grande. I set it carefully in the cup holder and drove across the parking lot to Pets-R-Us, where I parked and sipped my coffee until I saw that the small group of people gathered at the front door had begun to file into the store.

Depositing my cup in the trash can next to the entrance of Pets-R-Us, I followed the crowd inside and began wandering up and down the aisles. Dog beds, dog toys, dog apparel—these items all held appeal. I knew that I could design some cute dog beds, maybe one with appliqués and another with an attached pillow. As for dog toys, my experience with Bear had shown me that many of them just weren't too sturdy, especially for big dogs like Bear, who invariably destroyed any stuffed toys within a few minutes, but I thought that some type of very sturdy pull toy might work. Bear loves to play tug-of-war with a knotted rope.

Bear would never wear a coat. He loves cold weather, and with his thick undercoat, he doesn't need the extra coverage, but smaller dogs with thinner coats might wear a cute rain slicker or a coat decorated with faux fur. I tapped a few quick notes into my smartphone and emailed them to myself, just so that I wouldn't forget any of my ideas.

My next stop was the Paw-tisserie, a bakery that featured "Tasty Treats for Precious Pets," according to the large banner that hung over the glass counters, which were brimming with enticing snacks for dogs and cats. I bought Bear a few treats and browsed around the store. Treats containing apples seemed to be popular, so I decided to add apple treats to my list of possible projects. I'd need to either create a recipe myself, which probably wasn't going to happen, or I could ask Tracey to come up with one. My BFF was a genius in the kitchen, and she enjoyed experimenting and creating new recipes. Bear and I both really liked the yam chips that Tracey often made, but she hadn't had much time lately to bake.

In addition to all the goodies for canine companions, the Paw-tisserie was featuring Halloween costumes for pets. Although the pet parents undoubtedly enjoyed the costumes more than their pets did, I thought they were cute and appealing, and I knew that I could easily design a few Halloween and other seasonal canine costumes to include in my book.

Tucking Bear's snacks into my handbag, I headed for the nearest branch of the Center City Library, where I perused a magazine about dogs. One article concerned a backpacking trip the author had taken with his dog. A photograph of the two showed both of them wearing backpacks. The picture gave me the inspiration for a type of a carrier that a medium or large dog could wear with pouches for water bottles and toys or other items to take along on a walk.

My list of possible project ideas had expanded considerably, and I was pleased that my morning had been productive. Although I never copied anybody else's design, I often could find inspiration by looking at items currently being sold in retail stores, and my strategy was proving just as effective for DIY projects for dogs as it had for DIY fashion and home decorating projects in the past.

Arriving home, I could hear Bear barking as I exited my car and opened the door that led from the garage into the hallway. Bear rushed to greet me, and I reached down to pet him and tell him that he was a good boy. Panting, he ran to the back patio door, and I knew I couldn't escape playing a game of fetch-the-ball with him. We went into the backyard, where I found his ball lying on the patio and threw it across the yard for him to chase. He brought it back and hurled it to me with a toss of his head. After about fifteen minutes of nonstop play, I'd had enough, and I signaled to Bear to come inside with me so that I could have lunch and he could have a snack.

Dumping some bagged, prepared salad mix into a bowl, I added a chopped apple, some dried cranberries, and a few almonds to the mix before dotting the top with raspberry walnut salad dressing. I stowed the bowl of salad in the refrigerator until Bear had cooled down and stopped panting. Then I delighted him by giving him a couple of the treats I'd purchased at the Paw-tisserie before I ate my salad while scrutinizing my project list and categorizing the various projects. I now had a very workable total of two dozen possible projects, and I'd be able to start on the introduction and book outline to send Jenna.

My phone rang, and I picked it up, assuming that Luke was returning my call, but it was Liz with an invitation to dinner, which I promptly accepted. After promising to bring wine, I told her that I'd see her at seven. *Good,* I thought. A conversation with Liz was something else I'd planned to do today that I was actually going to get done.

Now I just had to find out whether Bessie wanted a party and ask her for her dog biscuit recipe. I thought it was odd that Luke hadn't returned my call. It had been several hours since I'd tried to contact him, so I tried again, but there was still no answer. This time, I didn't leave a message. I called the community center's main number and talked to Cassie, the fulltime receptionist, who said that she hadn't seen Luke all day, but that it wasn't "her day to watch him." I certainly wasn't going to ask Patty if she knew where Luke was, so I decided to drive to the community center and look for him myself.

Bear had settled down for his afternoon nap, and although he gave me his usual pleading look, designed to make me have a guilt trip for leaving him, I knew from experience that he'd go back to napping soon after I left the house. Bear's a creature of habit, and a long afternoon nap is part of his daily routine.

The community center's lobby was empty when I arrived, and it was easy to bypass the administrative offices, where Patty ruled the roost, and slip down the hall to Luke's office, which was empty. I decided to leave a message on his desk, but the door was locked, so I quickly scribbled a brief note to him and slid it under the office door. As I went back past the HOA's administrative offices, I heard angry voices, and, through the windows that separated the offices from the hallway, I could see that Luke and Patty were arguing. Only Patty and Luke were there, both standing behind the counter in the reception area, rather than in Patty's office. The clerks and receptionist must have gone out to lunch, I figured, leaving Patty alone, and Luke must have come along from the lobby while I was leaving him a note.

Curious, I ducked back beside the wall and sat on a low bench in the hallway, where neither Patty nor Luke could see me, but I had no problem hearing them.

"I can't approve this. You're requisitioning $500 for a party for that old crone? Ridiculous!"

"That 'old crone,' as you call her, has been a loyal employee of Hawkeye Haven for over ten years."

"If she'd been doing her job, her gun never would have been stolen, and she wouldn't have ended up in the hospital."

"That's not fair. Anyone could have been the victim of a surprise attack."

"I doubt it. Your entire security staff must have an average age of about seventy. Why don't you hire some people who can take care of themselves?"

"I'm going to ignore that remark, Patty. My staff does a good job, and I'm proud of them. And by the way, I don't work for you. I report directly to the board. That means I don't need your approval on the requisition. The new board president, Rachel Casswell, has already okayed the party for Bessie."

"If that's true, she's a bigger fool than I thought she was."

"You might not want to spread that around, Patty. She's your boss, too, now that Victor is gone."

"You sound a little too happy that Victor's dead, Luke. You never did get along with him, and we both know he was about ready to fire you. It seems awfully convenient that you don't have to worry about that anymore. Where were you when he was shot?"

"As I already told you, I don't report to you. You're the one who should be worrying about losing her job now that Victor's dead. He was the only reason the board contracted with your management company in the first place."

Cautiously, I sidled up to the window and peered inside. The look on Patty's face said it all. Luke's last comment had hit home. If Patty and her management company were on the way out, I didn't know anyone who would be the least bit sorry about it. I really hoped that Luke was right and that the HOA board would look for a different management company to replace Patty's as soon as her year-long contract expired. I figured she probably had about another six months to go—six months in which she could wreak considerable havoc if she chose, and since she was such an ill-natured and vindictive person, I had no doubt that she would do it. Of course, the board members could rein her in if they wanted to, but they'd all seemed like such milquetoasts at the HOA meeting that I wondered whether they'd exert their authority or just let Patty do as she pleased until her contract expired.

I slid back onto the bench just as Luke exited the office, shutting the door with mock precision as he left. When he saw me, he motioned me to come with him, and we headed back towards his office. Although he'd exchanged angry words with Patty, he didn't seem too upset by the encounter.

"I suppose you heard all that, Laurel?"

"Sure did. I didn't realize that you reported to the board and not the management company. That's great!"

"In this case, it certainly is. I'm sorry I didn't get a chance to return your call, Laurel. I came in late this morning because I covered for one of our rover drivers who was sick last night. I didn't even get a chance to check my messages until just a few minutes ago. Then I had to go out to the main gate, and about that time, Patty summoned me to her office. Even though I don't report to her, I still have to put up with some of her nonsense."

"That's a shame, Luke. She's such an unpleasant person."

"That she is. Anyway, Bessie's son Tom brought her in a little while ago just as I was arriving, and they both liked the idea of having a going-away party for her. She was so overwhelmed that I thought she might start crying. I'm glad she didn't, though. If there's anything that really makes me uncomfortable, it's a woman's tears."

"I'm really happy that she wants to have the party. When will we be having it?"

"Wednesday at six, if that'll give you enough time to issue invitations and have some food catered."

"All right. I can do that. Is there anyone Bessie wants to invite? Besides her son and daughter-in-law, I mean."

"Well, I guess I was right to ask for help on this. I didn't even think to ask her."

"No problem. I can call to ask her, if you'll give me her number."

"Sure. Let me see." Luke rifled through some papers on his desk and copied a number onto the back of one of his business cards, which he handed me.

"I assume you'll want to invite the board members and the security team. I'll send you an e-vite that you can forward to all of them, and it would be a good idea to mention the party to people you see in person, especially since we're not giving them much notice. I'll take care of inviting the residents that Bessie knows and anybody else Bessie would like to invite."

"That's great, Laurel. You're already more organized that I'd ever be. Don't forget that we have $500 for food or anything else you'll need. I'll have the cash here for you tomorrow. I'll just need receipts to back up our records."

"Okay, great. I can probably get everything we need at Costco. To keep it simple, we'll probably stick with subs, snacks, and desserts along with coffee, water, and soft drinks. We have that big coffee maker here for meetings, so that'll be handy. I'll get some of my friends to help me with the decorations and make party favors."

"Good. Is there anything else you need me to do?"

"Yes, give a short speech to honor Bessie, and I'll make a nice certificate to commemorate her ten years of service to the community that you can present her. Then, we should also give her some kind of a gift. We could solicit donations for the gift, but we don't have much time, so we should probably just pay for it out of the $500 budget. I can juggle the food budget so that we have enough to buy her the retirement present," I said, feeling less confident than I sounded because I knew that the budget was already tight.

"Now I'm happier than ever that I asked you to help. I never would have thought about that. Maybe I should get her some flowers, too."

"That would be nice, but a plant might be easier for her to take home, and it'll last longer."

"Okay, maybe I better have my wife help me pick something out."

"Good. I think we're all set. Can you meet us in the meeting room at five on Wednesday to set up the tables? A little muscle would sure be welcome."

"I'll be there, and I'll have Kenny there to help, too. Thanks, Laurel."

"You're welcome. I'm glad Bessie's going to have some positive recognition. She seemed so down just a few days ago, and I'm hoping the party will cheer her up a bit."

"Head injuries can be dicey, but she seems to be doing okay, as far as I can tell. She looked better this morning."

"That's good." I hesitated, uncertain that I should bring up something Patty had said, but my curiosity pushed me ahead. "Uh, Luke, I know it's none of my business…." That was an understatement, but I pressed on. "But I heard Patty say earlier that Victor wanted to fire you?" I made it a question, rather than a statement, but I could tell that Luke was irritated at me for asking him. He gazed coolly at me, and I squirmed uncomfortably.

"You're right. It is none of your business," he sighed, "but I suppose Patty will be spreading that story around, and once something hits the Hawkeye Haven grapevine, it's all over the community. It's true. Victor threatened to fire me. According to the HOA's bylaws, firing the head of security requires a majority of the board members to vote for removal. Luckily for me, Victor didn't schedule that vote for last week's meeting, so I'm off the hook for now. Of course, the remaining board members can do whatever they like, but I get along with all of them, so there's no reason to think they're going to fire me. The reason Victor didn't schedule the vote for last week's meeting was precisely that I do get along with everybody on the board. Victor's the only one I didn't see eye-to-eye with, and he would have needed some time to convince the other board members to vote to oust me."

"It doesn't sound as though Victor had the votes to fire you anyway."

"He seemed to have a lot of influence with the board members, though. I always suspected that he had something on each of them because he always seemed to get his way eventually, so I'm sure I'd be a goner if he hadn't been murdered."

"I'm sorry, Luke. I shouldn't have brought it up. If anyone spreads the word about Victor's wanting to fire you, it'll have to be Patty. I won't say a word to anyone."

Luke shrugged. I could tell he still wasn't happy with me for bringing up an unpleasant subject. I hated to leave things between us on a sour note, especially because I thought Luke was a good guy.

"Seriously, Luke, I do apologize."

Luke smiled weakly. "That's okay, Laurel. Don't worry about it. I shouldn't be worrying about it either, anymore. It's over and done with, so let's just go on and get ready for Bessie's party. I just want to forget about Victor and all his nonsense, but sometimes it's hard to do that because Patty's still here."

"I predict that the board won't renew her contract."

"Let's hope they don't," Luke agreed. "Well, I should go now. I need to make my rounds. I'll be sure to tell Kenny to be on deck to help with the room set-up on Wednesday."

"See you then."

Waving, I left Luke's office. Although he no longer seemed upset with me, I knew that what I thought of as curiosity, other people regarded as nosiness, a trait which could put people off. I really didn't want Luke to be one of those people, not only because I liked him, but also because he's Liz's grandson. I had to admit that learning about Victor's desire to fire Luke had shaken me a bit, especially because I now realized that Luke had a motive to kill Victor. Although I didn't think Luke was a killer, I didn't really know him well. Could his relationship to Liz, my dear friend, be coloring my vision? Whether or not she ever revealed to Luke that she's his grandmother, she would certainly be devastated if he turned out to be a murderer. No, I told myself; don't let yourself think that way, but my mind kept whirling with thoughts about the possibility that Luke could somehow have been involved in Victor's murder.

Okay, I had to sort this out, not only for Luke's sake, but for Liz's, too. I might as well start with the three crime basics that Cynthia had mentioned yesterday— means, motive, and opportunity. Last one first— opportunity. Was Luke in the community when Victor was killed? I didn't know the answer to that question. With his job as head of security and his 24/7 access to Hawkeye Haven, he very well could have been on the scene. Nobody would think of the rover vehicle as suspicious, either, so driving it could have been a good way to approach Victor's house. Even though I didn't know exactly what time the murder had taken place, the window of opportunity for the killer might include Courtney's night shift hours and the time it took her to drive to and from work. Too bad the police weren't likely to share the estimated time of death. I remembered that Luke had told me that he'd arrived at the crime scene about the same time as the Center City police had shown up. I decided it might not be significant, anyway, given the ten-hour time frame during which the murder could have occurred, but maybe there was some way I could find out whether or not Luke had worked that night.

Second—motive. Luke had one, but was the prospect of being fired from his job as head of security for Hawkeye Haven enough to make him want to kill Victor? Luke seemed convinced that Victor would have eventually succeeded in getting rid of him, but I wasn't really sure how harmful that would be to Luke's career, and I knew that, as a twenty-year military man, he received a monthly pension. Unless there was some other factor I didn't know about, Luke's motive didn't seem extremely strong to me, but I knew that people who had much weaker motives than Luke had been convicted of murder.

Last—means. Did Luke have the means to kill Victor; that is, did he somehow gain control of Bessie's weapon and use it to kill Victor? That brought up another question. Could Luke himself have attacked Bessie, taken her gun, and used it to kill Victor? Luke had certainly arrived at the scene quickly after Bessie had been attacked, but that didn't mean much since he could have easily driven there in the rover in just a few minutes from any location in Hawkeye Haven. What had Bessie said about her attacker? Whoever it had been had seemed familiar. Although Luke would qualify, Bessie had also said that the person seemed to be a few inches taller than she is. At five feet, six inches, I'm about four inches taller than Bessie myself, so if Bessie was right, whoever attacked her was about my height. That certainly would eliminate Luke, who stands over six feet tall. However, assuming that he had not attacked Bessie, he still might have been able to find the weapon the attacker stole and use it to kill Victor. That seemed a little far-fetched, though. Wasn't it Luke who had told me that the murder weapon was Bessie's gun? What if he'd been lying about that? It didn't seem likely, given the fact that there was really no reason I could think of that he would make up information to feed me. After all, I wasn't involved in the investigation.

Despite telling myself that it seemed highly unlikely that Luke could be Victor's killer, I couldn't help worrying that Patty would share her opinions with a resident or employee of Hawkeye Haven, and then the rumor would fly all over the community. Once that happened, Liz was bound to hear it, and she'd be terribly upset that her grandson was suspected of being a murderer. As I'd pledged to Luke, I wouldn't tell anyone that Victor had been planning to fire Luke, but Patty couldn't be counted on for discretion.

I figured that I should concentrate on the tasks I needed to accomplish so that we could have the party for Bessie Wednesday evening. Hurrying home, I called Bessie as soon as I placated Bear with another special snack from the Paw-tisserie. Bessie gave me a list of ten relatives and friends that she wanted to invite to the party. I chatted with her briefly, mentioning that I'd like to use her recipe in my new book if she had no objection. She liked the idea of the book, and she was excited that her recipe and her name as its author would appear in it. I gave Bessie my email address, and she said that she'd have her granddaughter send me the recipe because she and computers didn't get along.

Since I had to get the invitations out as soon as possible, we didn't talk long. Back at my computer, I merged Bessie's list with my own list of several residents who know Bessie and a couple who had never met her; namely, my cousin Tracey and Liz, both of whom had agreed to help with the party. Then I quickly added some tweaks to a template I'd used for e-vites in the past and filled in the details of the event with an RSVP notation and my email address. Even though I requested an RSVP, I knew that everybody wouldn't contact me, but at least I could get some indication of interest in the event, and I'd just have to guesstimate how much food to buy. As promised, I forwarded the e-vite to Luke, reminding him to send it to the board members and security team. Although we didn't have much time to plan the event, I knew we could pull it off. Besides Tracey, Liz, and Cynthia, Amy had also agreed to help. She was just waiting for me to let her know that the party was a "go" before she started getting the table decorations together, so I called her and gave her the go-ahead. We decided to use a burgundy and gold color scheme with dried flower centerpieces at each table because Amy had made quite a few of them for an event that had been cancelled at the last moment, and she was happy that her handiwork wouldn't go to waste.

Bear had started his early evening dance for his dinner, and I knew I'd have no peace until I fed him. He jumped up and down and pranced around in circles, throwing in a couple hearty yelps for good measure, all in his attempt to let Mommy know it was time for his doggy din-din. After I fed him, he settled down and soon fell asleep, his head flopping over the side of the dog bed I'd made for him and resting on the hard tile. His position looked very uncomfortable to me, but it was one he often assumes, so I guess it suits him.

Since I was due at Liz's for dinner in ten minutes, I quickly changed from the shorts and tee shirt I'd worn all day into a short-sleeved cotton print dress. After swiping on some mascara and lipstick and brushing my hair, I grabbed the bottle of wine I'd promised to bring and tiptoed toward the front door, but despite my efforts to be quiet, Bear heard me, jumped up, and ran to me, but he looked at me in resignation after I told him to stay home and be a good boy. If he'd known I was headed to Liz's, he'd really have raised a fuss.

"Laurel, just in time!" Liz exclaimed, as she answered my knock on her front door. She looked lovely in a turquoise chiffon caftan that was embellished with sparkling silver bugle beads. As usual, her hair and make-up were perfect. "We're having a nice salad for dinner."

My face undoubtedly registered my disappointment at this announcement because Liz laughed at me and said, "Just kidding, Laurel. You know I wouldn't do that to you. You get plenty of salad at home. Salads and sandwiches seem to be your mainstays."

Relieved, I grinned and nodded. "That's for sure. I'm one of the world's worst cooks, and I won't inflict my cooking on anyone, even myself." I followed Liz into her dining room where she had set out lighted candles and a vibrant orange floral arrangement as a centerpiece.

I noticed that there were only two place settings at the table. "Wow, Liz, is it just the two of us? Why so fancy schmancy?"

"Just felt like using my china and silver, but I'll admit to an ulterior motive, too. I'm trying out a different recipe for chicken cordon bleu, and I need your opinion."

"Before you make it for the colonel?" I guessed.

"Yes, he thinks I'm a good cook, and I want to keep it that way."

"Liz, you're a fabulous cook. I've loved every dish you've ever made."

"Thanks, Laurel, and thanks for bringing the wine, too. Now I'm almost ready. Could you pour?"

"Sure." While Liz plated the chicken and carried it to the dining room, I used the opener that Liz gave me for the wine, pulled the cork out of the bottle, and poured us each a glass of Chardonnay.

"This looks scrumptious, Liz," I said, taking a bite of chicken. "Tastes scrumptious, too."

"You think Bobby'll like it?"

"He'll love it. Your romance must be going pretty well. You'll have to bring me up to speed. We really haven't had a chance to talk since your big date on Saturday night."

"We had a great time, and I saw him again last night, too."

"Ah, yes." I remembered hearing their voices when I'd sat outside on my patio the night before.

"I really like him, Laurel. He's steady and reliable, but he's not stuffy. He's been all over the world and has some wonderful stories to tell. I think even my son Leonard might approve of him, although that could be wishful thinking on my part."

"Have you told Leonard about Luke yet?" I queried.

"No, but he's taking me out to lunch tomorrow, and I'm going to tell him then."

Knowing that the lunch would be stressful for Liz, especially because Leonard probably wouldn't take the news too well, I shuddered. I was afraid that Leonard might be more concerned about sharing his inheritance with his newfound nephew than with his mother's happiness, but perhaps I was mistaken about him. I certainly hoped so.

"And then you're going to tell Luke?"

"Yes, I think I'll tell him and very soon, too. He may not welcome the news, and it could upset him, so I'm definitely going to wait until later in the week, at least. I don't want anything to interfere with the party you two are planning for Bessie."

"I really hope it all works out well. I can't imagine that Luke wouldn't want to know his grandmother, especially since his grandmother is one of the sweetest ladies I know." Again, I wanted to deny the possibility that Luke could ever be considered a suspect in Victor's murder. After all these years, Liz had decided to reveal her secret, and it would be truly horrible if her only grandson turned out to be a killer. Of course, I said nothing to Liz about it, and I hoped Patty would keep what she knew to herself.

"I hope so, too, Laurel. I've been living with my secret for decades. It's time to put my past mistakes right."

Patting Liz's hand, I murmured, "Don't be too hard on yourself, Liz. You were just a kid when you had your son, and, with your husband gone, you were on your own with no resources."

"Yes, that's true." Liz paused, and we sat in silence for a while. I could tell Liz was thinking about everything that had happened long ago, so I didn't interrupt her reverie. After a few minutes, she was back.

"How about some dessert, Laurel? I made chocolate cheesecake."

"Yummy! That sounds great, Liz. I can't pass up cheesecake, even though I probably should."

"Well, I probably should, too, but I'm going to indulge," Liz said, as we carried our dishes to the kitchen. "Coffee? It's decaf."

"Sure, sounds good."

While Liz sliced the cheesecake, I poured decaffeinated coffee into the delicate, light blue, china cups that she had set out on the kitchen counter, and then we carried our coffee and calorie-laden desserts back to the dining room table.

"By the way, I meant to tell you that a couple of police detectives stopped by on Saturday," Liz said.

"A tall, good-looking guy and a pudgy blonde woman with an attitude?"

"Yes, did they talk to you, too?"

"They came to my house on Friday, and then on Saturday morning, I saw Detective Wesson at the community center when I was leaving after my DIY earrings class was over."

"Wesson—which one is that?"

"The guy."

"Oh, well, he seemed pleasant enough, but his partner sure didn't. She insinuated that Bobby could have killed Victor. Of course, Bobby's an expert marksman, and he was in the military for years, but that certainly doesn't mean that he murdered Victor. The lady detective said that Bobby threatened Victor at the HOA meeting, but I told both cops that Bobby calmed down after he left the meeting."

"That's what I told Detective Wesson, too. I suppose they talked to the colonel?"

"Oh, yes. He said the same thing. Anyway, he has an alibi, so he's not a suspect."

"He has an alibi for the whole night?"

Liz blushed and a cat-that-got-the-canary smile crept over her face. "He spent the night with me."

Chapter 11

"Liz!" I said. Honestly, I was a little shocked at her revelation, knowing that the two had just met for the first time at the HOA meeting the night before Victor's body had been discovered.

"Oh, no, no, no, Laurel. I didn't mean *that*! We just really hit it off, and we stayed up all night talking. You know what a night owl I am. Bobby's such a gentleman that when the police questioned him, he refused to say where he was when Victor was murdered, even though he had a solid alibi. So I told the cops myself that we were together all night. I couldn't have them thinking that Bobby had killed someone when he was right here in this house with me at the time of the murder."

"Thank goodness the colonel's not a suspect. I guess maybe I can understand why the detectives focused on him, though. With all his years in the military, he's more than a little familiar with firearms. He yelled at Victor when Victor had him thrown out of the meeting, and I suppose what he said about Victor's regretting the day he tried to get the colonel to take down his flagpole could be construed as a threat, even though we both know that the colonel was just blowing off steam. Another thing is that the colonel's often out and about early in the morning."

"Yes, I can see it from the detectives' viewpoint, too, but, strange as it may seem after only knowing Bobby for a few days, I have no doubt that he's an honorable man. If he were going to pick a fight with Victor, he'd do it right out in the open, like he did at the meeting, not sneak over to Victor's house in the middle of the night or early morning to shoot him when nobody else is around."

"I agree with you, Liz. The colonel's a good man. If it weren't for him, I probably wouldn't be here today. I swear that mountain lion we saw the day I met the colonel would have torn Bear and me to shreds if he hadn't come along and scared it away."

Liz shook her head. "I shudder to think about it. So much has happened around here in the past week; it's truly frightening."

"That's for sure. I guess the mountain lion incident was just a fluke, but what's scary is the attack and murder, both right here in Hawkeye Haven. I hope the police can find the killer soon because everybody's really on edge." What I didn't say was that I hoped against hope that Luke wasn't involved, especially now that Liz had finally made the decision to reveal to Luke that she's his grandmother. "By the way, thanks for helping Amy put the finishing touches on the decorations for Bessie's party. Considering that we've had only a few days to organize it, we're going to have a good turnout. The plans are coming along well, except that I need to think of what to buy for Bessie's retirement gift. Do you have any ideas about what we should get her?"

"Let me take care of that, Laurel. I saw some exquisite hand-painted silk scarves at Mimi's Boutique last week when I was shopping. What do you think?"

"Sounds good to me. You have wonderful taste, Liz."

"I'll pick out a nice one and gift wrap it, and I'll bring the present with me when Bobby and I come to the party, so you won't have to take it. You have enough to do without worrying about bringing the gift."

"Great! Thanks for helping. And thanks for dinner, too. I guarantee that the colonel's going to love your special chicken cordon bleu."

We embraced and air kissed good-bye, and I walked the few steps back to my own house next door.

Bear heard me rattling the key in the lock and came running to greet me as I opened the door. I hugged him, and he followed me to the kitchen, where I had inadvertently left my smartphone. After tossing Bear a couple of baby carrots, I checked my phone for messages. I had a text message from Tracey and a voice mail from Lynn, my cousin in Seattle, asking me if I'd had a chance to test her recipe for pumpkin dog treats.

Feeling guilty that I hadn't yet acknowledged her contribution to my book, I called Lynn and thanked her for sending the recipe. After telling Lynn that I'd make some pumpkin treats for Bear to test the recipe later in the week, we chatted briefly. Hearing her baby Emma's cries in the background as well as Barkley's howls, and knowing that Lynn's husband Sam had a night school class on Mondays, I promised to keep her posted about the progress of my *DIY for Dog Lovers* book and said good-bye. Lynn hadn't mentioned a word about the murder in Hawkeye Haven, so I felt positive that Aunt Ellen and Uncle Bill hadn't found out about it, and that meant neither had my parents. So far, so good on that score. The last thing I needed right now was my parents' helicoptering, well-intentioned though it might be.

Scanning my phone for the text, I saw that Tracey had confirmed that she had been able to change her schedule and take Wednesday off so that we could go shopping for the food for the party. I was really happy to hear that she wouldn't have to go to work that day because it would have been difficult to do all the shopping and deliver the food alone. I texted her back with a big "thanx" and spent the rest of the evening watching a thriller on TV.

My mind kept wandering so that I missed key elements of the convoluted plot, and, finally, I turned off the movie before it ended and went to bed. Unfortunately, I kept dreaming about Victor's shooting, and a montage of familiar faces, all potential suspects, swam around in my head so that by the time I woke up in the morning, I felt more confused than ever.

After a brisk morning walk with Bear and a strong cup of coffee, I felt the clouds begin to lift, and I was prepared to face the day. I worked on my book notes for a couple of hours before checking my email messages. I was pleasantly surprised to find that quite a few people had already responded to the RSVP notation on my party invitation. Because I hadn't noticed any responses from anyone on Luke's lists, I decided to check with him. I hoped he hadn't forgotten to forward the e-vites, especially since we were sending them so close to the party.

I had to go to the community center, anyway, to get my rosters for the following week's classes, so I could drop in on Luke while I was there. Patty, whether because of incompetence, nonchalance, or just plain orneriness, refused to email me the lists, so each week I had to retrieve them in person from the office. Hoping to avoid Patty, I deliberately waited until noon, when I knew Patty usually went out for lunch, before I left the house.

As I pulled into a parking space outside the community center, I saw Patty leaving the building. Taking no chances of an encounter with her, I waited until she got into her car and drove off before I went into the building. I sincerely hoped the board would get rid of her, although I supposed they probably would have to wait out her contract before doing so.

"Hi, Cassie. I'm here to pick up my class lists for next week."

Without bothering to respond, the receptionist looked up from the romance novel she was reading, handed me a folder containing my class lists, and went back to reading her book. She and Patty made a great team—rude and ruder. I felt sorry for Linda, Liz's friend, who worked as a part-time receptionist at the community center, that she had to put up with both Patty and Cassie.

"Thank you," I said, emphasizing the "you," but this time Cassie didn't even look up. "Must be a fascinating book," I commented. Still no answer. "Yes, well, I'll just be going now." Relieved to end the one-sided conversation, I left the office and walked down the hallway to Luke's office.

"Knock, knock."

Startled, Luke looked up from his laptop.

"Oh, sorry, Luke. I didn't mean to startle you."

"That's okay, Laurel. I was concentrating on making next month's schedule for the security team, and I didn't hear you coming down the hall. What can I do for you?"

"Well, I wanted to let you know that we should have a good turnout for the party tomorrow. I've already received a lot of responses to the e-vite I sent out yesterday. I was wondering whether you'd had a chance to forward it to the security staff and board members because I haven't heard from any of them."

"Uh, oh. Was I supposed to leave your email address on the RSVP line? I put mine there instead."

"That's fine. Any responses?"

"Yes, ten so far. Let me double-check here." Luke turned to his computer. "Another one just came in, so eleven now."

"Okay, that makes nearly forty at this point, and I know even more people will come, so we should have a nice crowd."

Luke nodded. "I hope $500 will cover the food and a gift for Bessie. That's all Mrs. Casswell would approve. Of course, if Victor were still the HOA president, we wouldn't be having a party for Bessie at all."

"Why did Victor want to fire you, Luke?" Surprised at my own audacity, I hastened to add, "You're the best security chief Hawkeye Haven ever had."

Luke looked at me thoughtfully. "Remember when I told you that I thought he had something on most of the board members?"

"Yes."

"A few weeks ago, I overheard him threatening Mrs. Casswell. He wanted her to vote his way to award the Hawkeye Haven landscaping contract to a new company, and he said that if she didn't do it, he'd tell everybody what he knew about her. Mind you, I have no idea what he knew or thought he knew about her, but she acted scared."

"Blackmail?"

"Right, I think he had some master plan, something that went beyond the landscaping contract that he mentioned to Rachel. There must have been some bigger reason that it was so important for him to sway a majority of the board's votes. Anyway, when he realized that I'd heard him, I knew my days here were numbered. He couldn't afford to keep anyone around who knew what he was doing. I might have been able to stay if he could have come up with some way to blackmail me, too, but I'm squeaky clean, so his dirty tricks wouldn't work on me. Victor was some piece of work. He probably thought that everybody had a dirty little secret. I wouldn't be surprised if he had a dossier on everybody, just like J. Edgar Hoover used to."

"Unbelievable! Victor was truly an evil man. It looks as though there could be another suspect for the police to investigate. If Victor was threatening Mrs. Casswell, she might have decided that Hawkeye Haven would be better off without him."

"Laurel, you know that I'm something of a suspect myself because Victor was planning to fire me, but, believe me, I would never murder someone over the possibility of losing a job. It's a good job, but I can always find another one. In fact, Foster Security has been trying to recruit me ever since I retired from the Air Force."

"Are you thinking of taking them up on their offer?"

"Not at this point. I'm satisfied here, especially now that Victor's no longer the HOA president, and I'm hoping the board will get rid of Patty when her contract's up. At this point, I'm planning to stay right where I am."

"That's good," I said, smiling. Luke's explanation sounded plausible to me, and the detectives could confirm the job offer from Foster Security easily enough. "Well, I'd better get going. I'll see you about an hour before the party starts tomorrow."

"Okay, Laurel, and thanks again for all your help."

"Glad to do it," I said, making my exit.

Home again, I looked over my list of party supplies, added a few items, and faxed it to Tracey at work, in case she wanted to add anything. After a quick game of fetch with Bear, I added the class rosters I'd picked up earlier to my notebook and double-checked my calendar to make sure the dates I had noted for the classes were correct.

I'd almost forgotten that I needed to prepare for a class on fall wreath-making that I was teaching the next week. I printed project handouts for the students who'd be taking the wreath-making class. Then, I unzipped the side pocket of my suitcase, removed the handouts from Saturday's DIY earrings class, and replaced them with the new project instructions that I'd just printed. Usually, if I had only a few left, I simply discarded them and printed a new batch if I decided to repeat a project, so I grabbed the earrings project instructions and dropped them into the wastebasket under my desk. Unfortunately, the receptacle was nearly overflowing before I added them, and the papers slid to the floor.

Muttering to myself, I stooped to pick up the papers and realized that one of them wasn't my project instructions at all. Now where had *that* come from? I must have picked it up somewhere by mistake. I remembered photocopying handouts in the office at the community center last week. Someone had left a paper on the photocopier's platen, and I'd set it aside without examining it. It wasn't an uncommon occurrence. The photocopy machine in the office had the bad habit of rejecting originals unless they were placed directly on the glass. It was easy to forget to remove the original. I'd done it myself a few times.

Looking at the stray piece of paper, I noticed a handwritten list containing the names of four of the board members of the Hawkeye Haven HOA. Beside each were scribbled notations. Although I had some difficulty making out the handwriting, it was clear that the notes beside each name indicated a reason to blackmail the person listed. Bingo! Hadn't Luke suspected as much?

Rachel Casswell's name topped the list. Although I didn't know her personally, I knew she'd been the vice-president of the HOA before Victor died, so according to the HOA's rules, if the president were no longer willing or able to serve, no new election would be held, and the vice-president would automatically take over as president. That meant Rachel was now the board's president. Luke had already told me that Victor had threatened to reveal something about her that she didn't want known if she didn't vote his way, and what she didn't want known was right in front of me in black and white. Rachel Casswell had had a felony conviction in Illinois. According to the note, she'd been convicted of embezzlement and had served a two-year sentence in the state prison. If that information were true, and I thought it probably was, Rachel wouldn't want anyone at Hawkeye Haven to know about it.

The next name on the list was Edna Elkins. I knew Edna. She'd taken several of my classes, and I remembered thinking, when I attended that HOA meeting with Liz, that Edna had never been a shrinking violet, yet she hadn't objected to anything Victor said or did during the meeting. Right in front of me was the reason for her silence. Edna, a retired nurse, had re-used a hypodermic needle when she'd given a patient an injection, and the patient had later developed hepatitis C. Edna had lost her job, her nursing license, and her malpractice insurance, and she had pleaded "no contest" to charges of criminal negligence and the reckless endangerment of her patients. She'd been lucky to receive a suspended sentence. *Strange,* I thought, she certainly hadn't lost her self-confidence because of the incident. I'd often heard her dispensing medical advice during class. I shuddered to think that the other students always listened to her with respect because they thought an experienced, retired nurse would know what she was talking about.

The third name on the list was Luis Cardoza. I'd never seen the man until the night of the HOA meeting, and he hadn't said a word during the time I'd been there, but I remembered what he looked like. Another quiet board member—quiet because Victor knew something that Luis Cardoza wanted to hide. Unlike the two women, Luis's secret wasn't a crime, but a personal matter. When Luis had decided that he no longer wanted to marry his fiancé, she had been devastated by his rejection. When he refused to relent, she threatened suicide, but he didn't take her threat seriously. Unfortunately, she took an entire bottle of sleeping pills and never woke up. Luis blamed himself for her suicide—a mortal sin, according to the Catholic Church. Having noticed a St. Christopher's medal hanging on a gold chain around Luis's neck, I believed that Luis was Catholic.

Peter Harvey, whose name was last on the list, sounded familiar to me, although I hadn't recognized him at the meeting. Now, where had I heard that name before? I couldn't remember, so I googled "Peter Harvey" and added "Center City" to see if any pertinent returns came up, and I saw that he was a member of the Iowa State Board of Commerce, which wasn't extremely high-profile, but made the news occasionally. No wonder his name sounded familiar. I must have heard it on a newscast. Since Peter Harvey was the only person on the list involved in the public sphere, whatever he was hiding could have ramifications that went well beyond Hawkeye Haven. I gasped as I read that he'd been fired from a management position in an eastern construction company after a building he was responsible for had collapsed. After unproven allegations that Peter had bribed a local housing inspector, he had resigned from his job and moved to Iowa. He was never charged. Perhaps he hadn't done anything wrong, but a cloud of suspicion could still hang over him, even though the building's collapse had occurred nearly twenty years ago, and, as a public figure, even one without an especially high profile, Peter Harvey undoubtedly wouldn't want the bribery allegations to become public knowledge.

   Good grief! The majority of the HOA board
members of Hawkeye Haven really did have something
to hide, and, according to Luke, Victor wasn't above
taking advantage of what he knew about each of them
to swing votes his way. I wondered who had left the list
sitting on the copy machine and whether or not the
person had realized that it was missing. Possibly, Victor
himself could have left it there, or perhaps he'd shared
it with someone—Patty?—who had made copies. The
list didn't seem like a document that Victor would leave
lying around in plain sight on his desktop, but someone
could have searched his files for it. Offices at the
community center were sometimes locked, sometimes
not, although it didn't seem likely that Victor would
have left his office unlocked if he'd kept such
inflammatory information in his files. Another
possibility was that someone with a master key had
unlocked Victor's office and searched it. I surmised that
Patty, Victor, Luke, and Max, the head of maintenance,
all had master keys, but maybe others did, too. It might
not be too difficult to borrow a master key and then
replace it, which caused the list of possibilities to
expand.
   Bottom line: unless someone admitted to leaving the
list on the photocopier, I'd probably never know who
had done it. But maybe it didn't really matter. What did
matter was that there were more suspects than ever in
Victor's murder, and I knew I needed to turn the list
over to the police.
   Searching my kitchen junk drawer for Detective
Wesson's business card, I located it wedged under a
rubber-banded stack of coupons that I'd clipped but
would probably forget existed. I might remember to use
a coupon at the supermarket a couple of times a month,
if that. Last year's savings from couponing probably
amounted to all of twenty dollars. Thumbing through

the coupons in the stack, I found that all except one had already expired. An extreme couponer, I was not. Plucking out the one current coupon, I stowed it in my handbag and deposited the rest in the garbage can.

I realized I was stalling because I didn't want to call Wesson. The last time I'd seen him, I'd flounced out the door of the community center without bothering to tell him good-bye. I'd been angry that he'd seemed to question my good faith. Although I'd had plenty of time to cool down since then, I still felt nervous about talking to him.

Giving myself a mental swift kick, I picked up my smartphone and called him. He answered on the second ring.

"Wesson."

"Lieutenant Wesson, this is Laurel McMillan."

"Yes, Laurel?"

"I called you because I've come across something that might help in Victor Eberhart's murder investigation."

"Go on."

"Well, I was sorting through some papers, and I found one that wasn't mine. I must have picked it up when I was photocopying some handouts for class last week at the community center." I felt as though I were babbling.

"What is it?"

"It's a list—a list naming four of the board members of Hawkeye Haven, along with reasons that they could be blackmailed. I think Victor was using the information to get them to vote the way he wanted, although I don't know why that would be so important to him, but maybe one of them tried to put a stop to it permanently."

"Hmmm. Interesting. I'll need to get that from you. If you'll be home later, I can stop by to pick it up."

"Okay."

"Around eight o'clock work for you?"

"That's fine."

Well, I'd done it now. I'd have to see Wesson again, but what choice was there? I felt obligated to turn over the list to the police. After all, there were four more people with possible motives for wanting to kill Victor. I supposed the only alternative might have been notifying his snotty partner instead of Wesson, but, despite my nervousness at the prospect of seeing the handsome detective again, I'd never for an instant considered calling Detective Smith.

Half an hour before Wesson was due to arrive, I was already pacing the floor. I'd changed my clothes three times, finally settling on a bright turquoise-colored sleeveless maxi dress, beaded brown leather sandals, and long earrings with sterling silver chain that brushed my shoulders. I'd applied make-up with more care that I'd taken in months, and I'd tamed my unruly auburn hair so that it fell in soft waves.

Although I'd scolded myself for dressing as though I were going on a date—Liz was the only woman I knew who dressed up and wore full make-up for lounging around the house—I wanted to look my best when Wesson showed up. I'd been trying to deny the fact that I felt attracted to the man, but I'd finally had to admit it, if only to myself.

The doorbell rang, startling me, and Bear barked and ran to the door. Unless someone else was there, Wesson was early. My stomach did flip-flops as I cautioned Bear to get back. I gazed through the peephole to see who was there. It was Wesson, all right. I took a deep breath and swung the door open.

"Hi, Lieutenant."

"Wes, remember?"

"I remember," I murmured, as I motioned for him to come in.

Blocking Wes's way, Bear danced around him, and he stooped to pet my canine companion. Bear responded enthusiastically by dropping to the floor, rolling onto his back, and holding his paws up under his chin.

"Oh, Bear," I sighed. "Give the lieutenant—uh, Wes—a break."

"That's okay, Laurel," Wes said, rubbing Bear's tummy. "He's fine. You like a belly rub, don't you, boy?"

As if to answer him, Bear panted his approval, and I couldn't help laughing at the dog's antics.

"Bear likes attention; that's for sure. Have a seat, Wes." Wesson sat on the sofa, and Bear plopped at his feet.

"He's a nice dog, Laurel. Have you had him a long time?" Wesson didn't seem to be in a particular hurry.

"Five years. I adopted him from an animal rescue society when he was just a pup."

"I wouldn't mind having a dog myself, but I work long hours, so I'm not home much. In fact, I have to go back to work tonight."

"Those *are* long hours. Have you had a chance to have dinner?" What was I saying? I was the world's worst cook, but I supposed I could at least offer a hungry man a sandwich. After all, he hadn't had to come to my house to pick up the list. He could have asked me to deliver it to the police station, or he could have had someone else pick it up for him. Thank goodness he hadn't asked Smith to do it. The thought of seeing that abrasive woman again made me cringe.

"Yeah, I grabbed a burger and fries at the Burger Inn on the way over."

"Would you like something to drink?"

"Would I ever, but I'm on duty." His eyes crinkled merrily, and I knew he was teasing me, but I played it straight.

"A bottle of water, then? Coffee, iced tea, a soft drink? Take your pick."

"Water would be great." I stepped into the kitchen, grabbed a bottle of designer spring water from the fridge, and handed it to him.

"Thanks. Guess I should get down to business. The paper you found?"

"Right there, on the end table." I nodded toward the table where I had left the list, and Wesson half stood to reach the paper that sat on the table at the other end of the sofa.

Glancing at the list, he seemed surprised. "You didn't tell me it was handwritten," he said sharply. A familiar wave of annoyance washed over me.

"You didn't ask," I said irritably.

"Sorry, Laurel, it's a policeman's curse—treating everyone as though they're suspects."

"Hmmph—how charming. You must be a very popular guy," I said sarcastically.

"Not very," He smiled disarmingly. "Honestly, I didn't mean to be rude." Frowning, he studied the list. "This handwriting is awful. It's almost impossible to read."

"Yes, it's pretty bad, but I managed to make it out. Want a translation?"

"Sure, that would be helpful."

Sitting beside him on the sofa, I took the list and pointed to the words as I read them to him. Sitting so close to him, I felt uncomfortably nervous, and my hand trembled slightly, but Wesson didn't seem to notice. At least, he made no comment. When I'd finished reading, I gave the list back to him and hurriedly moved from the sofa to the facing loveseat.

"Maybe one of the board members named on the list killed Victor," I said. "They wouldn't have been happy about Victor's using what he knew to get them to vote his way."

"How do you know he did that?" At least his question didn't make me feel as though I were being interrogated this time.

"I don't know positively about Edna Elkins, Luis Cardoza, or Peter Harvey, but Luke told me that he overheard Victor threatening Rachel Casswell, and he thinks Victor had some hold over others on the board because Victor always managed to swing every vote the way he wanted it to go. Other people noticed that, too, and wondered how he accomplished it."

Wesson was staring at me quizzically.

"You can confirm that with Luke," I offered.

"I'll talk to Luke about it, but not because I don't believe you, Laurel. It's just procedure."

I nodded. As annoying as it was, I was beginning to realize that much of Wesson's job consisted of dotting the i's and crossing the t's.

"Now, when you called me earlier, you mentioned that you found the list at the community center. Would you mind going over how you found it again?"

Everything with Wesson came down to an interrogation, but at least he'd asked if I "minded" this time.

"The only thing that I can imagine could have happened was that I accidentally scooped the list up with my class papers when I was using the photocopy machine last week. I remember finding a paper left on the photocopier—it happens all the time, so I didn't really think much about it. I set the page aside, and I didn't even realize that I had it until I was sorting through my class papers this afternoon. That's when I called you."

Wesson nodded. "Who has access to the copier?"

"Just about everyone. It's right out in the open, in the HOA office's reception area, and everyone who works in the office uses it. So do the instructors and anyone else who works in the building. It's available for the residents to use, too."

"No code or key card?"

"No. Like I said, it's pretty much wide open."

"As you suggested, the board members named may have had a motive for killing Eberhart, but the list itself doesn't prove anything. We don't know where it came from. We don't know who compiled it. We don't know that the information on it is accurate; in fact, the whole thing could be a total fabrication, someone's lame idea of a practical joke."

"I thought of that, but considering what Luke told me, I thought the list might shed some light on the situation."

"It could at that, and you did the right thing by turning it over. I never know where a lead might take me. We'll look into it." Wesson folded the paper and tucked it into his front shirt pocket. He leaned back on the sofa, picked up the water bottle I had given him, and drained it. "Guess I was thirsty."

"Would you like some more water?"

"No, thanks; I need to get back to the office. I'll be lucky to get home by midnight."

"All work and no play—"

"You got that right. It wouldn't hurt to take an evening off." He looked at me speculatively. "Would you like to have dinner with me tomorrow evening?"

Whoa! I hadn't seen *that* coming. The lieutenant had gone from Mr. Official Police Detective to Mr. Potential Boyfriend in a flash. I wasn't sure I was ready for the Miss-Potential-Girlfriend role, but Tracey's words came back to me, advising me that I needed to move on with my life, and that meant making room in my heart for romance again. Maybe she was right.

"I'm afraid that I can't tomorrow night." Seeing the disappointment on Wes's face, I hastened to add, "But I could go the following night. Tomorrow, I'm helping with a going-away party we're having for Bessie." I could tell that Wes hadn't recognized Bessie's name. "You know—the guard who was attacked."

"Oh, right." He hesitated only a second. "Well, Thursday's fine with me. How 'bout eight? I'll pick you up."

I smiled. "Eight's fine."

As Wesson stood, Bear, who'd fallen asleep with his chin on the detective's shoe, jumped up and trotted beside him to the front door.

"Good night, Laurel, and good night to you, too, Bear."

Chapter 12

With a parting pat on Bear's head, the lieutenant flashed me a 200-watt smile and strolled down my front sidewalk. When he reached the street, he looked back at me and waved. Feeling a bit light-headed, I raised my hand in a half-hearted salute and leaned on the door, closing it. What had I done?

I rushed to my smartphone and texted Tracey that I had a date with Wes on Thursday evening. Not surprisingly, my phone rang within seconds.

"I can't believe you texted me the big news! Why didn't you call?" Without waiting for my response, Tracey demanded: "Tell me everything."

I did exactly that, describing how I'd found the list mixed in with my paperwork and my meeting with Wes. By the time I finished, Tracey was gushing with uncontained excitement. At last, I was following her advice, and she was thrilled.

"So you think I did the right thing by accepting his invitation to dinner?"

"Why would you even ask that, Lo-lo?" she said, reverting to her childhood name for me. "He sounds totally hot! You go, girl! Does he have a brother?"

We laughed. Tracey may have been between boyfriends at the time, but that was a situation that never lasted very long. My BFF certainly didn't need my help where meeting men was concerned.

After discussing my new-found love life for an hour, we agreed to meet the next day to do the shopping for Bessie's party. I was glad that Tracey had been able to take the day off. As a top manager at a company that specialized in branding and the design of custom-made trade show booths and displays, she has some flexibility with her schedule. Not only that, but she also has a huge SUV. With her big vehicle and my smaller one, we would be able to transport all the food with no problem. After comparing notes on our expanding grocery list, we arranged to meet for brunch at our favorite breakfast hang-out, Cuppa Joe, before driving to Costco to buy the food for the party. I wasn't sure that our budget would cover everything that we needed to buy, but I had already decided to pick up the difference if we couldn't stretch the money far enough.

During the night, I tossed and turned restlessly, not sleeping much at all, and after I finally fell asleep, it seemed like only minutes before I felt a wet doggie kiss on my face, and I knew that it was already time to get up and take Bear for his morning walk. After a quick trip to the bathroom, I dressed in light cotton capris, a brown t-shirt, and my been-through-the-mill, lace-up walking shoes. A glance in the mirror told me all I needed to know about my appearance. My sleepless night showed on my face, dark circles shadowing my eyes. Oh, well. I knew there wasn't anything I could do about that now, and there'd be no time for a nap later, so I'd have to depend on caffeine, and lots of it, to get me through the day.

After Bear and I had our morning walk and I downed three cups of coffee, I jumped in the shower, then dressed for the day in a short denim skirt, flat sandals, and a lightweight voile top with an autumn-leaf-inspired print design. I added sterling silver teardrop earrings and a beaded sterling bracelet I had made and popped on a couple of turquoise and silver rings.

After Tracey and I shopped for the food, we planned to cart it directly to the community center's kitchen, which connected to the meeting room where the party would be held. Since I wouldn't be home until after the party in the evening, which would make a long day alone for Bear, I'd made arrangements for him to spend it with my neighbors, Fran and Brian Wells, a retired couple who have a friendly golden retriever. Bear loves to romp with Goldie, and the Wellses planned to take the doggie duo for a walk in the park, too. It's handy to have neighbors who want to trade dog-sitting duties occasionally.

Stowing his food and treats in a canvas bag, along with some extra goodies and a present for Goldie, I snapped on Bear's leash, tied his new Western fringed scarf around Bear's neck, and we walked three doors down the street to Bear's home away from home for the day. I knew Goldie had heard us approaching when I heard her barking, and before I had a chance to ring the doorbell, Brian opened his front door and greeted us. Goldie was right at his heels, creating a bottleneck in the small entryway, but we managed to plunge ahead into the living room.

"What a cute scarf you're wearing, Bear!" Fran said. "I need to take a picture." She pulled her phone from her pocket.

"Wait a second, Fran. I made a scarf for Goldie, too." I reached in the canvas bag, pulled out Goldie's leopard-print scarf, and tied it around her neck.

"They're adorable," Fran said as she took several pictures of Bear and Goldie posing in their scarves. "I'll post these pictures on Facebook."

"Great! I'll take a look as soon as I have a chance. Thanks so much for taking care of Bear today. I really appreciate it!"

"We're happy to have him," Brian said. "Goldie always likes to have company, and Bear's her favorite. They'll have a good time at the park."

I set the canvas bag down on the kitchen counter. "Here's a container with Bear's food for dinner and some snacks. I brought extras for Goldie."

"Are they those peanut butter treats you make, Laurel?" Fran asked. "Goldie really likes those."

"Yes, and I added a couple of pumpkin treats, too. I'm trying out a new recipe." After Wes had left, I'd spent some of my nervous energy making a batch of treats with the recipe my cousin Lynn had sent me. I'd been especially careful to follow the recipe exactly and monitor the baking time because I was famous for burning almost everything I attempted to bake.

"You're so talented, Laurel. Honestly, I can't imagine how you think up all those projects of yours."

"Thanks, Fran. Actually, I'm not much of a cook or baker. My cousin Lynn gave me her recipe for the pumpkin treats."

"Well, I'm sure Goldie will love them."

"I should be back around nine or so to pick up Bear. I need to stay after the party and help with the clean-up."

"Sounds like you're going to have a long day, Laurel. Would you like some coffee to take with you?"

"No, thanks, Fran. I've had three cups already this morning." I leaned over and patted Goldie with one hand and Bear with the other. "Be a good boy, Bear," I admonished him.

"Don't worry about Bear, Laurel. He'll be fine," Brian said.

"I know he will, Brian. Well, I'd better head out. I'm meeting Tracey in a few minutes. See you tonight."

"'Bye now."

Although rush hour had come and gone, the mid-morning traffic turned out to be unusually heavy, and I pulled into the parking lot of Cuppa Joe ten minutes late. I could see Tracey's white SUV parked near the restaurant's door, so I scurried inside and spotted her in a booth next to a window that looked out on the parking lot. Panting slightly, I slid into the seat across from her.

"Sorry I'm late. Traffic," I said, taking a sip of coffee to which I'd added a generous amount of the rich cream that Cuppa Joe features. "Thanks for ordering the coffee."

"That's okay. I figured you got hung up somewhere, so I ordered the food, too. The usual for you."

"Great!" I don't think I'd ever had anything except my usual brunch dish at Cuppa Joe. It's a scrumptious French toast made with extra-thick bread that has raspberry filling inside and a raspberry garnish on top. "Looks like it's coming out now," I observed as the cook set two platters on the ledge between the kitchen and the dining room. Our server immediately picked them up and whisked our plates to us.

"Another pot of coffee, ladies?" the server asked as she set our plates in front of us.

"Sounds good to me," Tracey said. She turned to me after the server left, admitting, "I had three cups while I was waiting for you."

I nodded. "Bring it on." As Seattle natives, both of us love coffee, the city's favorite drink. "Mmmm. Yummy. This French toast rocks! You really should try it sometime, Trace."

"I'm more salty than sweet, unlike some people I know." Tracey paused and winked at me. Honestly, she's the only woman I know who can pull off a wink. "I'll stick with my Canadian bacon and eggs; thank you very much."

"To each, her own."

"I'll bet your lieutenant likes sweets. He likes you!"

"We'll see, and he's not *my* lieutenant."

"It's only a matter of time," Tracey said confidently as she speared a morsel of Canadian bacon with her fork. "Well, I don't believe it," she said, peering out the window. "Look over there, Laurel," she said, pointing to a boutique on the other side of the parking lot. "Isn't that Eva Meyer going into Ooh La La? I thought Karl said that she hadn't been out of the house in over a year."

"Looks like her, all right."

"Maybe having Courtney stay with her and Karl has expanded her horizons and inspired her to get out of the house for a while. I don't see Courtney with her, though."

"How does she stand it, I wonder, being trapped at home all the time?"

"Beats me. I'd go batty after a day or so myself if I didn't get out of the house."

"I guess she must prefer it that way. Nobody's forcing her to stay inside all the time. It's not as though Karl prevents her from leaving home."

"That's true."

"Didn't you think Karl seemed frustrated with Eva's refusal to go out of the house when we talked to him on Sunday?"

"Yeah, now that you mention it. Poor guy. Oh, gotta get this," Tracey said as her phone beeped, signaling an incoming text message. "I can't ever leave the office without being bombarded with messages."

"That's because you're a VIP."

"No, that's because I'm too much of a pushover," Tracey said as she rapidly texted a response. "You wouldn't believe how many times the people at work bugged me last week when we were in the Ozarks. Mom and Dad really got irritated."

"Maybe you could turn your phone off for the rest of the day," I gently suggested.

"No can do. We're working with a new client who has a huge budget, but, unfortunately, he needs a lot of hand-holding."

"Poor you! I don't know how you stand it."

"Goes with the territory. You about ready to head out?"

"Yes, I am. I've had enough coffee today to float a boat," I said, pulling some cash out of my handbag and setting it on top of the check the server had left when she delivered our second pot of coffee. "My treat."

"Thanks, Lo-lo. When we get to Costco, let's park right next to each other. It'll be easier to load all the food."

"Okay, I'll follow you there, but I'd better make a quick pit stop first," I said as I headed to the restroom.

Although Costco turned out to be much busier than I'd anticipated on a middle-of-the-week day, we managed to forage through the huge store, loading our carts as we went. We each ended up with two full carts of party fare before we joined the long check-out line. The couple in line behind us groaned when they realized that all four carts contained one order, but we shrugged and pressed on. Such are the grocery wars. As I'd guessed, our total came to more than Luke had given me, so I added some of my own cash to make up the difference.

Loading all the boxes was a chore, and by the time we had them all stowed in our SUVs, I was feeling very glad that I'd been faithfully following my weight-lifting regimen, even though I worked out with only eight-pound dumbbells, far from the heaviest weights, for sure. Even so, I could definitely tell the difference. Before I began working out with the weights, it would have been much more of a struggle to lift heavy boxes.

The next few hours passed quickly as we returned to Hawkeye Haven, unloaded the food at the community center, and prepared for the party. With help from Luke, Kenny, Cynthia, and Amy, we finished setting up just as the first few guests began to arrive. Cynthia and Amy had volunteered to replenish the food and drinks, which we'd arranged buffet style, on three long tables set against the wall in the meeting room where we were having the party. That left Tracey and me free to mingle until after the party, when we'd both be on clean-up detail.

"Here's Bessie now," I told Tracey as Bessie arrived with her family. "Come on, and I'll introduce you." Actually, Bessie looked like a different woman in her beautiful purple lace cocktail dress, and I realized that the only time before tonight that I'd seen her wearing anything other than her security guard's uniform had been last week, when I visited her in the hospital.

"Hi, Bessie." I greeted her with a quick hug, and we made introductions all around. Bessie's son, his wife, and their two teen-aged daughters accompanied her.

"You look lovely, Bessie," I said, and I meant it. The wound on the back of her head wasn't visible at all. She must have noticed that I was looking at her hair, trying to figure out how the head wound had miraculously healed so quickly.

Bessie patted her hair and whispered to me," It's a wig. Debby fixed it for me."

"Wow, well, it looks great. I couldn't figure out how you'd healed so quickly. Sorry I was staring."

"If only I had healed quickly! My head still hurts, but it's getting a little bit better every day. I don't feel nearly as fuzzy as I did when you visited me in the hospital. I don't even feel bad about giving up my job anymore because I already got a new one."

"That was quick. I thought you were going to take it easy for a while."

"Don't know what I'd do, staying at home all day." Her comment made me think about how different Bessie is from Eva, who wants to stay home all day, every day. "Deb noticed that they were looking for a clerk at our neighborhood supermarket. I applied yesterday, and this morning, the manager called and told me I could start work there Monday. Not bad, huh?"

"I hope you like it, Bessie," I said.

"Oh, I will. All my friends shop there, and I know all the clerks, too. It'll keep me out of trouble," she joked. "Hey, Al!" she cried, as she spotted a white-haired man wearing the uniform of the Hawkeye Haven security guards. I'd noticed that quite a few of her co-workers had shown up to bid Bessie farewell. "'S'cuse me, Laurel; I'll see you again later," Bessie said as Al approached her and gave her a big hug.

Turning to Tracey, I suggested that we sample some of the food from the buffet that we'd helped Cynthia and Amy to set up. Luke and Kenny had placed several round tables in the center of the room where guests could sit although many of the attendees were milling about the room, balancing plates and cups while standing. Since we'd been on our feet for several hours, we decided to snag places at one of the tables so that we could sit down for a few minutes.

"Call me a wimp, but it feels good to sit down," Tracey said.

"It really does," I agreed. "I'm glad we're having a good turn-out tonight. It was nice of Luke to suggest having a party for Bessie. Too bad he had to hassle with Patty about it."

"Speak of the devil," Tracey said. I turned to see Patty approaching Luke.

"Oh, no, now what?" I groaned as Patty angrily grabbed Luke's arm. He shook her off, but she grabbed him again. I watched as Luke led her toward the kitchen and closed the door between the two adjoining rooms.

"Looks like it's time for me to replenish the veggie tray," I said.

"Amy and Cynthia will take care of that," Tracey said, looking at me as though I'd lost my mind. Then the light dawned. "Oh, I get it. I'm coming with you."

We discarded our paper plates and cups in the giant wastebasket Kenny had set next to the kitchen door and passed through to the adjoining kitchen. Although Amy and Cynthia were bustling about the room, there was no sign of Luke or Patty, so I guessed that they'd gone out into the hallway. Just as I reached the door to the hall, Luke burst through it, a big grin on his face. Certainly not what I'd expected.

"Luke, I'm surprised Patty showed up," I said.

"Anything to cause a problem. That woman is certifiable. Now she's complaining that I was supposed to have her authorization to book the room. I told her again that the board had approved this party and that she'd better steer clear or I'd remove her from the building. Just then Rachel, the new HOA president, happened to come by, and she backed me up."

"So Patty left?"

"She turned around and headed towards her office. I don't think we'll be seeing any more of her tonight."

"Let's hope not. I wouldn't want anything to spoil Bessie's party."

"What do you say we go back in, ladies? I'm going to present Bessie with her ten-year service certificate in a minute."

"Could you wait just a little while longer before you start? Liz said that she'd bring the going-away gift, but

I haven't seen her yet. I need to find her so that you can give her the present along with the certificate."

"Sure. Just say the word."

Returning to the party, we scanned the room looking for Liz. Tracey spotted her sitting with the colonel at a table in the corner at about the same time Liz saw us and waved. We made our way through the crowd to their table.

"Hi, girls," Liz greeted us. "Would you like to join us?"

"Sure," Tracey said, grabbing the chair next to Liz.

"I bet you're looking for this, aren't you, Laurel?" Liz pulled a beautifully wrapped gift box from a shopping bag that she had stashed beside her on the chair that Tracey now occupied.

I smiled. "Sure am, and that's a fantastic job of gift wrapping. Did you do that, Liz?"

"Wish I could claim credit, but I'm not nearly as crafty as you are. Mimi, the lady who owns the boutique where I bought the scarf, wrapped it for me when I told her it was for a special occasion. I hope Bessie likes the scarf I picked out for her."

"I'm sure she will, Liz. You have exquisite taste. Thanks for getting it. Let me just drop this off to Luke and I'll be right back."

I found Luke chatting with a man I recognized as one of the HOA board members. Except for Edna Elkins and Luis Cardoza, I couldn't match names with the faces of any of the other board members I'd seen at last week's meeting, but when Luke introduced us, I knew that the name of this man wasn't on the list I'd found on the HOA's photocopier.

Leaving the gift with Luke, I detoured past the tables where we'd set up the desserts and assembled a plateful of cookies to take back to our table.

"Cookies, anyone?" I offered as I set the plate in the middle of the table. "These cookies aren't from the store. Cynthia made the raspberry chewies herself, and Amy made those pinwheel cookies," I said, helping myself to a chocolate and vanilla pinwheel.

"Don't mind if I do," the colonel said, taking one of each.

"I'll have a couple, too," Tracey said.

"Might as well make it unanimous," Liz said.

"Anybody need some coffee or something else to drink?" I asked.

"Let me go get the drinks, Laurel," the colonel said. "You've had a busy day. Why don't you sit down here and relax for a while." The colonel pulled out the chair beside him, and, thanking him, I plopped down in it. "What would you all like to drink?" We gave the colonel our drink orders—coffee for Tracey and me and iced tea for Liz—and he headed off to fetch them.

Before the colonel could return with our drinks, the squeal of feedback and electronic screeching signaled Luke's first attempt to use the microphone that was set up in the front of the room for board meetings. After a few seconds of testing, Luke managed to adjust the microphone so that the sound came through loud and clear. Luke beckoned Bessie to stand next to him as he gave a short, but flowery speech, wishing her well, thanking her for her ten years of service to the community, and saying that he was sorry to lose such a valuable member of the security team. He presented her with the certificate I'd made in recognition of her ten years of employment at Hawkeye Haven and then gave her the gift as a "small token of our appreciation." Preserving the lovely gift paper, Bessie carefully unwrapped the present, and she seemed genuinely thrilled when she saw the scarf that Liz had selected for her. Draping it around her neck, she petted it as though it were a soft cat's fur. Her voice quavering, she thanked Luke and everyone for coming to the party. The crowd clapped, and Bessie started to step away when Luke called her back and asked her son Tom to come up. Luke reached under the draped table next to him and pulled out a huge plant, which he presented to Bessie. She grinned and gave Luke a hug, and her son was left with the task of carrying the heavy plant out to his car as several of the partygoers gathered around Bessie to chat.

"Here we go, ladies," said the colonel, who had returned to our table balancing a tray holding our drinks. "Sorry I took so long, but I didn't want to disrupt the proceedings."

"Thanks," Tracey said, taking a sip of coffee. "That hits the spot."

"Mind if I join you?" I hadn't noticed Luke making his way over to our table until he spoke.

"Have a seat, Luke. How about some cookies?" I picked up the platter and put it in front of him as he sat next to me. He selected one of Cynthia's raspberry chewies, and began to munch it.

"Laurel, I want to thank you for all the work you did to put this party together. You too, Tracey. I know it was a lot of work on a tight budget."

"We're happy to do it, Luke. I think Bessie's having a good time, and I can tell she really appreciates the recognition," I said. Out of the corner of my eye, I could see Liz's hands trembling, but they were in her lap, so I doubt that anyone else noticed.

"You're right, Laurel. Ms. Dawson, I wanted to make sure I thanked you, too, for selecting Bessie's gift. My wife can tell you I don't have a clue when it comes to picking out something appropriate for the ladies."

"Thank you, Luke, and please call me Liz." Liz paused. "Is your wife here with you tonight? You showed me her picture the other day, and I'd like to meet her."

"No, she was planning to come, but our babysitter cancelled at the very last minute, and it was too late to find someone else to watch the girls."

I could tell that Liz really wanted to talk to her grandson, so I suggested that Tracey and I were needed in the kitchen, and we left Liz and the colonel at the table with Luke.

"What's up this time?" Tracey asked me.

"I can't go into the details because I promised Liz I wouldn't say anything to anybody, but, trust me, you'll know about it soon."

"Hmmm. Very mysterious. I thought you told me everything."

"I do. Well, unless I've promised to keep a secret."

"Ah, ha, so it's a secret?"

"It is, but not for long."

"Guess I'll just have to wait to find out," Tracey grumbled but without irritation. I could tell that she was more intrigued than annoyed. As we passed through the crowd, I spotted Edna Elkins leaving the group that had gathered around Bessie.

"There's Edna. Let's go talk to her and see what we can find out."

"Find out about what? Oh, no, you're not going to ask her about that list, are you? I thought the cops were going to handle that."

"I doubt that she knows that a list exists, but I am going to ask her about the reason her name appears on it."

"Lo-lo, I don't think that's such a good idea. What if she freaks out?"

"We'll see."

"Ooh, you're making me very nervous."

"Don't worry, Trace. Nothing's going to happen in the middle of the party, but maybe I should talk to her alone. Why don't you stay here for a minute? I'll be right back." Before Tracey had a chance to answer or talk me out of what was probably going to be a disastrous encounter, I hurried over to Edna, leaving Tracey anxiously standing next to the dessert table.

"Hi, Edna."

"Hi, Laurel. Nice party. Rachel told me that you helped Luke put it together."

"Yes, but I had a lot of help, too."

"Oh?"

"Tracey, Cynthia, Amy, and Liz all lent a hand."

"Well, that's nice. Be sure to thank them on behalf of the board members, although I can't say I was consulted about it in the first place. Rachel agreed to the party without mentioning it to anyone else. I just hope she doesn't turn out to be as high-handed as her predecessor."

"I guess nobody liked Victor."

"You can say that again. I don't know how he managed to get elected as board president."

"Maybe he used some of the same tactics he used to sway the board members his way."

Edna's smile was instantly replaced with a frown. "What would you know about that?"

"I've heard rumors."

"Just exactly what are you implying, Laurel?"

"I'm not implying anything. I heard that Victor coerced some of the board members into voting the way he wanted them to. That's all."

Edna eyed me suspiciously. "And where did you hear that?"

"I'm really not at liberty to say." I certainly wasn't going to tell her about Luke's suspicions or about my finding the list.

"You don't know what you're talking about."

"I know that it would have been easy for Victor to resort to blackmail. He knew things about people that they didn't want to be made public. Like losing your nursing license and your brush with the law." I knew I was pushing it with Edna. Her face contorted with anger, but her rage didn't stop her from trying to turn the tables on me.

"Really, Laurel, you should be ashamed of yourself for spreading gossip."

I ignored her remark, which was laughable given that the Hawkeye Haven grapevine was so active, and Edna had never before objected to participating in some juicy gossip about her neighbors.

"So you deny that you injected a patient with a dirty needle?" I was on thin ice, and I knew it. Although Edna's secret had been listed on the paper I found, there had been no notation about where the incident had taken place, and I hadn't been able to find any information about it when I searched online. I suspected that Edna had probably changed her name and moved to Iowa sometime after the lawsuit had been settled, but I really had no proof.

"Laurel McMillan! You have no right to accuse me of anything. You'd better watch yourself, missy, if you want to keep teaching those silly little classes of yours. The board could cancel them at any time, you know."

Her face flaming, Edna turned and stalked out of the party. It didn't escape me that she had maintained her the-best-defense-is-a-good-offense strategy right to the end of our conversation. I'd noticed something else, too. Edna had never denied that she'd gotten into legal trouble or that she'd lost her nursing license. I'd hit a nerve, and I'd made an enemy, but I still had no idea how far Edna would have been willing to go to keep her secret. Far enough to murder Victor?

168 Death by Association

Chapter 13

"What did you say to Edna, Lo-lo? She took off out of here like her hair was on fire," Tracey said as she joined me.

"Oh, not much. I just suggested to her that Victor may have been trying to coerce her votes on the board, and she didn't like that very much. Then I asked her about the dirty needle incident, and she threatened to cancel my classes."

"Oh, no!"

"Not to worry, Trace. Edna may think she can cancel my classes, but she's wrong. I have more than two years left on my contract to teach the DIY classes, remember?"

"That's right. I'd forgotten about the contract. Your lawyer looked it over, if I remember right."

"Yes, and he said it's ironclad, so I'm not too worried. I doubt that Edna even realizes that I have a contract with Hawkeye Haven because she wasn't a member of the HOA's board when I signed it. Edna may think she frightened me, but she's wrong."

"Well, I hope she drops the matter."

"So do I. I guess she figures the best defense is a good offense. It was pretty bold of Edna to threaten me, though. I think she's scared."

Tracey nodded. "Maybe you should back off. You're not going to talk to the others on the list, are you?" Reading my expression, Tracey exclaimed, "You are!"

"Maybe I'm thinking about it. Tonight the opportunity just seemed to present itself."

"Be careful, Lo-lo. You could be talking to a killer. Why don't you let the police ask the questions?"

Why, indeed? At first, my interest in Victor's murder had stemmed from mere curiosity, but when I realized that there might be a link between Bessie's attacker and the murderer, and that the killer was very likely one of my neighbors, I had been drawn into the puzzle. I felt uncomfortable in my own community, and I knew that my friends did, too.

"I guess I should, but after finding that list, well, I can't help but wonder whether one of our HOA's board members could be the killer," I said.

"I suppose they hated Victor as much as anyone, maybe more since he was blackmailing them."

"Four of them, anyway, including Rachel, the new HOA president. I guess Victor couldn't come up with anything on the other two."

"Rachel seems like a nice lady. After all, she agreed to let Luke have this party for Bessie, and she backed him up when Patty objected to it."

"Hopefully, her life of crime is over. She's the one who was convicted of embezzlement."

"Didn't you tell me that she went to prison?"

"A two-year sentence, according to the info on the list. Not exactly something she'd want to include on her résumé when she ran for the board and probably not something she'd especially want her neighbors to know."

As we talked, Tracey and I had drifted toward a corner of the room. We'd kept our voices low so that nobody could overhear what we were talking about. I'd been so engrossed in our conversation that I hadn't noticed that the crowd had begun to thin out.

"It looks as though the party's winding down," Tracey observed. "Look at the buffet tables. They're practically empty."

"I'd better pop into the kitchen and touch base with Cynthia and Amy, but it looks as though we can probably start cleaning up now."

"Right. Say, maybe we should send the leftovers home with Bessie," Tracey suggested.

"That's a good idea."

I looked around the room and saw Bessie talking to Al, the security guard, she'd greeted earlier.

"There she is," I told Tracey. "Let's check with her and find out if she wants to take the rest of the food home."

After confirming with Bessie that she'd be happy to have any leftovers, I went into the kitchen to let Cynthia and Amy know, and Tracey began clearing some of the trays from the buffet tables. Because we'd used disposable plates and plastic utensils, only the serving trays, pitchers, and the huge coffeemaker needed to be washed. I set to work at the sink, washing the serving pieces while Tracey continued to clear the buffet tables. Cynthia and Amy packaged the leftovers so that Bessie could take them home with her.

With only the coffeemaker yet to wash, I thanked Cynthia and Amy for their help and told them that Tracey and I would finish cleaning up and that they might as well go home. They didn't object, and we waved good-bye as they went into the meeting room to wish Bessie good luck.

After I washed the coffeemaker, Tracey dried it and returned it to its usual place on the kitchen counter. For good measure, we wiped all the kitchen countertops one last time before calling Bessie's son to carry the big box of leftovers to his car.

The rest of the crowd had departed, leaving only Bessie, her family, Luke, and Rachel in the meeting room. Kenny was supposed to help Luke move the tables and chairs to set up the room for the next meeting, but I didn't see Kenny. I suspected that he was hanging out in the janitor's closet, puffing on a cigarette, just as he had been when I'd needed to find a key to enter my locked classroom on Saturday. I figured that the only reason Rachel was staying was that she was waiting to give her son a ride home.

I heard Luke tell Rachel that it was time to move the furniture, and he left in search of Kenny. Although I was tempted to talk to Rachel, as I had Edna, Bessie had rushed to thank me and Tracey for our help with the party, so I couldn't speak with Rachel alone. Just as I was giving Bessie a good-bye hug, Luke returned with a reluctant Kenny in tow.

"Hurry up, Kenny," his mother commanded. "You still have homework to do, you know."

Acknowledging his mother's admonition with a grunt, Kenny slunk into the room. Dressed in a black sweatshirt and worn jeans, he wore a red baseball cap pulled so low over his face that it hid his eyes. Luke directed him to one of the tables we'd used for the buffet, and as the two of them reached down to fold the metal legs of the table, the right sleeve of Kenny's sweatshirt rode up, revealing a hideous-looking tattoo of a fire-breathing dragon. Suddenly, Bessie gasped and pointed to Kenny.

"It's him! He's the one who attacked me!"

Everybody froze as Bessie's trembling finger continued to point at Kenny, but the teenager didn't wait to hear any more. Kenny sprinted from the room, leaving his wide-eyed mother sputtering in confusion. Luke took off after Kenny, and although the teenager had the advantage of youth on his side, Luke managed to grab him before he ran too far, and he hauled Kenny back into the room. Hanging his head, Kenny refused to look in Bessie's direction.

"Bessie, how do you know it was Kenny?" I asked.

"It's his tattoo. I remember it now—that red dragon tattoo."

"What do you have to say for yourself, Kenny?" Luke demanded, a scowl on his face. He was still panting from the chase to catch up to Kenny.

"Answer the man, Kenny," Rachel demanded.

"I didn't mean to hurt the old lady," Kenny said. "I was just after the gun."

"Oh, no, Kenny," Rachel said. "Whatever possessed you?"

"I couldn't be a Dragon without a gun."

"Are the Dragons a gang at your high school?" Luke asked.

Kenny hung his head and nodded.

"Where's the gun now, Kenny? Did you give it to someone else in the gang?"

"No, after the old lady fell and cracked her head, I got scared and dumped it. So I still couldn't join." Incredibly, Kenny appeared to continue to covet membership in the Dragons even though he'd committed a felony in the process of trying to obtain the price of membership.

"This is serious business, Kenny," Luke said. "I'm going to have to turn you over to the police, and you're going to stay right here until they come to pick you up," Without releasing his grip on Kenny, he turned to Rachel. "I'm sorry, Rachel."

While Luke pulled his smartphone out of his pocket and called the police, Rachel sobbed openly. Kenny, eyes downcast, at least had the decency to look ashamed for disgracing himself and his mother.

"Uh, Kenny, you said you dumped the gun. What exactly did you do with it?" I asked.

"Threw it in a trash can on the way home."

"Kenny, that's enough. Don't say anything else," Rachel cautioned her son. "I'm going to get you a lawyer. Don't say another word, do you understand?"

"Yeah."

"I mean it, Kenny. You're in big trouble. Don't make it any worse," Rachel reiterated.

Although I could understand that Rachel wanted to protect her son, I wished she hadn't thought of it quite so soon. Once Bessie had identified Kenny as her attacker, he hadn't tried to deny it. Maybe we could have found out more about precisely where he'd disposed of the gun if Rachel hadn't switched into mama-bear mode. That is, *if* he really had disposed of the gun, and that was a big "if."

Assuming that Luke was correct, the gun Victor was shot with was Bessie's gun. Kenny admitted stealing Bessie's gun, so it wasn't a leap to think that there was a possibility that Kenny could be Victor's murderer. It didn't make much sense that he would have grabbed the gun and then disposed of it, especially because the price of admission to the gang he wanted so much to join was a gun. Maybe Kenny had lied about getting rid of the gun. After all, he'd confessed to the attack on Bessie to take her gun. It was only a step further to connect him to the murder itself.

If he did it, why did he do it? Kenny worked part-time at the community center. Perhaps Victor had reprimanded him for shirking his on-the-job duties. Still, that seemed a bit far-fetched, especially given that Kenny was a known slacker, one whom both his immediate boss and Luke had warned to shape up. His mother had gotten him the job, probably in the hope that it would keep him out of trouble and that he'd learn some responsibility. Despite his less-than-competent job performance, he hadn't been fired because his mother was a board member.

Maybe it had nothing to do with Kenny's job at the community center. Maybe it had everything to do with Rachel. Could Kenny have found out that Victor was blackmailing his mother? If so, he may have decided to solve Rachel's dilemma by killing her tormentor. Protecting a loved one could be a powerful motive. I was having trouble believing that Kenny could be a murderer, though. It was difficult to picture the whiny teenager shooting Victor, but I reminded myself that he'd attacked Bessie, if only accidentally, since he claimed that he hadn't intended to harm her.

We waited for the police to arrive—Rachel dabbing at her eyes with a limp tissue, Kenny hanging his head, Luke maintaining a firm grip on the juvenile delinquent, Tracey and I standing silently next to Luke—as Bessie and her family moved away from Kenny to the far side of the room. Within a few minutes, two uniformed officers arrived and took Kenny into custody after they spoke briefly with Luke and Bessie, both of whom agreed to go the station to make a statement. Although Tracey and I had heard Kenny confess, too, the policemen took our names, addresses, and phone numbers, saying that we'd be contacted if necessary, although we all assumed it wouldn't be necessary because Kenny had admitted attacking Bessie and stealing her gun.

I was a little bit disappointed that Wes hadn't responded to Luke's call, but I knew he'd hear about the wayward teenager soon enough. Anyway, even if Wes had come to arrest Kenny, he would have been all business, and worse yet, his pugnacious partner might have accompanied him. Still, I wouldn't have minded seeing Wes. He certainly wasn't too hard on the eyes, I thought dreamily before I willed myself back to reality, and the reality was that even though I had a date with the handsome detective tomorrow night, that didn't necessarily make him my Prince Charming. Since Tim's tragic accident, my love life had been woefully short on princes, and there had been little charming about it, either.

Chapter 14

"Some party, huh?" Tracey said as we walked through the community center's parking lot to our cars.

"A lot more excitement than we anticipated, that's for sure. I'm glad Bessie's memory has come back, and so has her spunk. Can you believe that she recognized Kenny by that awful dragon tattoo of his?"

"Now that we know he's the culprit, I can understand why Kenny was acting so strangely."

"What do you mean?" I asked.

"He seemed to be making an effort to stay away from the party, hiding out the way he did. Then when Luke made him come back to help take down the tables, he avoided looking at Bessie, and he had his cap pulled down over his face. Not only that, but who wears a sweatshirt on a hot day like today?"

"You're right. I didn't think much of it at the time because I know from experience that Kenny tries to avoid work, but the baseball cap disguise was a new wrinkle, and it's way too warm to be wearing a sweatshirt."

"That kid's in for a rough time."

"He deserves it. He could have killed Bessie, even though he says he didn't mean to hurt her."

"Well, I don't envy him or his mother. I think they'll throw the book at him, lawyer or no lawyer," Tracey said.

"Most likely. It was interesting to see Rachel in action. Obviously, she's really upset with Kenny, but she's still the protective mom."

"She's done time herself, if the information on that list you found is real. I can't imagine how she must feel, knowing that her son could be sentenced to prison, too."

"Yes, it would be awful. As far as I know, Kenny's her only child."

As we were saying good-bye, Tracey's phone rang, and she mouthed that she had to take the call. Since she'd turned her phone off during the party, it didn't surprise me that she'd received a call as soon as she'd turned it back on. I'd be willing to bet that her voice mail had filled with several messages during the last few hours, too. With a wave to Tracey, I started my engine, and I waited until she pulled out of her parking space before I did the same.

I knew I'd be late picking up Bear and that Fran and Brian must be wondering what was keeping me so long. As soon as I rang their doorbell, I could hear Bear and Goldie both barking, and as Brian opened the front door for me, they rushed past him to greet me. Goldie settled down quickly, but Bear bounced around for a while as I slowly inched my way into the house, patting my enthusiastic Lab at the same time.

"Settle down, Bear," I said. "We're going home in a minute."

"How was the party, Laurel?" Fran asked, wandering into the living room from the den. She'd been watching television, I knew because I'd heard the unmistakable sound of a laugh track as I'd entered the house.

"It was great, but we had a big surprise at the end." I proceeded to fill Fran and Brian in on the latest news. The Hawkeye Haven grapevine was probably already humming with the story of Kenny's confession.

As it turned out, I wasn't the only bearer of news. Fran told me that she'd received an email message earlier in the evening that Patty had sent to all of the residents of Hawkeye Haven, informing them that Victor's funeral would be held on Friday morning at the Meadows Funeral Home. I figured that Patty had probably come to her office in the community center after hours to send the message, and then she'd decided to take the opportunity to object again to Bessie's party. Strange that Patty really hadn't seemed much affected by Victor's passing, especially since Victor had hired her, they'd worked together at IFI, and they seemed to have some kind of a scheme planned at Hawkeye Haven. Still, Patty had insinuated that Luke might have been involved in the murder, so maybe she had been shaken by Victor's murder, after all.

"Are you going to the funeral?" I asked Fran and Brian.

"No, can't say that I thought much of the man," Brian answered. "Victor substituted in our golf foursome a couple of times when one of the guys was in the hospital. That's the only way I knew him, and I can't say that I cared for his constant bragging about what a great golfer he was and how much money he had made. Last time our group needed a sub, we found someone else to fill in. When Victor ran for president of the HOA, we didn't vote for him, either. In fact, I'm surprised he was elected."

"Are you planning to attend?" Fran asked me.

"I'm not sure yet, but I may go. I know his daughter slightly because she's attended a couple of my classes, and I have the feeling she may need the moral support. The only time I ever saw Victor myself was at the HOA's meeting last week, and he was very rude to a couple of my friends, so if I go to the funeral, it won't be because I held him in great regard."

"It's a sad commentary on his life, but, from everything I've heard, he wasn't much of a man," Fran said as Goldie nuzzled her side, and she turned to talk to her dog. "Okay, Goldie, sweetie, we'll go night-night in a few minutes."

"I can take a hint," I joked. "Come on, Bear, let's head for home. Thanks so much for taking care of him, and let me know when I can dog-sit Goldie for you."

"Oh, we will! We're planning on a short trip to Omaha in a couple of weeks, and it would be great if she could stay with you," Fran said.

"We'll be happy to have her, won't we, Bear? 'Bye now, and thanks again."

Bear was tired after his day with Goldie, so as soon as we reached the house, he headed straight for the bedroom, where he flopped down on the cushy bed that I had made for him. The dog bed was a DIY project that I intended to include in my book because it was so easy to make, and it required no sewing at all. I'd made three beds for Bear so that he could have one in the bedroom, the den, and the office, and he takes full advantage of all of them, although when the weather is hot, he often likes to lie on the tile because it feels cooler.

He fell asleep promptly, and he didn't even wiggle as I brushed my teeth and prepared for bed. Even though it had been a busy day, I didn't feel very tired, so I decided to read in bed for a while. My book club's next meeting was two weeks away, and I knew I should probably be reading the book designated as September's selection, but I hadn't even made it through the first chapter the last time I'd attempted to read it. Instead, I settled on a historical romance that the club members had voted to read so that we could discuss it at our October meeting. The novel held my interest through the first several chapters, and the time slipped away. It was closer to one than midnight before I realized it. I knew Bear would be up before six the following morning, which meant that, with luck, I'd have only five hours of sleep. Actually I know several people who seem to function just fine on five hours of sleep, but, unfortunately, I'm not one of them. Groaning, I thought about how awful I was going to look for my date tomorrow night—no, make that tonight—with dark circles under my eyes. Before I turned out the light, I checked Bear and saw that he hadn't even moved since he'd fallen asleep. Maybe he wouldn't get up so early, after all.

That hope turned out to have been in vain. Eager for his morning walk, Bear woke up at the usual time. Reluctantly, I tumbled out of bed, quickly dressed, took him for his walk, and returned home to make a big pot of coffee. Caffeine would have to carry me through the morning, and I'd depend on a rare afternoon nap to revive me before my date with Wes.

Although it would be several hours before Wes came to pick me up for dinner, I was already feeling nervous at the thought of going out on a formal date. It had been more than a year since I'd even gone out with a man. I'd doubled with Tracey and Liam, who'd been her boyfriend at the time. Rick, my date, was a friend of Liam's, and although Rick seemed like a nice guy, we didn't hit it off, so it was a chore just to get through the evening. After that, I told Tracey absolutely, positively, no more blind dates for me. I had learned my lesson. I had to keep telling myself that tonight was no blind date. Wes already knew me—at least a little bit—and liked me—at least a little bit—or he'd never have asked me to dinner.

To distract myself, I got busy with household chores, cleaning the kitchen and both bathrooms and washing some clothes. When I'm tired, I have trouble focusing, and I make a lot of mistakes, so it definitely wouldn't have been a good time to work on my book proposal or a slide presentation for next week's DIY class, Make Your Own Autumn Wreath.

By early afternoon, I felt satisfied that I'd at least accomplished something. Slathering on sunscreen, I grabbed a floppy hat to wear and took Bear out to the backyard to play fetch with him. He chased his hard rubber ball again and again until we both grew tired. It seemed like the perfect time to take the nap I'd promised myself, so I unplugged my landline, turned off my smartphone, and lay down on the sofa in the den. Bear curled up on his bed next to the sofa, and we both slept soundly for over an hour. After catching up on sleep, I felt refreshed and ready to decide what to wear for my date with Wes.

Turning my smartphone back on, I texted Tracey to ask her opinion, and she texted me back, inquiring whether or not I knew where we were going. In fact, Wes had never mentioned a specific place, and I hadn't heard from him since he'd asked me out. Before I could answer Tracey, she called me.

"Hey, I would have called you back right away, but a client was in my office when you texted. Mr. Super Picky just left. Thank goodness. I guess I must have looked really serious when I picked up my phone to read your text, so he took that as a cue. Boy, am I glad he's out of here. He's the biggest pain ever, trying to micromanage everything. I can't imagine why he bothered to hire us in the first place. Uh, sorry for the rant, Lo-lo. The guy really gets to me sometimes."

"I don't know how you do it, Tracey, having to put up with all the whims of your clients."

"We try to keep them happy, and most of them are reasonable people. But now that you mention it, I guess a few of them are a little hard to take at times. This guy, for instance. We've bent over backwards trying to accommodate him, but he wants to change everything we do. It's like he's got to have his own personal stamp on even the slightest detail, or he's not happy. Ugh! He's driving me crazy!"

"He sounds awful."

"He's the guy I mentioned the other day—the one with megamillions."

"And you want him to spend some of those millions with your company."

"That's the general idea, but sometimes it doesn't seem worth it, and this may be one of those times. Unfortunately, that's not my call. But, anyway, enough about him. Where did you say you two are going tonight?"

"Don't know. Wes didn't mention any place in particular."

"Okay, so dinner. That could mean anything from a hamburger at Burger Inn to gourmet cuisine at a five-star restaurant."

"I guess so, although Burger Inn is probably out," I said, laughing at my own tiny joke. "That's what he had just before he came over to my house the other night—a hamburger and fries from Burger Inn. It might be his go-to fast food place."

"Yeah, I was kidding about the fast food. I'll bet he's going to take you someplace nice. Why don't you wear that cobalt blue silk dress you made? It really looks stunning on you."

"You don't think it's too dressy?"

"No, it's okay to be a little dressed up. Just don't wear glitzy jewelry or carry an evening bag. Then you'll be on safe middle ground—nice but not too dressy."

"Hmmm. I was thinking of wearing that sundress— the one I wore to the buffet Sunday."

"Too beachy, I think."

"Well, you're probably right. I guess your pick makes more sense. I'll wear the blue silk dress."

"Atta girl. The color's perfect with your red hair and fair complexion. And don't you dare put your hair in a bun. It makes you look too severe."

"Really? That's exactly how I was planning to wear it."

"No way! Wear it down—loose and flowing. Guys like that. One more thing, Lo-lo. Past relationships almost always come up on a first date. If he dwells on his, run like the wind. The last thing you need is a boyfriend who's still hung up on his ex, so make sure he's really available."

"Yes, coach. I'll bow to your expertise. You know how long it's been since I've been on a date. I don't know what I'm doing. I'm an incompetent dater."

"Not for long, you're not. Just go and have a good time. Don't try to over-analyze the experience or the man. And remember, he isn't Tim. No man can replace him. Wes is a different person. Appreciate him for who he is."

"Okay, okay, you make a good point."

"Don't forget to call me and fill me in on all the details."

Assuring Tracey that I'd tell her all about it after my date, I wished her good luck with her client, Mr. Super Picky.

Tracey was right, of course. I needed to stop thinking that Tim had been the only man I could ever love, and I should stop comparing every man I met to my late husband. I knew it wasn't fair, and maybe it was my way of keeping love away. After all, in my experience, love hurt, and I didn't ever want to be hurt again. My self-imposed avoidance of the dating scene and men, in general, had served its purpose, and I kept asking myself if I wanted to be vulnerable again. On the other hand, I was already analyzing the situation— doing just exactly what Tracey had told me not to do.

She knew me too well. I couldn't seem to stop looking at all the angles and wondering whether this first date would lead to a second and a third.

Enough! I forced myself to stop thinking about it and, instead, concentrated on what I needed to do to get ready. I spent a long time styling my hair, as Tracey had suggested, and playing with my make-up so that it would be just right. Honestly, I didn't know how Liz could do such detailed make-up every single day, even when she never left the house. I'd never have the time to spend so long on my face each morning, but Liz had had plenty of practice, and she probably was much faster at it than I was.

Although it seemed to take forever, I finally put the finishing touch of lip-colored gloss on, just as the doorbell rang.

Bear beat me to the door, but I made him sit and stay back a ways so that I could greet Wes before my dog did. I opened the door and smiled at Wes, who looked handsome in a navy blazer, conservative striped tie, and gray trousers.

"Wow, you look beautiful, Laurel."

"So do you," I said and blushed furiously. "I mean handsome," I murmured, but before Wes had a chance to respond, Bear rushed over to us, unable to contain his excitement at having a visitor.

"Oh, Bear, you're not minding very well. He was supposed to sit and stay," I explained to Wes.

"So he's in the dog house?" Wes laughed.

"Not too much, I guess. He has an over-indulgent pet parent; that's for sure."

"How are you, boy?" Wes patted Bear, and the attention pacified the eager dog.

"Wes, shall we go and leave him to his nap? We could be here all night, the way Bear soaks up attention. He'll settle down as soon as we leave."

"Sure, that's fine."

"Stay here and be a good boy," I told Bear as we quickly departed. Bear looked forlorn, as usual, and it was difficult to ignore his doggie version of a guilt trip, but I knew that he'd settle down and nap most of the time while I was gone.

As we left the house, I spotted a large black pickup truck parked at the curb, and fearing that it belonged to Wes, I panicked momentarily. I certainly wouldn't look very graceful trying to climb up into such a big truck.

"That's not your truck, is it, Laurel?"

"No," I said, relieved that it obviously wasn't Wes's, either. "Must be somebody visiting one of the neighbors."

Wes led me to a late model silver Toyota Camry, parked across the street, and opened the door for me. Nice. We were off to a good start, I thought.

"Where are we going?" I asked, glad that I'd worn my blue silk dress.

"Arnold's. It's a relatively new place that my sister recommended. She told me that Chef Arnold left a ritzy, five-star restaurant to open his own place on the east side of town. Denise is a foodie, so she's up on the local restaurant scene."

"Do you have other relatives living here?"

"Just Denise and her husband Jack. They have two grown daughters, but the girls are both attending college in California. How about you, Laurel? Any family here?"

"My cousin Tracey, who's my very best friend in the world—she lives in Hawkeye Haven, too—but the rest of our family all live in Seattle."

"Have you lived in Center City long, Laurel?"

"About three years now."

"Coming from Seattle, you must've gone into shock with our humid summer heat and freezing winters."

"Uh, huh. My first winter here I thought I would die. I'd never been anyplace so cold in my life. I do miss Seattle's moderate climate sometimes."

"Iowa weather can be brutal, and don't let the natives kid you. They don't like it any more than the transplants. I know I don't."

"So you're from Center City?"

"Yup, born here, went to school here, and then college at the University of Iowa in Iowa City."

"Did you always want to be a cop?"

"No, I had no idea what I wanted to do. I majored in business, mostly because I needed to declare a major in something, but when I graduated, the police department was recruiting. I had no other prospects, so I applied."

"And here you are—a detective."

"And here I am with the DIY Diva."

"How did you know that's my handle?"

"I'm a detective, remember? It's on the cover of your books. I bought the only two the Book Nook had left in stock."

"I'm flattered, but I can't imagine any of my books being too interesting for a guy. Which ones did you buy?"

"Uh, something about earrings—that's one, and the other one's about Christmas decorations."

"*The DIY Diva's Guide to Making Your Own Crystal Earrings* and *The DIY Diva's Guide to Holiday Decorating*."

Wes nodded. "You're a very talented lady. Is there anything you don't know how to make?"

"Food," I laughed. "I'm the worst cook in the world. Ironically, I'm going to include a few recipes in my next book. Actually they're for dog treats. I have one recipe I thought of myself, but I'm relying on my friends and relatives to give me some of their recipes to include in the book. Oh, darn, that reminds me—I never did get an email with Bessie's recipe. I guess she forgot to have her granddaughter email it to me."

"Bessie—that's the security guard who was attacked, the one you were having the party for?"

"Yes, with all the excitement at the party last night, I totally forgot to ask her about the recipe again." I paused, switching gears. "Do you think Kenny killed Victor?"

"Let's just say he's a person of interest at the moment."

"I know he confessed to stealing Bessie's gun, but he claimed that he didn't mean to harm her. According to what Kenny told us last night, he's all hung up on joining some gang at his high school, and they told him he had to have a gun to become a member. That's the only reason he stole the gun. Somehow, I just can't see Kenny shooting someone. He seems like such a cowardly, little weasel."

"You'd be surprised what people will do."

"I suppose so. So you think Kenny shot Victor?"

"Let's just say he's a person of interest at the moment," Wes repeated. His bland expression gave nothing away.

"Okay, you win. You can't talk about it, right?"

"Right, not while it's an active, unsolved case, but, believe me, it will be solved. With as many leads as we have coming in, I know from experience that something will break. But I don't blame you and your neighbors for being concerned."

"Our crime wave has really affected the residents; that's for sure. Everybody's jumpy. I guess we all assumed that we were safe because we live in a guard-gated community."

"I can understand that. In fact, murder in a guard-gated community is rare. Here's the thing: most killers have a close personal connection with their victims. In

Victor Eberhart's case, you know as well as I do that a lot of people Eberhart dealt with harbored a grudge, so it's likely that whoever killed him won't go after any other residents."

"But that's not a certainty."

"No, and, in any case, it never hurts to be on your guard. Seriously, Laurel, be very careful. Take Bear with you when you're walking around the community, and never open your door to someone you don't know."

"Victor wouldn't have opened his door unless he knew his killer, and he wasn't afraid of whoever it was."

"That's a logical assumption."

"Scary when you think about it."

"If there's one thing I've learned from being a homicide detective, it's that there are no guarantees in life."

"That's for sure," I sighed.

"Ah, here we are," Wes said as he turned into the parking lot of a strip mall on a busy east-side street.

After he parked, I waited while he came around the car and opened the door for me. Since he'd opened the door for me when we left home, I figured he'd do the same when we arrived at the restaurant, so I curbed my inclination to open the door for myself. I'd become so used to doing everything for myself since I'd become a widow that I'd almost reached for the door handle myself.

Although Arnold's didn't look like much on the outside, the tiny restaurant was cozy and inviting inside. Its tables, each one with a single rose in a bud vase, were spread with white linen tablecloths and set precisely with china, silver, and crystal. The lighting was low—a perfect setting for a romantic dinner.

"Tonight I'm not on call, so we can enjoy dinner without any interruptions from the office," Wes told me after our waiter had presented us with menus and recited the chef's special of the evening—seared Atlantic salmon with lemon-dill butter. The salmon sounded good to me, and Wes barely glanced at the menu before deciding on steak. Following the waiter's suggestions for wine, we both ordered a glass—a white for me and a red for Wes, both of which were delivered promptly along with the chef's bread basket, filled with two warm mini-loaves of savory bread that smelled heavenly.

After the waiter took our order, Wes said, "You're not the only one who doesn't cook. I practically live on fast food. A good steak will be a welcome change, but it's probably not too great for my cholesterol, or so my son tells me."

"How many children do you have, Wes?" Here was the opening to talk about past relationships. I intended to follow Tracey's advice and avoid getting bogged down in that discussion.

"Just one. My ex-wife and I split when Derek was still a pre-schooler. She didn't want to live on a cop's salary, and I didn't want to go to work for her father, selling used cars. We both did our best with Derek, though. A few weeks ago, he started his first year in medical school at Johns Hopkins."

"Wow, that's a top medical school."

"So they tell me."

"You must be very proud of him, Wes."

"I am. He's smart, but he worked hard to get in, too. He's always been kind of a serious, studious kid. How about you, Laurel? Any kids?"

"No, I was married, but my husband died in an auto accident a few years ago."

Tears sprang to my eyes, just mentioning it, and Wes gently covered my hand with his and said simply, "I'm sorry, Laurel."

"Luckily, our waiter arrived just then asking if we'd each like another glass of wine, and I took a moment to compose myself before going back to Wes's question.

"We didn't have any children."

"I thought you probably didn't, or, young as you are, you'd have kids still at home with you."

"Uh, thanks. How old do you think I am?"

"My best guess—thirty. Am I right?"

"I wish. I'm thirty-eight."

"Laurel, honestly I'm not saying this just to flatter you, but you really do look much younger. It's a relief, though. Now I don't feel as though I'm a forty-five-year-old cradle robber."

We both laughed. I realized that we'd gotten past the topic of past relationships, only spending a couple of minutes on it, and I certainly didn't intend to bring up the subject again on our first date. I also realized that I was now thinking of this dinner as our first date, meaning that I thought there'd be more to follow, but maybe I was getting ahead of myself. As I'd told Tracey, I'm an incompetent dater.

When he wasn't busy questioning me as though I were a homicide suspect, Wes was down to earth and easy to talk to. I thought it best not to mention that I'd asked Edna Elkins about the end of her nursing career because I was sure that he'd warn me off, but if I didn't say anything about it, Wes wouldn't have the chance. Wes probably didn't want to discuss it with me any more than I wanted to discuss it with him, although our reasons were different. I didn't want a lecture, and I knew that he wouldn't approve of my snooping around in an official murder investigation. As I'd hoped, the crimes at Hawkeye Haven didn't come up again the rest of the evening.

Wes's sister had made a good choice in recommending Arnold's. Our dinners were superb, and we enjoyed meeting Chef Arnold, who made the rounds of each table to chat with his customers, making sure they were happy with their meal selections. I had planned on skipping dessert, but when our waiter offered a scrumptious tray of sweet confections, both Wes and I succumbed to temptation. We lingered over dessert and coffee. Having neglected to order decaf, I drank three cups of regular coffee, and I was sure I'd regret it when I tried to go to sleep. I noticed Wes was drinking regular coffee, too.

When we'd finally finished our dinner, Wes paid the bill, which I knew must have been steep, with cash, leaving a generous tip for our waiter. We were at the front door, ready to step outside, when our waiter came up to us and presented me with the rose that had been in the vase on our table.

"It's for you, Miss. I meant to tell you earlier. We always give the ladies a rose."

"Oh, thank you," I said, surprised as I took the flower gingerly to avoid the thorns. "That's really nice."

"Thank you," Wes repeated to the waiter.

"Our pleasure, sir."

From my point of view, the evening had been a success. I worried about what to do when we arrived back at my house. Should I invite Wes in for a nightcap? I realized that it would be nearly midnight by the time we got back to my house, but then I told myself the time didn't matter—nobody was going to turn into a pumpkin at the witching hour. We'd been at the restaurant for three hours. In fact, there had been only one other couple still there when we'd left. The staff had probably wanted to push us all out the door so that they could go home.

Wes and I chatted easily on the way home, and when we arrived, Wes escorted me to the front door. I asked him if he'd like to come in for a drink, but he declined, saying that he had to get up early the next morning.

"Well, thanks for a lovely evening, Wes. I had a good time."

"You're welcome. It was fun." We could hear Bear barking on the other side of the door. "Bear's up and at 'em," Wes observed.

"Yes, and he'll be bright and alert and ready to go for a walk by six tomorrow morning."

"So you have to get up early, too. I'd better shove off." Wes leaned down and brushed his lips against mine. It happened so quickly that I was caught off guard, even though I shouldn't have been surprised. But, as I said, I was an incompetent dater.

Wes stepped back, smiled at me, and strode down the sidewalk, whistling as he walked to his car.

Chapter 15

Considering how much caffeine I'd consumed at dinner the night before, I slept remarkably well, and I almost managed to match Bear's eagerness for our morning walk. My date with Wes had gone much better than I'd anticipated, and I was wondering when I'd see him again. Then I remembered. Victor's funeral was scheduled for Friday morning. I'd put off deciding whether or not I would attend, but I couldn't put it off any longer. If I went to the funeral, I'd have to start getting ready soon after breakfast.

Based on Courtney's behavior at the DIY Earrings class she'd attended a few days earlier and the fact that she hadn't been arrested for her father's murder, I felt certain that her alibi, which the police had had ample time to confirm, was rock solid and that the shooting had happened while she was at work. Although Victor had been an unpleasant, perhaps even an evil man, his daughter Courtney, whom he hadn't treated very well, clearly had some daughterly feelings for him, and she'd be even more distressed than she was already if there weren't very many people at the funeral. Not only had Courtney lost a father, such as he was, but she had also discovered his bloody body lying in the doorway of their home, a traumatic experience that she'd never forget. I decided that going to the funeral was the right thing to do, much as I would have preferred to avoid it, and I might just have the opportunity to find out more about the information on the mysterious list if some of the board members attended.

Would Wes be there? He hadn't mentioned Victor's funeral during our date, but I'd watched enough true crime shows on television to know that detectives sometimes attended a homicide victim's funeral. Although I wanted to see Wes again, I wasn't sure I wanted to see him at Victor's funeral. Having him there could definitely cramp my style if I got the chance to talk to one of the board members whose name appeared on the list I'd found.

Taking my time getting ready—I wanted to look nice just in case Wes showed up—I rushed out the door only a few minutes before the funeral was scheduled to start. I'd deliberately chosen not to wear black because it washed me out, so much so that I might have looked like the corpse myself had I worn the fashionable, but gloomy, color. I decided to wear a sleeveless, dark brown sheath dress, figuring it would suffice as appropriate funeral attire, and, on the plus side, it didn't necessarily look as though I were dressed for a funeral.

When I arrived at the Meadows Funeral Home, I recognized a few other stragglers from Hawkeye Haven parking their cars, too. I followed them inside where a somber usher in a black suit greeted me at the door to a chapel-like room and handed me a memorial program. For a man who was pretty much universally despised, there was a respectable turnout. In the front of the chapel, Victor's body was laid out in a satin-lined casket, surrounded by several floral arrangements. Seeing Victor in artificial repose gave me the creeps. For some reason, I couldn't help thinking about the hole in his chest caused by the deadly bullet that had ended his life.

From my vantage point at the side of the aisle in the back of the room, I could see Courtney seated in the front row with Karl on her right side and two couples I didn't recognize sitting on Courtney's left. Patty sat alone in a pew a few rows back, and the HOA board members occupied another pew, although Rachel Caswell wasn't among them. I looked for Wes, but he wasn't there. After spotting Cynthia and Amy, sitting in a pew a couple of rows from the back, I joined them.

Thankfully, the service was short. The officiant, an elderly white-haired man, opened the service with a brief prayer and then read Victor's short biography, which I recognized as the same one that had run in the newspaper. The two men sitting next to Courtney turned out to be a couple of Victor's cousins, and I assumed that the women accompanying them were their wives. When he spoke, one of Victor's cousins mentioned that he and his relatives had driven over from Des Moines, where he and Victor had worked at the same company for several years. The other cousin reminisced about some of his vacations with Victor when they were children, and one of Victor's golf buddies talked about Victor's love of the game. Patty, mercifully the last speaker, spun a yarn about Victor's having made outstanding contributions to community life in Hawkeye Haven. Reading the expressions on several faces as Patty told her fairy tale, I knew that neither the residents present nor the board members were buying any of her malarkey. Wondering whether Wes might have slipped in late, I glanced surreptitiously over my shoulder a few times during the service, but I didn't see him. I guessed that he'd had more pressing business to take care of.

To end the service, the officiant intoned another short prayer. Classical violin music wafted from hidden speakers while the attendees filed by Victor's open casket and then stepped out into the hallway, where Courtney, supported by Karl, and Victor's cousins were accepting condolences. Circling back through the door I had entered and down the hall to avoid passing by the casket, I joined the receiving line, where I nodded to Karl, gave Courtney a quick hug, and shook hands with Victor's cousins and their wives.

Cynthia and Amy were waiting for me near the front door.

"Courtney seems to be holding up pretty well, considering what she's been though the past week," Cynthia said.

"I think so, too," Amy agreed. "I'll never be able to get that image of Victor lying dead in his own doorway out of my mind, and I doubt that Courtney will, either. I've had nightmares ever since it happened. It's so scary to think about a killer running around loose in Hawkeye Haven. I lock up tight every night, and I'm really careful when I come into the house after I've been gone. I even had Cynthia come in with me and look around when we came home after dark the evening of the party for the security guard." Amy shuddered as though the very thought of a murderer lurking in the community was too much for her to bear. "You're lucky, Cynthia, you have Pete to take care of you, but my Jim's gone."

Tears rolled down Amy's cheeks, and she dug through her purse, eventually pulling out a tissue to wipe them away. Cynthia put her arm around Amy while I patted Amy's arm, but I doubted that we provided much comfort for her. I knew exactly how she felt. After a few minutes, Amy straightened. "I'll be all right," she whispered.

"I can run you home now, if you like," Cynthia offered. We don't have to go to the cemetery or the reception."

"No, no, I think we should do what we came to do," Amy protested. "After all, we've been the Eberharts' neighbors for years, and I don't want to let Courtney down. She needs all the support she can get at a time like this."

"Are you sure, Amy?" I asked.

Amy nodded. "I'm sorry."

"Nothing to be sorry about," Cynthia said and together the three of us walked across the parking lot, following the small crowd of attendees into Meadows Cemetery, where Victor's body would be buried in a few minutes. I noticed that fewer people were gathered at the grave site than had been at Victor's funeral, but there was still a sizeable group. After the casket had been set in place for the graveside service, the officiant offered brief remarks and prayers. The board members stood together in the back, and I noticed that Luis Cardoza, one of the board members Victor may have been coercing, crossed himself after the final prayer. He looked sad, although whether he felt sad about Victor's passing or he felt sorrow for another reason, I didn't know. Certainly, it wasn't an unusual reaction. Even though I had attended the funeral to support Courtney, rather than to mourn her father, the pervasive reminder of death as life's final destination that the cemetery represented was impossible to escape. Courtney wept at the sight of Victor's casket being lowered into the ground, and Karl put his arm around her to comfort her. Other than Amy—the only other person crying—nobody seemed especially upset, not even Patty, and I was sure that Amy's tears fell for her late husband, rather than for her unpopular neighbor.

As we turned from the grave to walk back to our cars and proceed to the reception, I saw Wesson's partner, Smith, standing several yards away, surveying the crowd. She had been in back of us during the graveside service, so I hadn't spotted her earlier. No way did I want to talk to Detective Smith, so I ignored her, hurried to my car, and headed back to Hawkeye Haven, where I was surprised to find out that the funeral reception was being held in the same meeting room where we'd held Bessie's farewell party just two days earlier.

For Victor's funeral reception, the room had been set up with an elaborate buffet luncheon presented artistically on long tables that ran almost the length of the room, surrounded by several round tables, where people could sit down to eat. At the end of the room, a drink station had been set up with wine, beer, coffee, tea, and bottled water. Servers wearing long, bright blue aprons bearing their catering service's logo discreetly embroidered at the hem, bustled about the room. I knew that Pizzazz, a catering service owned by a celebrity chef, specialized in pricey delicacies. The catering for this event must have cost a small fortune, and I couldn't help wondering whether Courtney was paying for it or whether Patty had authorized the payment to come from the Hawkeye Haven HOA. I suspected the latter, and it made me angry to think about Patty's strenuous objections to Bessie's party while she was probably planning a grand send-off for her cohort on the HOA's dime. Edna Elkins would know whether or not the HOA was footing the bill. Despite our run-in at Bessie's party, I thought about asking Edna, but she pointedly avoided me. When I walked to one side of the room, she made her way to the other, and when I started towards her, she retreated, so I gave up my attempts to intercept her when I saw that Cynthia was motioning for me to join her and Amy, who were sitting at a table with some other women who often took my DIY classes.

"Sit here, Laurel," Cynthia said, patting the chair next to her. "We saved you a seat."

"Laurel, dear, don't you want to get something to eat? This is a real good feed," Alice Sandstrom, who sat across the table from me, observed.

"Hi, Mrs. Sandstrom; yes, everything looks good. I'll go through the buffet line as soon as it thins out a little." I was surprised to find Alice at the reception. I hadn't seen her at the funeral or the cemetery, and, as far as I knew, she wasn't acquainted with Victor. Since she lived several blocks away from his house, she was his neighbor only in the loosest sense. Curious, I asked, "Did you know Victor well?"

"Oh, I didn't know him at all, dear, but I saw his daughter last Saturday at class, and the poor girl seemed so upset that I thought I should come. But then I got turned around and couldn't find the funeral home, so I came back here. Made it just in time, too."

"Uh, Alice, you drove yourself?" Cynthia asked.

"I did," the ninety-year-old admitted. "I know what you're thinking, Cynthia. An old lady like me shouldn't be driving at all, and you're right. My neighbor Amber's been giving me rides all week, but she had a doctor's appointment this morning, so I decided to drive myself. I really can't see too well, though. I guess I shouldn't have done it."

"I'd be happy to give you a ride home, Alice," Cynthia volunteered, "and Amy could drive your car to your house for you, couldn't you, Amy?"

"Sure, and please give me a call when you need a ride, Alice. Since Jim passed away, I have nothing but time on my hands," Amy said.

Poor Amy. Her husband's death had been a devastating blow to her, and she was looking for ways to fill the void, just as I had when my husband Tim had died.

"I'm going back to the buffet," Cynthia said. "Alice, may I bring you some dessert?"

"Oh, yes," Alice said enthusiastically. "I'll have a couple of those little bar cookies—the ones with the pink frosting and the raspberry on top—and some carrot cake. Oh, and maybe a slice of chocolate meringue pie." Obviously, Alice had a sweet tooth and had surveyed the desserts earlier. Although the oldster's request took Amy aback for a moment, she quickly recovered her composure and nodded.

Jumping up, I said, "I'll go with you, Amy." I couldn't help smiling. At least, Alice was enjoying herself.

As Amy and I approached the buffet tables, I saw Luis Cardoza detaching himself from a group of people and heading for the buffet. "Be back in a few minutes, Amy," I whispered and intercepted him before he had a chance to reach the food.

"Mr. Cardoza?" Puzzled, he looked at me, and I could tell that he was trying to figure out who I was. "Hi, I'm Laurel McMillan. I teach some classes here at the community center."

"Miss McMillan? How can I help you?" he asked politely.

"I wonder if I could speak to you for a moment."

"Certainly. I've heard good things about your classes."

"Thank you. I appreciate that." This was going to be more difficult than I'd anticipated. I didn't know this man, and there was no reason he should answer any of my questions. "My neighbors here in Hawkeye Haven are really quite concerned that Victor's murder hasn't been solved yet. Frankly, we're frightened."

"That's understandable. We're all concerned."

"Yes, well, I didn't know Victor myself. The only time I ever saw him was at the HOA meeting last week, but from what several of my students and other residents have told me, he wasn't very popular."

"No, he wasn't," Luis agreed. He had yet to give me some kind of an opening.

"Maybe someone who had a grudge against him killed him."

"Maybe."

"Do you know anyone who could have hated him enough to shoot him?"

"Hard to say."

This was like pulling teeth. Luis wasn't giving an inch.

"Did you hate him, Mr. Cardoza?"

"Just what is it you want, Miss McMillan? Out with it."

"Okay," I murmured. "I understand that Victor influenced the votes of some of the board members by means of blackmail—threatening to reveal something he knew about them that they wouldn't want known publicly. Is that true?"

"Oh, I see where you're leading." The sad look returned to Luis's face. "You think he blackmailed me."

"Did he?"

"He tried," Luis sighed.

"Did he succeed?"

"No, as a matter of fact, he didn't. My fiancé took her own life after I told her I didn't think we should get married. I blame myself for her death. I knew she was upset, but when she said she was going to kill herself if I left her, I didn't believe her at first. By the time I checked on her, it was too late. She'd taken an entire bottle of sleeping pills. It was my fault. If I'd taken her threat seriously, she'd still be alive today. My priest says God has forgiven me, but I've never forgiven myself. I'm not proud of what happened, but give in to blackmail? Never."

"What about the other board members? Do you think Victor succeeded in coercing any of them?"

"I don't know. I can't speak for anyone else."

"But you have your suspicions?"

"As do you, Miss McMillan."

"Well, thank you for speaking with me, Mr. Cardoza."

"Just a minute. You didn't seem surprised by what I told you. You must have known about it already. How did you know?"

"I didn't know for sure until you confirmed it. I came across some information purely by accident. I felt duty-bound to tell the police, but don't worry. I have no intention of spreading rumors. I know how far and fast the rumor mill at Hawkeye Haven goes. As I said before, I'm concerned about the residents' reaction to Victor's murder. We don't feel safe in our own homes anymore."

"Be careful, Miss McMillan. Whoever shot Victor won't appreciate knowing that you're nosing around. It could be dangerous."

"I suppose so."

It was interesting that Luis Cardoza had warned me not to "nose around," as he put it. Had he been threatening me under the guise of concern for my welfare? If he truly hadn't been influenced to change his vote by Victor's threats to expose his indiscretion and guilt over his girlfriend's suicide, then maybe he really thought that I could be in danger. Frankly, I didn't believe that I had anything to worry about. After all, I'd only spoken to a few people, and I thought I had been discreet. I looked around for Peter Harvey, the board member who had been suspected of involvement in a building's collapse when he'd worked as a construction company manager, but I no longer saw him in the room and wondered whether he'd already left. If so, I might not have another chance to talk to him. I decided to stay at the reception for a while in case he returned.

As long as I intended to hang around, I decided I might as well have lunch. I wandered over to the buffet and helped myself to a lovely spinach salad and some asparagus quiche that looked inviting. As I picked up a setting of silverware wrapped in a large white linen napkin, I heard a strident voice coming from across the buffet table. Although I'd heard her speak on only two occasions, I'd know that voice anywhere. It was Wes's partner, Sergeant Smith, the one person in attendance whom I'd wanted to avoid. Holding a plate piled high with a lavish lunch, she stood glaring at me from the other side of the buffet table.

"Surprised to see you here, Red," the detective said.

If there was anything I hated, it was being called Red, not that I minded having red hair, but, for some reason, the nickname had always irritated me. It also irritated me that Smith acted as though she knew me, which she most assuredly did not.

"Oh, why's that?" I asked, trying to keep the annoyance out of my tone.

"Thought you told us you didn't know Eberhart." Here we go with another ridiculous interrogation, I thought. Crazy the way the detectives could twist my words. I felt sure it was a deliberate technique that they'd picked up at some Detective-Daring-Do training session.

"That's right. I said that I didn't know him personally, and I didn't. I do know his daughter, however."

"Uh, huh," Smith said sarcastically. What had I done to this woman that she disliked me so much? Her reaction to me, which at first I'd attributed to Bear's unwanted deposit of fur on her clothing, seemed altogether out of proportion with the dog's unintended offense. Too bad Smith had shown up at the funeral, instead of Wes. Simultaneously, I wished that he'd call me, and I wished that he'd get a different partner, one who could qualify as half-human, at least. Not in the mood to tangle with Smith, I left her standing there and, without another word, I retreated to friendlier territory, rejoining Cynthia, Amy, and the others, who were all now enjoying their desserts.

We chatted for several minutes before Cynthia and Amy departed with Alice Sandstrom in tow. I hoped that Alice would leave the driving to Amber or Amy from now on. I remembered how grateful Alice had been the first time Amber had volunteered to drive her car the day that Bessie had been attacked, and she hadn't objected today when Cynthia offered to drive her home and Amy had volunteered to take her wherever she needed to go if Amber wasn't available to drive.

As I waved to my friends, I decided it was time for me to leave, too. I looked around to make sure that Detective Smith had gone. No way did I want to have another encounter with the pugnacious investigator. Aware that courtesy demanded that I stop to say a few words to Courtney before departing, I approached her as she stood by the door with Karl and her out-of-town relatives.

"So sorry for your loss," I murmured as I gently touched Courtney's arm and nodded to Victor's cousins and their wives.

"Thank you for coming, Laurel," she said, wiping a tear from her cheek with a soggy tissue. "It means a lot to me."

"Please let me know if there's anything I can do to help," I said, although I realized that Courtney was unlikely to ask me for any help; nevertheless, I believed that I should make the offer.

"That's nice of you, but I think I can manage. I'd been planning to move in with my friend Mia who has a condo on the east side of town, anyway, so I'm going ahead with the move tomorrow. I've taken advantage of Karl and Eva's hospitality too long."

"Nonsense, my dear," Karl said. "We're happy to have you stay with us." Karl put his arm around Courtney's shoulders in a protective gesture. I remembered that he'd been afraid that the police might target Courtney as a suspect. "There's no need to be in a rush."

"I appreciate everything you and Eva are doing for me; really I do, but I can't bear to stay right across the street from the house where my father was murdered any longer. I keep having nightmares about finding him there in the doorway," Courtney shuddered at the memory of her grisly discovery. Although Karl looked as though he wanted to protest, he didn't say anything. I left quietly, glad that he hadn't insisted that Courtney continue to stay with him and his wife. I could certainly understand why she seemed eager to move away from Hawkeye Haven and the scene of her father's shooting.

Before I left the community center, I stopped at the mail room next to the administrative offices where small cubby holes, each marked with the recipient's name on a peel-and-stick label, served as mail boxes for the instructors and other employees of Hawkeye Haven. Usually the mail consisted of nothing more than flyers promoting community activities, sundry advertisements, and the HOA's newsletter. I quickly leafed through my mail, tossing everything into the trash can except a long, business envelope with my name neatly printed on the front.

Occasionally, my reimbursement checks for class supplies were left there, so I ripped open the sealed envelope, expecting to find a payment for the materials

I'd used in last month's classes. Instead, I found a sheet of standard-sized, white printer paper with letters, obviously cut from a magazine, pasted onto the page, spelling out a message: BACK OFF OR U WILL B SORRY. However, the message had the opposite effect on me than its author likely expected. I almost laughed because I knew exactly who had put the message there, and I wasn't one bit afraid of her. It had to be Edna Elkins. She and Luis Cardoza were the only people I'd questioned about their backgrounds, and even if Luis Cardoza had wanted to send me another message—I remembered that he had already warned me to be careful—he wouldn't have had time to put this cut-and-paste-DIY-project-gone-wrong together. Although I found Edna's attempt to frighten me rather amusing and definitely pathetic, I also felt annoyed at the retired nurse, who probably feared that I'd share her secret with the entire community, although I had no intention of doing so. I returned the message to its envelope and stuffed it into my handbag, unsure whether I'd confront Edna about it or just ignore her feeble attempt to scare me.

The sound of chimes startled me for a moment until I remembered that I'd been playing with the ring tone on my smartphone and had reset it. Digging into my purse, I grabbed the phone and answered it, although I didn't recognize the number on the caller ID display.

"Laurel McMillan," I said in a formal tone, aware that it could be a business call.

"Hi, gorgeous," came a voice that I immediately recognized. "It's Wes," he added as if I didn't know.

"Well, thank you, kind sir," I said, pleased with the compliment. I'd never thought of myself as gorgeous, but if Wes thought so, it was fine with me.

"I'm not catching you at a busy time, am I?"

"No, as a matter of fact, I'm just about to leave the community center. Victor's funeral reception was held here in the meeting room."

"You went to his funeral?" Wes sounded surprised. "I thought that you didn't know the guy."

"I didn't, but I know his daughter Courtney. She attended a couple of my classes, so I thought I should go to her father's funeral for her sake."

"That was a kind gesture. Were many people there?"

"More than I expected—that's for sure. I saw your partner. I think she hates me."

"She doesn't hate you. She's—well, let's just say she's a little grumpy sometimes."

"Grumpy doesn't begin to cover it."

"Don't pay any attention to her, Laurel." Wes said and promptly changed the subject. "I had a great time last night. I was hoping that maybe you're free tomorrow night. We could go to the Greek Food Festival, or if that doesn't appeal to you, we could go someplace else."

"The Greek Food Festival sounds good. I've gone to it with Tracey each year since I moved here."

"Oh, I don't want to intrude."

"You're not intruding. You'd be welcome, in any case, but Tracey had to cancel because she has some bigwig client in town, and she'll be tied up in meetings all weekend. So anyway, I'd really like to go with you."

"Good, but I have to warn you that, even though I'm not on duty tomorrow, I'm on call. There's always a chance that I might have to go to work."

"Oh, okay, I understand."

"Let's hope that doesn't happen, but I thought that I should give you a heads-up, just in case. Pick you up around six?"

"Six is fine. Fingers crossed then."

"See you tomorrow, Laurel."

"See you then, Wes, and thanks for asking me."

"Believe me, it's my pleasure."

Smiling, I dropped my phone back into the depths of my handbag. Tracey had texted me to cancel our planned outing to the Greek Food Festival earlier in the day, and I'd been trying to decide whether to tag along with some of the neighbors or hope that Tracey might be able to go on Sunday, instead of Saturday. I love Greek food, and I didn't want to miss the annual event, so I was happy that Wes had invited me to go with him. I really hoped that he wouldn't be called to go to work in the middle of our date.

"Somebody looks happy," Luke observed as he came into the mail room.

"Oh, hi, Luke," I said without acknowledging his comment. My relationship or whatever it was with Wes was too new for me to feel comfortable talking about it, except to Tracey or Liz.

"Have a class today?"

"No class today. I thought I'd just stop in to check my mail box as long as I was already here. I went to Victor's funeral this morning and the reception here in the meeting room afterwards."

"I'd have felt hypocritical going myself, so I stayed away."

"I went to support Courtney. She's been a student in my classes a couple of times, and I know she's pretty upset."

"Understandable, although I heard Victor wasn't much of a father."

I nodded. "I heard the same thing, but he was her father, even if he wasn't a very good one, and it's obvious that she still had feelings for him. She was crying at the funeral."

"Poor kid," Luke said. "Some people should never have children, and Victor was one of them. Say, I want to thank you again for putting Bessie's party together. I would have done an awful job of it without your help."

"Thanks, Luke. I was glad to do it. Who would have guessed that Bessie's attacker would be at the party and that he'd turn out to be Kenny? I was floored when she recognized him."

"Kenny's not the sharpest knife in the drawer. You would have thought he'd have done anything to avoid seeing Bessie since he knew the party was for her. His cap pulled down over his eyes wasn't much of a disguise."

"No, it wasn't, but his dragon tattoo gave him away. If she hadn't seen the tattoo, Bessie might not have known he was the one who attacked her. He admitted stealing her gun, but do you think he'd shoot Victor?"

"Can't think of any reason why he'd want to kill Victor."

"I can think of one, but somehow I just can't picture Kenny as a murderer. He said he didn't mean to hurt Bessie, and I'm inclined to believe him."

"You said you could think of a reason. What is it? Victor never had any interaction with Kenny here. His mom got him the job, but his supervisor and I were the only people who kept track of him and his work."

"I suppose if Victor had been giving him a hard time at work, that could have been a motive, but I was really thinking more of his mother."

"Rachel? You think he was defending her honor or something?"

"Maybe her reputation. You mentioned that Victor was holding something over her so that she'd vote his way."

"Yes, that's true, but how would Kenny know about that? I doubt that she'd have told him."

"Maybe the same way you knew. He could have overheard her talking to Victor."

"Mmmm. Could be, but I tend to agree with you. I doubt that he did it. He doesn't strike me as someone who has much initiative. He wanted that gun so he could join the Dragons' gang; otherwise, I don't think it would have occurred to him to steal a gun. The last I heard on the local news was that "a juvenile" had been charged with the attack, but there was no mention of a murder charge, and you know if he'd been charged with murder, it would have been all over the media, maybe even on the national news since it happened in a guard-gated community."

"That's true. I guess we'll just have to wait to see if anything breaks. Well, I'd better be off and tend to my dog."

"'Bye, Laurel."

Out in the parking lot, I had already unlocked my car and tossed my handbag onto the passenger seat when I heard the snap of car locks from the black Acura SUV, parked next to my car, and saw Peter Harvey approaching. Maybe I could complete my mission after all. I walked around his SUV and waved at him as he loosened his tie, pulled off his blazer, and deposited them in the back seat. A short, balding man with a florid complexion, he was perspiring profusely.

"Mr. Harvey? I'm Laurel McMillan. I live here at Hawkeye Haven, and I'm also an instructor at our community center. Could you spare a moment?"

"If you have a complaint to bring to the board, you should put it in writing or come to the next meeting to have your say." Harvey had pulled the driver's door open.

"No, it's not a complaint, but it does have to do with the board," I said as Harvey climbed up into the driver's seat. Fearing that he would leave before I could continue, I plunged ahead. "I understand that Victor

Eberhart subjected several of the board members to coercion so that he could get them to vote with him."

"No comment."

"I'm not a reporter, Mr. Harvey, just a concerned resident. If it's true that you were responsible for a building's collapse several years ago, Eberhart could have been threatening to expose you."

"Who told you that?" Harvey said, gritting his teeth.

"It doesn't matter, does it? I can't imagine that someone in your position would want that information to become public knowledge."

Harvey sighed. "It isn't true. My boss tried to blame me for the building's collapse, but he's the one who approved using sub-standard materials for the job. It happened a long time ago, but somehow Eberhart found out, and he threatened to go public unless I went along with him on some things. He already seemed to have the majority on his side, anyway, so it didn't make much difference how I voted."

"So you voted his way?"

"I didn't say that. Are you trying to get me thrown off the board?"

"No, although you might consider resigning if your votes can be influenced, Mr. Harvey. Where were you last Thursday night and Friday morning?"

"What? Oh, no, you're not going to pin that on me, young lady. I was in Des Moines at a Board of Commerce meeting. I didn't come back to Center City until Sunday evening."

"I suppose you can prove that."

"If I have to, but since you're not a cop, I think I've said all I'm going to say." Peter Harvey slammed his door before I could say anything else. He started the black SUV and peeled out of his parking space, his tires squealing, leaving me standing there alone.

Well, well, well. Peter Harvey certainly hadn't been happy to learn that I knew about his past, but I also noticed that he seemed more annoyed than frightened. Unlike Edna Elkins and Luis Cardoza, he hadn't issued me a warning, and if he had been in Des Moines when Victor had been shot, he couldn't be Victor's killer.

Thus far, my inquiries hadn't produced much of anything, and as I mentally reviewed my list of possible suspects, I realized that I seemed to have eliminated most of them, even though they all had motives, mainly because they didn't seem like the type of people who could walk up to Victor's door and shoot him right on the spot. But what did I really know about murderers? I remembered Wes's words: "You'd be surprised what people will do." I guessed that applied to me, too. A couple of weeks ago, I'd never have dreamed that there'd be a murder in my usually calm and peaceful community, let alone that I'd have the nerve to question any of the suspects.

Chapter 16

I knew that I should probably tell Wes what I'd learned, but I rationalized that it wouldn't hurt to keep it to myself a while longer. If the police solved the murder soon, I might never tell him I'd talked to the board members. Sooner or later, the detectives would question the board members whose names had appeared on the list, but I surmised that they might try to confirm that the information on the list was accurate before that happened. Based on my conversations with Edna Elkins, Luis Cardoza, and Peter Harvey, I felt sure that the information on the list was true. I hadn't talked to Rachel Caswell, who was dealing with her son's crime now, but Luke had overheard Victor threatening her. Each one of the four board members whose names appeared on the list had had reason to fear Victor, and a lot of other people had reason to hate the man, but only one person had acted, and whoever that person was had gained possession of Bessie's gun. Kenny had admitted to stealing it but claimed that he'd dumped the gun after the attack. If Kenny hadn't shot Victor, then the killer must have found the weapon. Had the murderer, already planning to kill Victor, stumbled upon an opportunity to pick up a weapon? Or had the killer decided to shoot Victor solely because he or she had conveniently found a gun that had been stolen?

Confused by the numerous possibilities, I drove home to pacify Bear, who began to bark loudly when he heard the garage door going up. He stopped barking and ran to me as soon as I entered the house, giving doggie yelps of joy that he was no longer home alone. Opening the back door, I let Bear out into the backyard to romp while I changed from my dress to shorts and a t-shirt. I could hear my smartphone chiming from the depths of my handbag, which I'd left on the kitchen counter, but I decided to ignore it for now. After we'd played Bear's favorite games of fetch-the-ball and tug-of-war for half an hour, I called it quits, and we went into the house, where Bear ran to his water bowl and slurped away until it was nearly empty. Panting, he plopped down on the tile floor.

"You're hot, aren't you, boy?" I said, patting his back.

I checked the setting on the air conditioner, turned it down a few degrees so that we could both cool off, and poured myself a glass of iced tea. Remembering that the phone had rung earlier, I fished it out of my purse and checked for messages. I saw that Liz had called but hadn't left a message, so I returned her call.

"Hello, Laurel."

"Hi, Liz. I saw that you called. What's up?"

"I'm getting forgetful in my old age, Laurel. I was planning to go to Victor's funeral this morning, but I forgot to set my alarm clock last night, and by the time I woke up, it was too late."

Since I'd known her, Liz had never been an early riser. She was definitely a night person. She liked to stay up until the wee hours and sleep until mid-morning or later.

"I thought you might be planning to go to the funeral since you and Victor's wife were such good friends. I didn't decide to go until this morning."

"I should have been there, too. I'm sorry I let Courtney down. I'm going to send her some flowers with a note."

"That would be a nice gesture, Liz—flowers just for Courtney, rather than a funeral arrangement. By the way, she mentioned that she's moving tomorrow. You could probably get Floral Creations to deliver a bouquet later this afternoon to her at Eva and Karl's house, though."

"That's a good idea. I'm going to call them right away. How about bringing Bear over this evening for a swim?"

"Sure, he'd love it. We'll see you later."

"Okay, I'm going to call the florist right now before I forget about that, too."

For the rest of the afternoon, I busied myself with my notes and project plans for my upcoming *DIY for Dog Lovers* book, pausing just long enough to feed Bear his dinner. Still full from all the goodies I'd consumed at the reception, I skipped dinner and continued working. I was writing how-to project instructions for making a dog bed of thick memory foam with a soft, washable cover, like the ones I'd made for Bear, when Liz called to ask me whether I still planned to bring Bear to her pool for a swim. I explained that I'd lost track of time and that we'd be right over, and Liz said that she'd unlock her backyard gate for us.

I woke a groggy Bear from his after-dinner nap, but once he saw me bring out his leash, his energy level increased considerably. By the time I opened Liz's back gate, he was bouncing around me in anticipation, and I had to hold him back long enough to close and latch the gate.

"Bear's raring to go, I see," Liz observed as I took the big Lab's collar and leash off and he dashed for the pool. By the time I'd settled myself next to Liz on the patio, Bear had swum the length of the pool.

"He does love the water," I said, watching my dog splash about in the pool.

"Iced tea, Laurel?" Liz asked. She set a tray with two glasses and a tall pitcher of iced tea with lemon slices on the table between us.

"Sure, thank you," I said, as she poured tea over ice cubes in one of the glasses.

"I'm still gathering the courage to tell Luke that he's my grandson. We had a nice talk at the party Wednesday night, and I can tell that he's a good man, but I can't help wondering whether he's going to be happy to find out that I'm his grandmother. After Leonard's reaction to the news, I'm not so sure Luke will welcome it, either."

"I remember that you were planning to tell Leonard. So he didn't take it too well?"

"Not at all. He's very angry. You know, Laurel, my son has never quite approved of me. He's always thought of me as an embarrassment to him. Now that Leonard knows that I had a child long before he was ever born, and I gave my baby up for adoption, he's even more embarrassed that I'm his mother."

"That's such a shame, Liz."

"Even when he was a little boy, he acted ashamed of me. He's never liked the way I dress or the way I look."

"You always look fabulous, Liz."

"Not to Leonard. He'd prefer me to look mousy."

"That's too bad," I murmured. I'd been afraid that Leonard wouldn't react well to learning that he had a nephew he'd never heard of. I also suspected he was afraid that Liz would leave Luke some of her money.

"Guess I'm too old to change now," Liz sighed. "I'm determined to concentrate on what comes next—telling Luke that he's my grandson. There's nothing I can do to pacify Leonard, anyway."

"When are you going to tell Luke?"

"Monday, I hope. I had planned to try to catch him today, but I chickened out, and it's too late now. I checked with the office, and he's not scheduled to work this weekend, so I'm going to invite him to come over after work on Monday."

"Liz, I don't know Luke too well, but he certainly comes across as a fine man. It might be a bit of a shock to him, but I hope he'll be happy to know you're his grandmother."

"I'm so nervous. He may take the news worse than Leonard did. You never know. Anyway, I thought I'd tell him about his grandfather and me and maybe show him some of my photo albums if he wants to see them. I was looking through some of them before you came." Liz motioned to a stack of albums lying on top of the cabinet behind her.

"May I?" I asked, picking them up.

"Of course. Let me show you Luke's grandfather. This is the only picture I have of him." Liz picked up one of the albums and flipped to a large glossy black-and-white photo of a young Liz and a tall, good-looking, teenager, his arm casually draped around her.

"Why, Liz, Luke looks like an older version of his grandfather! I remember you told me how much alike they looked, but seeing this picture really brings it home. How old was your husband when the picture was taken?"

"Seventeen, and I was fifteen. Scandalous, I know, but we were in love. Of course, we lied about our ages so that we could get married. I told the justice of the peace that I was nineteen, and Dennis said that he was twenty-one. At our ages, we were supposed to have permission from our parents to marry, but the JP never questioned our story."

"You've been through a lot," I said, thumbing through the rest of the album.

Bear had finally tired of swimming and jumping in and out of the pool. Stretching, he shook off the water and trotted towards us, but I met him with a thick towel before he could reach us and wiped him vigorously. He followed me back to the patio, where he lay between Liz and me and promptly fell asleep.

Liz looked at the sleeping dog and said, "I wish I could fall asleep so easily. I battle insomnia most nights."

"He does make it look easy, doesn't he?"

"Life's simpler for our pets. Miss Muffet spends most of her time snoozing. Maybe if I wasn't so worried about how Luke might react to what I'm going to tell him, I could sleep better."

"I hope it'll all work out, Liz."

"Me, too," Liz sighed, picking up an album that looked much less worn than the first one I had seen. "I want to show you someone else, Laurel," she said as she slowly turned the pages of the album. "Ah, here it is. This is a picture of Diana—Victor's wife—and me taken a couple of months before she died. We dressed up and went to high tea at the Hotel Excelsior. Even though she was quite weak at that point, she really wanted to go to tea one last time. I know it must have cost her great effort. Our waitress took that picture for us in front of the hotel's tea room."

"Oh, yes, I see the silver tea service in the background on that little table."

"It didn't occur to us to take our own picture with one of our cell phones. Nobody'd ever heard of a selfie back then."

"It's a good picture, Liz. Something about that brooch that Diana is wearing looks familiar. I could swear that I've seen that same brooch somewhere." The large brooch, set with hundreds of sparkly, tiny red rhinestones, black jet, and small white pearls, all set in silver, was shaped like two pistols placed at an angle facing each other with their barrels crossed.

"It was one of Diana's favorites. She won it, along with a huge trophy, at a local shooting match. She wore it quite often."

"I can see why. It's so distinctive."

Little yelping noises interrupted us. We looked at Bear, who was still sound asleep, although his legs were moving. Deep in dreamland, he barked so loudly that he woke himself up, looked confused for a moment, stood up, and nuzzled my hand. I scratched him behind his ears, just the way he liked, and he lay back down at my feet while Liz and I sipped our iced tea.

"Where's the colonel tonight, Liz? I'm surprised you don't have a date."

"His hiking club's on an overnight camping trip, but they should be back sometime tomorrow evening."

"So that's why you two didn't get together tonight. You didn't want to go with them?"

"Me? Hiking? Camping? No, I'm afraid I'm a city girl. Anyway, it's strictly a men's club—they're all retired military guys."

"Maybe you and the colonel can do something Sunday."

"Yes, we're planning to go to the Greek Food Festival Sunday afternoon."

"No kidding? I'm going tomorrow."

"With Tracey?"

"No, she's tied up with work, but I have a date."

"Don't tell me. Let me guess. Could it be with that handsome detective who knows more about me than he should?"

"Uh, huh. He took me to dinner last night."

"And you two already have another date? I'll bet he's smitten."

"Well, I just hope he can make it. He warned me that he's on call tomorrow night."

"If he has to cancel because of work, you could always go with Bobby and me on Sunday."

"Thanks, I'll keep that in mind. I guess it's about time for Bear and me to head home now. Good-night, Liz."

Once in bed that night, I couldn't stop thinking about Liz and her plan to tell Luke that she was his grandmother. I'd all but eliminated Luke as a suspect in Victor's killing, but what if I was wrong? It would be terribly hard on Liz, not to mention Luke's wife and children, if he were the killer. The police didn't seem to be making too much progress on the case, not that Wes would tell me if they were, and I hadn't learned much from questioning the board members.

Kenny remained a wild card in the mix, but thinking about Kenny and what he'd revealed before his mother had told him not to say another word, I knew what I had to do, and I knew that I had to do it early tomorrow morning.

Chapter 17

Before I went to bed, I sorted through my file of paperwork from the Hawkeye Haven HOA, finally finding the most recent annual directory of residents of the community. Scanning the last names that start with C, I located Rachel Caswell's home address, 3826 Lily-of-the-Valley Lane. Surprised, I hadn't realized that the new president of the HOA and her son Kenny lived on the same street where my cousin Tracey lived, the very street where Victor Eberhart had resided before he'd been murdered. Kenny wouldn't have had far to go if he'd shot Victor.

Somehow, I couldn't quite picture the lazy high school student and part-time janitor as a killer, despite Wes's having labeled him as "a person of interest." Although I wasn't sure whether or not the teenager had been lying about discarding the gun in a trash can on the way home, he'd sounded sincere. Kenny hadn't had a chance to explain any details because his mother had suddenly told him to keep quiet, and that's exactly what he'd done.

Combining my fact-finding mission with Bear's Saturday morning walk might net some interesting information about where Kenny had disposed of Bessie's gun. Armed with my smartphone, plastic bags for doggie pick-up duty, and my house key, I left the house with Bear a few minutes before sunrise. We headed for the back gate. I planned to retrace Kenny's path back to the Caswell house after his attack on Bessie. Surely, Kenny hadn't lingered after he'd shoved

Bessie and she'd fallen, injuring her head. He must have pulled her gun from her holster and run away as quickly as possible, taking off his ski mask and making a beeline for home. Because all the houses in Hawkeye Haven had six-feet-high walled backyards, I thought it unlikely that Kenny would have tried to hide by taking that route. The fastest way for Kenny to reach his house would have been to sprint straight down Hawkeye Haven Way, the wide maple-tree-lined main street, which snaked through the community, the front gate and main guardhouse on one end and the back gate and its smaller guardhouse on the other end. Two blocks from the back gate's guardhouse, he would have turned left onto Lily-of-the-Valley Lane, the four-block long street where he lived with his mother. I had written down Rachel's house number, and, by comparing it with Tracey's, I knew that the Caswell home was in the fourth and last block of Lily-of-the-Valley Lane, which ends in a cul-de-sac. Anyone visiting a home on Lily-of-the-Valley Lane or an intersecting side street would have to come in and go out at the intersection of Lily-of-the-Valley Lane and Hawkeye Haven Way because there is no other outlet.

Planning to start at the guardhouse and walk directly to Kenny's house, I urged Bear to hurry up, but he had spotted Goldie coming out of her house with Fran, and I knew my chocolate Lab wouldn't be satisfied unless I let him greet his pal. I waved to Fran and crossed the street. Tails wagging, the two dogs nuzzled each other.

"Hi, Fran, taking Goldie for a walk?"

"No, a ride. I forgot to buy coffee at the grocery store yesterday, and we're totally out. I'm just going to buzz through Starbucks and pick up a couple of grandes while Brian fixes us some breakfast. Goldie kept bugging him, so I thought I'd take her along." As if to confirm her pet mommy's declaration, Goldie barked sharply.

"Sounds as though she's raring to go."

"She loves to ride in the car. Say, have you heard the latest?"

"Ummm. I don't know. What?"

"Rachel has hired Gerard Foster as Kenny's attorney. I just heard it on the early morning news."

"No kidding! Gerard Foster, the celebrity lawyer?"

"That's the one. Anytime Hollywood stars get into trouble, they hire him."

"Kenny's defense must be costing Rachel a fortune. I didn't realize that she was so wealthy."

"She isn't, but her ex-husband is, and I'm sure he's the one footing the bill for his son. He'd do anything to keep that kid out of prison, and if anyone can help Kenny get out of this mess, it's Gerard Foster."

"Kenny hasn't been charged with Victor's murder, has he?"

"Not yet, I guess, but it could happen any time. That's probably why Kenny's dad hired Foster. The report I heard this morning said that the gun used in the murder was our security guard's stolen gun, and everybody at Hawkeye Haven knows that Kenny's already admitted to taking it."

Evidently, Luke had been right about the stolen gun's being the same gun that the killer had used to shoot Victor. I wondered why the police had released that bit of information to the public. Perhaps, as Fran assumed, Kenny was about to be charged with the murder.

"Well, I'd better hurry. Brian will be getting grumpy without his morning coffee. Come on, Goldie." Goldie hopped into the back seat of Fran's car, and Bear tried to follow her, but I held him back. "See you later, Laurel."

"'Bye," I called to Fran, before tugging on Bear's leash to turn him around. "Let's go this way, Bear." When we approached the guardhouse at the back gate, Bear pranced and wagged his tail in anticipation of his usual treat. Luckily, I had remembered to bring a dog biscuit to pacify him, but I felt sad that Bessie would never be there again to greet us on our daily walk.

Pulling my smartphone out of my pocket, I activated the voice memo function so that I could make a record of my findings. I planned to note the address of each house where a trash can had been set out. Wednesday and Saturdays are the regular trash pick-up days for Hawkeye Haven, so the residents usually set out their garbage the night before or sometimes early in the morning (HOA Regulation 89a states that "trash must not be set out until after dark on Tuesday and Friday.").

Kenny had said that he'd dumped the gun in a trash can. Many residents simply used trash bags, rather than cans, because they wouldn't have to worry about bringing them in from the curb within the HOA's mandated twelve-hour time limit after the garbage had been collected. There'd be a limited number of trash cans set out, and I intended to learn where they all were.

We proceeded along Hawkeye Haven Way, where only four garbage cans were set out in the two blocks from the gate to Lily-of-the-Valley Lane. I noted the address at each place on my voice memo. We turned left at Lily-of-the-Valley Lane, and I continued noting trash cans and addresses until we reached the end of the street. Rachel Caswell's house turned out to be one of the last homes on the street, sitting on the cul-de-sac. There was no trash at all in front of the house. Rachel had probably been too busy dealing with Kenny's legal problems to worry about trash pick-up.

We circled the cul-de-sac and headed back, switching to the east side of Lily-of-the-Valley Lane. We'd passed Tracey's house when we came in, but I didn't go to the door or text her because I hoped that she'd still be asleep. Undoubtedly, she could use some rest after the week she'd had at work—the week that had become never-ending. I knew that her rich-but-in-your-face client had proven to be even more indecisive and unreasonable than Tracey had first anticipated, and she and her team were going to have to spend the entire weekend trying to come up with a plan of action and branding strategy that he would approve. He was the reason she'd had to cancel our plans to go to the Greek Food Festival together.

Just as we were about to pass her house on the other side of the street, Tracey's garage door opened, and she slowly backed her white SUV into the street. She spotted us, stopped, and opened her window. Bear jumped up on the door and poked his head in the window to greet Tracey, but I quickly pulled him back. She was on her way to work and didn't need to take any stray dog hairs along with her.

"Lo-lo and my best buddy Bear! I wish I could go walking with you instead of heading to work."

"You're going in early today—and on a Saturday, too. I hope this client comes through for you."

"So do I. We haven't spent this much time courting a client in years, but it'll be worth it if he buys into our plans for his company's branding. He's insisted on taking us all to dinner tonight, so I knew there was no way I'd be able to go to the Greek Food Festival this evening, but I'm glad you're going to be able to go with Wes."

"So am I. I'll pick up some baklava for you."

"My favorite. That'd be great!"

"Good luck with your client."

"Thanks, I'll need it. Keep me posted on Mr. Wonderful."

I smiled. "I will."

"And I promise I'll make Bear some yummy yam chips just as soon as my client leaves town."

Wagging his tail, Bear woofed his approval as though he knew what Tracey had said, and maybe he did. He probably recognized the word "yam."

Tracey drove off as Bear and I continued down Lily-of-the-Valley Lane. As we walked, I wondered whether or not tracking the residences where the trash cans were used was an exercise in futility. Since I didn't know most of the people along the route, I wasn't sure that I'd be able to garner any clues, but I was certainly going to try. So far as I could tell, nobody was paying much attention to what Kenny had said about getting rid of Bessie's gun.

That was probably unfair of me. More likely, the police hadn't yet been able to question Kenny. After all, thanks to his father, Kenny had a high-powered attorney who would use every legal maneuver in his repertoire to obtain the best possible outcome for his client. Anyway, if Kenny hadn't shot Victor, he would still be accountable for the attack on Bessie, but his celebrity attorney might well be able to wrangle a favorable deal for Kenny. I was sure Bessie wouldn't like that. Even if Kenny hadn't deliberately injured her, the attack had altered her life significantly. Without the hapless teenager and his desire to join the Dragons, Bessie would still be on the job at the guardhouse.

Once home, I settled myself on the patio with a cup of coffee, my laptop, and Hawkeye Haven's directory of residents while Bear wandered around the backyard. Spotting a harmless little garden snake that lived under one of the dense bushes along the back wall, he raced to the spot where the snake had slithered out from beneath the bush, but the snake, easily taking cover under another bush, proved much faster than Bear. Still alert, Bear sat under the bush awaiting the small reptile's return while I pulled my smartphone from my pocket and transferred all the addresses where I'd spotted trash cans during our morning walk to a spreadsheet on my laptop. Listing each address first, I then looked up the name of the residents who lived there and entered those names in the second column. I created a third column for notes, or more accurately, speculations about each entry.

There were three addresses that I didn't have to look up in the directory because I already knew who lived there; in fact, they lived within a few houses of each other—first, Cynthia and her husband Pete; second, Amy; third, Karl and Eva. They all lived close to Victor's house, so close that Karl had heard Courtney's screams when she'd found her father's body lying in the doorway and had run to help her. Amy evidently hadn't been far behind.

There were five names on the spreadsheet that I didn't recognize at all along with another name of someone I knew—one of the ladies who often attended my DIY classes. But the final two entries on my spreadsheet were the ones that gave me pause and might very well mean that I should narrow my list of suspects to three.

Chapter 18

One of the two residences that had strongly grabbed my attention belonged to Tommy and Sonya, and the other belonged to Luis Cardoza and his wife. I hadn't realized that Sonya and her angry husband or Luis Cardoza, who'd warned me that it could be dangerous to "nose around" in the murder investigation, lived on Lily-of-the-Valley Lane. Well, well, well. Although I realized that this information might mean nothing, it was equally possible that it might mean everything.

Abby, my student, had described Sonya's behavior as "weird" when she'd attended my DIY Earrings class the day after the murder. I remembered the reason for the comment: Sonya had been acting as though nothing had happened after Victor had been shot, and she'd mentioned the detectives' visit to her in an almost breezy way. She'd been more concerned about extending her babysitter's hours so that she could run errands than with Victor's murder. Something about her attitude had struck the other students as odd, although I hadn't paid much attention at the time, having been mainly worried that Sonya would blame me for pointing the detectives in her direction. Of course, that worry had subsided when I learned that I hadn't been the only person Sonya had told about her problems with Victor and the HOA. She'd confided in quite a few other residents, too.

Tommy, Sonya's husband, hadn't exactly played it cool, either. Several men had heard his locker-room threats against Victor, including Cynthia's husband

Pete, who'd witnessed the scene in the locker room at the golf course and had concluded that Tommy might very well be Victor's killer.

Then there was Luis Cardoza. At Victor's funeral reception, he'd admitted that he felt responsible for his fiancé's suicide, but he'd denied allowing Victor to blackmail him. He'd certainly sounded believable, I thought. When he'd ended our conversation with a warning, I hadn't known quite how to interpret it. Had he threatened me, or had he warned me because he'd felt concerned for my safety? His meaning was ambiguous, at best.

Any one of the three could have seen Kenny put the gun in their trash cans as he fled from the guardhouse. Any one of the three could have taken advantage of the opportunity such a weapon had presented, especially if they could have retrieved it from the trash can without anyone's observing their actions. In that case, there'd be nothing to connect the stolen gun to the killer. All three had a motive to kill Victor, but which one had acted?

So far as prime suspects were concerned, I was leaning toward Tommy myself, mainly because Luis had seemed somewhat credible to me, and Sonya didn't seem the type of person who would resort to violence. Still, I couldn't discount either Luis or Sonya. Maybe I could eliminate one, two, or all three of them, if I could just find out whether or not they had alibis for Thursday night and early Friday morning, the time frame during which Victor had been shot. I'd had the opportunity to ask Luis Cardoza where he'd been the night of the murder, but I hadn't done so. I could have kicked myself for failing to ask the question. I'd seen Sonya in class the day after the murder, where I could easily have asked her what she'd told the detectives about her and Tommy's whereabouts that night, but I hadn't done that, either. I'd have to try to think of a way to ferret out the information because, thus far, the sum of my sleuthing amounted to very little.

My smartphone's chiming interrupted my reverie, and I could see that Amy was calling me.

"Hi, Amy. How goes it?"

"Better than yesterday, that's for sure. Funerals make me feel so depressed that I avoid them whenever possible, but Cynthia didn't want to go to Victor's alone—of course, Pete had to work—so I agreed to go with her."

"Well, some good came out of it. I'm sure Alice appreciated the help you and Cynthia gave her."

"That's true. She's a sweet lady. I made her promise that she'd call me anytime she needs a ride. It's not as though I have no free time now that Jim's gone," Amy said, sighing deeply.

"It's nice of you to volunteer to drive her, Amy," I said, somewhat at a loss for words. Amy was having a terrible time trying to adjust to life as a widow, and I didn't know how to comfort her. Mere words, I knew, didn't help much.

"I'm happy to do it. The reason I called, Laurel, is that I was wondering whether you might be interested in going to the Greek Food Festival with me this evening. Cynthia and Pete asked me to go with them, but, honestly, whenever I tag along with a couple, I feel like a third wheel."

"Oh, thanks, Amy, but I have sort of a date."

"It's not firm?"

"Right. My friend warned me that he's scheduled to be on call tonight."

"Oh, is he a doctor?"

"Noooo. He's a policeman, actually." I hadn't planned to tell anybody except Tracey and Liz about

Wes, but, on the other hand, I didn't see any need to hide it.

"I didn't realize you were dating anyone, Laurel. That's great." Amy liked nothing better than to play matchmaker, but when she was too late for that role, she loved to hear all about a romance.

"Well, I wouldn't exactly say we're dating. Tonight would be our second date."

"At least there *is* a second date—sounds promising to me. Where did you meet your cop?"

"He's one of the detectives investigating Victor's murder."

"The tall, handsome guy, I'll bet."

"That's the one."

"Lucky you! Well, I definitely don't want to interfere with a budding romance."

"Remember, Amy, there's a chance he may have to cancel. If he does, I'll call you, and we can go together."

"That's nice. Yes, let me know; otherwise, I think I'll just curl up with my latest romance novel this evening. I can always go to the Greek Food Festival with my neighbor Lisa and her kids tomorrow afternoon if I don't go tonight."

Naturally, I was hoping Wes wouldn't have to work that evening, but just an hour before he planned to pick me up, the phone rang, and I had the sinking feeling that it was Wes. Sure enough, there'd been a multiple homicide, and he'd been called in to investigate. Ah, I thought, the joys of dating a policeman. If we continued to see each other, there would probably be lots of cancelled dates along the way. In this case, at least I could offer Amy some company for the evening. I knew how terribly lonely she was, so a little distraction, even for a few hours, would do her good.

As usual, Saturday night was the busiest time at the three-day Greek Food Festival, held annually in Center City at St. John the Baptist Greek Orthodox Church. Streets around the church were packed with parked cars as hundreds of people flocked to the event. Amy had offered to drive, and she knew better than to try to park close to the church, so she found a spot several blocks away, and we walked, skipping a ride on the roving shuttle bus that regularly collected people going to the festival who'd parked blocks away. Once at the church, we joined the long line of people waiting to pay their general admission fee, but the line moved quickly, and we soon moved past the crafts vendors and out onto the grassy lawn in back of the church where tables were set out in the center and tents with Greek food lined the sides. There was a stage at one end, where costumed members of the church's youth groups performed Greek folk dances and Greek bands played.

"Do you think we'll be able to find a place to sit?" Amy asked. "It looks really crowded."

"Over there," I said, pointing to a table close to one of the food tents. "Those people are leaving."

We almost ran to the table to grab chairs and sit down. Although we could have stood to sample the food, we both planned to eat dinner, and it would be much easier to enjoy our Greek goodies if we had a place to sit. A couple with several children sat at the same table. Although they greeted us, they didn't try to engage us in conversation. They had their hands full, feeding and taking care of their little ones, none of whom looked older than five.

"We were lucky to find a spot." Amy said. "Shall we take turns going to the tents to get dinner? That way, we won't lose our seats."

"Sure, you go ahead, Amy, and I'll wait until you get back."

As Amy rose, I took off my light cotton jacket and draped it over her chair to signal that the seat was taken. The aroma of cooking food wafted my way on a light breeze, and I thought about which dishes I'd select for dinner. Spanakopita, the Greek version of spinach pie, topped my list of favorites, along with dolmades or stuffed grape leaves, and saganaki, a Greek flaming cheese dish.

Amy returned, setting her plate filled with pastitsio, a baked pasta dish, and a gyro on the table. She reached into her roomy denim shoulder bag and pulled out two bottles of water.

"I bought some water for us. I didn't know if you wanted anything else to drink, but I figured we can't go wrong with water."

"Thanks for picking that up. Water'll be fine."

The antics of the children at our table kept us entertained while we ate our dinner, and the family was still there when we departed so that we could move closer to the stage and watch the dancers. It was crowded at the foot of the stage, but we persevered long enough to watch several folk dances.

"Ready to look through the booths?" I said after the dance group finished and was making way for one of the bands to take the stage.

"Sure, I always like to look at the crafts and especially the jewelry. The dessert tables are right next to the arts and crafts, so we can pick up something on the way out."

I agreed, and we wandered over to the vendor booths in the bazaar area that was set up close to the festival's entrance and exit area. Although we spent some time looking through the various wares, we didn't find anything we wanted to buy, the Greek food being the main attraction at the festival.

"Well, I think I'll get in line for the baklava," I said. "Should I pick up some for you?"

"No, I'm going to go for the honey puffs; I think they're called loukoumathes in Greek. I love those things, and this is the only place I can get them."

"Okay, well, it looks as though the lines are pretty long, so this might take us a while. Let's meet next to the exit when we're done."

"See you there." Amy went off toward the booth where the honey puffs were sold, and I joined the line for the baklava. I'd promised to pick up some for Tracey, so I had the church member who took my order prepare two boxes, each with several pieces of the small traditional baklava, chocolate dipped baklava, and mocha caramel baklava. The pieces were small, I reasoned, so the calorie count couldn't be too high. Even as I thought about the calories, I knew I was fooling myself, but I figured a little splurge once in a while wouldn't hurt. After all, the festival happened only once a year. I paid for my purchase and moved out of the way as the people in line surged forward.

Amy hadn't come yet when I arrived at our meeting place, but a familiar figure in the crowd caught my eye. Although her back faced me, I would recognize that long, black ponytail anywhere. It had to be Sonya. She stood next to a big blonde man. Both were dressed casually in t-shirts, shorts, and sandals—nothing too unusual there—typical attire for festival-goers. What was most noticeable about the couple was that they had their hands all over each other, embarrassingly so for a public venue. As I watched them, the man leaned down, swooped Sonya into his arms, and planted a passionate kiss on her lips as her arms circled his neck. Amy had joined me while I watched this scene and saw the surprised looks the couple was drawing from the crowd.

Nudging Amy, I asked, "That *is* Sonya, isn't it?"

"Yep."

"Who's the big guy with her?"

Amy shot me a look. "It's her husband Tommy."

"Really? I've never seen him before, so I didn't realize he was her husband. I thought they weren't getting along. In fact, she told me he had actually threatened to divorce her. Guess he must have changed his mind."

"Now that Victor's no longer around to harass them."

Sonya whispered something to Tommy, and the couple disentangled as Tommy strode off toward one of the tents, leaving Sonya sitting on a ledge under a tree, but only after the duo had exchanged another passionate kiss. What was going on? Not ten days earlier, Sonya had confided that she and Tommy were at each other's throats because he blamed her for their swimming pool fiasco. Now a piece of paper couldn't pass between them.

"Let's go say 'hi' to Sonya," I suggested.

"You go ahead. I'll wait for you here," Amy said. "I see Cynthia and Pete coming this way."

"Okay, I'll be back in a few, I promise."

I walked away, hurriedly joining Sonya so that we could talk before Tommy returned.

"Hi, Sonya."

"Hi, Laurel. It's a fun festival, isn't it?"

"Yes, I always enjoy it."

"Tommy's gone to get us some ouzo. It's not my favorite, but he loves the stuff."

I'd only sampled ouzo once myself, and I hadn't cared for the characteristic licorice flavor of the drink, but I knew it was Greece's most popular alcoholic beverage.

"Oh, the two of you must have reconciled?" My inflection suggested a question. I really wondered what had happened to change the situation between the two.

"We have. Tommy has a hair-trigger temper, and I guess he thought the mix-up with the HOA's approval of our backyard project was all my fault. In his mind, there was plenty of reason to be angry, but once Victor died, he calmed down quite a bit. He said that he was sure we could get the HOA to back down now that Victor's dead, even if we have to plead our case before the full board to do it. Tommy said that whoever shot Victor did us and everybody else in Hawkeye Haven a huge favor."

"Sonya, you don't think that Tommy could have…."

"No way—my husband didn't shoot Victor! He doesn't even own a gun."

"The person who murdered Victor used a stolen gun."

"Well, it wasn't Tommy! He has an alibi."

"Oh?" Sonya was easy to interview. She answered questions before I ever asked them!

"That's right. Last Thursday night, Tommy had been drinking, and things got a little heated at home, so I called the cops. Tommy spent the night in jail, and the kids and I went over to my parents' house. They didn't want me to bail him out the next morning, but I hoped that a night in jail had cooled him off, and I knew he'd really be furious if I didn't post his bail. Just after we arrived home, we heard that Victor had been shot, and Tommy's mood improved tremendously."

"Well, I hope everything works out for you."

"See you in class next week."

I walked back toward Amy, who stood near the exit chatting with Cynthia and Pete, before Tommy returned with the ouzo. If Sonya were telling the truth, there was no need to ask Tommy about where he'd been when

Victor had been shot. As Sonya had said, her husband had an alibi, one that would have been simple for the police to confirm immediately. When she'd attended my last class, Sonya hadn't seemed too concerned that the detectives had questioned Tommy and her. Now I understood the reason, although her breezy attitude towards the entire situation puzzled me a bit.

"Hi," I greeted Cynthia and Pete. "It looks as though you're taking some goodies home with you."

"Too many, but I can't resist delicious food," Pete said. "Every time we go to the buffet on Sunday, I feel as though I'm rolling out of there."

"I remember Karl mentioning the same thing when we saw you there."

"We like to kid ourselves that playing eighteen rounds of golf makes up for stuffing ourselves at the buffet every Sunday. We haven't missed a Sunday since he hired a manager for his landscaping company."

"My downfall has always been sweets," Cynthia added. "I've never met a dessert I didn't like."

Amy nodded in agreement. "Me either. I like the baklava well enough, but these honey puffs are to die for," she said, holding up her bag of pastries.

"How about you, Laurel?" Cynthia asked. "I see that you bought something, too."

"Yes, baklava for Tracey and me. She had to go to dinner with a client tonight, so I promised I'd bring her some."

"Say, I noticed you were talking to Sonya a minute ago," Pete said. "I've always thought that Tommy might have been the one who shot Victor. I thought he was going to kill him right there in the locker room the other day."

"According to Sonya, Tommy has an air-tight alibi. She just told me that Tommy spent that night in jail because she called the police after they had a big argument."

"Well, what do you know about that?" Pete asked. "If he was in jail, he sure couldn't have shot Victor. I wonder if we'll ever know who the murderer is."

Chapter 19

"See you later, Amy, and thanks for driving. It was fun."

As soon as I closed the car door, I could hear Bear barking inside. He knew Mommy was home. Jumping up and down in excitement, my big Lab blocked the doorway, making it difficult for me to enter the house, but I finally managed to nudge my way inside and deposit my boxes of baklava in the refrigerator before I stooped to give him a hug.

"I suppose you want a treat, huh, Bear?" He panted his assent. "Of course, you do. Here you go, boy," I said, tossing him a pumpkin treat. "That's all now." Both of us had had ample food for the day. I still felt full—all that spinach pie had had plenty of calories, not to mention the stuffed grape leaves and the saganaki.

While I tried to read the boring novel that my book club was scheduled to discuss at our September meeting—the one that had put me to sleep the last time I tried to read it—Bear plopped down on his bed in the den, curled up, and was soon snoring softly. This time I managed to read the first two chapters. I was a few pages into the third chapter when my attention began to flag.

I kept thinking about what I'd learned that evening. I'd considered both Sonya and her husband Tommy strong suspects before I'd learned that they had alibis for the time of the murder. Feeling sure that the police had confirmed those alibis, I'd crossed them off my mental list of possible killers.

Now what? I had the nagging feeling that I had missed a significant clue somewhere along the line. Snippets of all the information I'd gathered whirled around in my head like pieces of a jigsaw puzzle, and I felt the need to put each piece in the right place for the whole picture to emerge. As midnight approached, I could only hope that the cobwebs would disappear by morning. I decided to stop trying to solve the puzzle until after I'd had a night's sleep.

Somehow, in my dreams that night, my subconscious mind made a crucial connection that had eluded my conscious mind. I remembered where I'd seen the unusual brooch that I'd noticed Diana wearing in the photo in Liz's album, and I remembered who had been wearing it. I thought that I just might know who the killer was. Now, I needed to decide what to do about it.

As I dutifully walked with Bear that morning, I reviewed my options. I could call Wes and tell him what I knew and how I'd interpreted it. I'd missed the chance to see Wes again when he'd been forced to cancel our date for the Greek Food Festival, and I hadn't received a call or a text message from him in the meantime. He must be tied up with his most recent case, and I hated to bother him with speculation. To be honest, I had to admit that I was a teensy bit disappointed that I hadn't heard from him later in the evening. Was he really so busy that he couldn't take the time to send me a brief text message?

I also resented the fact that he expected me to share any information I picked up with him, but, on the other hand, he refused to share what he found out with me. Okay, I knew I was being unreasonable because he was a Center City detective who had to follow the police department's procedures and stick to its policies, but that didn't mean that I liked his mum's-the-word strategy when it came to Victor's murder.

Then there was the issue of my snooping around, which was sure to spark the handsome detective's ire. Wes's official-Mr.-Detective attitude might work wonders on suspects, but it left me with feelings of guilt and anger, not the emotions most conducive to a new romance. I liked Wes a lot better when he was being a human being, rather than when he was being a detective. So, maybe my first step in seeking to confirm my theory shouldn't be sharing my suspicions with Wes.

If I hadn't known that Tracey was tied up in a breakfast meeting, I would have asked her what she thought of my deductions, but I couldn't interrupt her while she worked, especially since I knew how hard she'd been trying to land her money-bags client's business.

Why not go ahead and ask my suspect a couple of seemingly innocent questions? I could find a pretext for my curiosity and perhaps confirm my suspicions in doing so, probably without the murderer ever realizing the purpose of my inquiries. At the moment, this plan seemed to be the best course of action. If I could ferret out pertinent answers, I'd turn all my evidence over to Wes and let him and his obnoxious partner take it from there. The more I thought about it, the more my plan appealed to me. If I was wrong, no one would be the wiser. If I was right, I'd have solved a murder.

As soon as Bear and I returned home from our morning walk, I fortified myself with some strong coffee before showering, styling my hair, applying sunscreen and make-up, and dressing in navy capris and a sleeveless, cotton blouse with an abstract brushstroke print design in different shades of blue on a white background. I'd made the button-down blouse the previous spring, and it was one of my favorites. I slipped on my tan thong sandals and grabbed my digital camera, which I deposited in my handbag. With a pat on the head to Bear, along with an admonition for him to be a good boy, I left through the door to the garage. I'd decided to drive to my suspect's house, even though I could have walked, since it was only about a mile from my own home. I'd driven about half a block down the street when it occurred to me that maybe I should let someone know where I intended to go. I dug my smartphone out of my purse and sent Tracey a terse text message. She replied immediately urging me to wait and telling me that I shouldn't go to the suspect's house alone because it could be dangerous. I replied with a "don't worry" before turning off my phone and returning it to my handbag. I had my plan, and I was going to see it through.

As I turned on Lily-of-the-Valley Lane, I felt hopeful that my little ruse would work. I'd find out in a few minutes, I thought, as I parked in front of my suspect's house and hoisted my handbag onto my shoulder. I walked to the front door and rang the doorbell. I stood there for a while, knowing that the person inside was probably peering at me through the peephole and trying to decide whether or not to open the door. Finally, the door opened, and I was staring at the person I thought had killed Victor.

"Laurel?" she said, a puzzled look on her face.

"Hi, Eva," I replied. "I'm working on a project, and I was hoping you might be able to help me."

Eva didn't look exactly thrilled as I advanced over the door sill without waiting for her to invite me to come into the house, but she stepped aside and allowed me to enter. Remembering that her husband Karl had said that Eva didn't always let her own therapist into her home, I knew that I was probably lucky to make it that far. Eva didn't invite me to sit down, nor did she offer me coffee, although she did close the front door. We both stood there awkwardly in the small foyer, Eva with an expectant look on her face.

"What do you want, Laurel?" she asked bluntly.

I went into my spiel then, explaining that I'd been asked to give a lecture about unusual costume jewelry to a local women's group—a fabrication, but I had to come up with some plausible story so that Eva would let me come into her house—and that I needed some pictures of jewelry to illustrate my talk. I explained that I planned to give a PowerPoint presentation, just as I did in class when I was presenting project instructions. Eva raised her eyebrows, a skeptical look on her face, as I prattled on. I was beginning to fear that she might not want to cooperate. As an agoraphobic, she may have resented my invasion of her home—the only place where she felt safe.

"And so I was hoping that you'd let me take a photo of that unique brooch—the one with the two pistols crossed—that I saw you wearing in class last year," I continued, as I pulled my digital camera from my bag.

"Well, I don't know," Eva said, hesitating.

"It's such a stunning piece, and it'll only take a few minutes to take a picture of it. I could even take a picture of you wearing it."

"Oh, no. I wouldn't want to be in the picture."

"Then it's okay if I take a picture of the brooch?"

"I guess so," Eva said reluctantly.

"The light's good in the living room. Maybe I could put it on the coffee table and use that as the background." I repeated my earlier maneuver, stepping forward into the living room without Eva's invitation.

"I don't know, Laurel. I don't think this is a very good idea."

Uh, oh. I'd pushed too far, and now Eva was backtracking. Desperately I tried to think of a way to pacify her, but pleading seemed to be the only strategy left.

"Please, Eva," I begged, "a picture of your brooch would really add a lot to my presentation, and I know that the ladies would really enjoy seeing your unique pin."

"I don't think so. I'd like you to leave now. You're acting strange."

Clearly, I'd overplayed my hand. Knowing that I might never have another chance to talk with Eva, I laid my cards on the table.

"All right, Eva. I'm leaving, but not before you tell me why you have that brooch."

"I don't know why you'd care, but someone gave it to me." Eva said, looking confused. "It was a gift from Courtney."

This bit of information didn't surprise me. In fact, it made perfect sense.

"Why did Courtney give you that particular brooch, Eva?" I asked.

"Oh, I was there when Diana won the brooch and a trophy at the Annie Oakley Shootout Competition several years ago."

"But why give it to you? Why not Liz or one of Diana's other friends? Was there a special reason?"

Eva shrugged. "Maybe because I earned it. I'd have won that competition myself if my gun hadn't jammed during the final round."

What Eva had just told me certainly confirmed my suspicions. Eva was a crack shot. Her neighbors had mentioned her habit of looking out the front window to keep track of what was happening in the neighborhood. She could easily have seen Kenny drop the gun into her trash can, retrieved it while her husband showered or slept, and taken the opportunity to shoot Victor. Victor knew Eva, so he wouldn't have hesitated to open his door for her. However, I'd heard that agoraphobic Eva hadn't left her house for more than a year. If that were true, I wouldn't have considered Eva a suspect, but Tracey and I both thought we had seen her at a shopping center the day we picked up the supplies for Bessie's party. If so, Eva had overcome her agoraphobia enough for a foray outside her house, and that bit of information clinched it as far as I was concerned. Eva had to be the killer, I believed.

Her motive? Strictly self-preservation. According to Luke, Victor planned to replace Hawkeye Haven's current landscaping company, and Eva's husband Karl stood to lose the lucrative contract. Unless I missed my guess, KM Landscaping—it had finally dawned on me that KM stood for Karl Meyer—had only one major client, Hawkeye Haven, and Victor was ready to cancel KM's contract. If that happened, Eva, who was solely dependent on her husband, could lose her precious home. Even if she had ventured out a few times, she was still an agoraphobic, and her house remained her sanctuary.

I couldn't stop myself from pressing forward.

"I guess it must have been an easy shot—close range and all."

"What are you talking about?"

"Come off it, Eva. You shot Victor, didn't you?"

"You're crazy!" Eva's voice trembled.

"Am I? You were protecting your own, weren't you? That's why you shot him."

"No, no, no! Nothing you're saying is true," Eva shouted. "Get out of my house!"

"Hey, what's going on here?" While Eva and I were mixing it up, Karl had come into the house so quietly that neither of us had heard him.

I'd been sure that Karl wouldn't be home when I arrived, and I'd been right about that, but I'd also been sure that he'd be away from the house until at least early afternoon. I knew that he played golf with Cynthia's husband Pete every Sunday and that, after the golf game, Cynthia joined the men for brunch at the buffet. Karl shouldn't be home now, yet here he was. Eva hadn't admitted anything, and now that Karl was on the scene, I figured that she never would.

Eva ran to Karl, who protectively put his arm around her. "She must be insane," Eva moaned. "She accused me of shooting Victor."

"Oh, she did, did she?" Karl said, looking at me quizzically.

"Laurel's all mixed up. She said something about protecting my own. I have no idea what she's talking about."

"Just what *are* you talking about, Laurel?"

"Your wife killed Victor to save your contract with Hawkeye Haven."

"What would you know about my contract?"

"I know that Victor was on the verge of cancelling it and hiring a different landscaping company."

Karl glared at me, a calculating expression in his eyes. In a flash of insight, suddenly I realized I'd targeted the wrong spouse. Eva hadn't shot Victor, but her husband Karl had. My new-found knowledge must have been written all over my face. Unfortunately, I wasn't very good at hiding my feelings.

Karl took one look at me, and, in that instant, I knew that he'd realized I'd figured out that he was the murderer. I bolted toward the front door, but Karl intercepted me, gripping me firmly by the arms and pulling me back into the living room. Although I struggled, I couldn't loosen Karl's hold on me. Despite his rotund middle section, the man had muscles like steel.

Eva screamed while Karl tried to shush her.

"Karl, what are doing? Let her go!" she pleaded.

Karl shook his head. "No, she knows too much. I have to think." He tightened his grip on me, pinning my arms behind my back so that I couldn't move. Slowly, he began dragging me toward the kitchen. Eva followed in our wake, her eyes wide with shock at her husband's reckless behavior.

"What do you mean—she knows too much?" Eva croaked, still not fully comprehending the significance of Karl's uncharacteristic actions.

"Shh, shh, shh, Eva." Karl said, not answering her question. "Leave us alone. I'll take care of this."

"He shot Victor, Eva!" I yelled. "Help me! Make him let go of me!" I wiggled in Karl's vice-like grip, but I couldn't break free.

"Karl? No, he wouldn't do that."

"Then why's he acting this way, Eva?" I asked.

"Shut up!" Karl shouted. "Don't listen to her, Eva. You said yourself that she was all mixed up."

Her eyes darting back and forth from her husband to me, Eva finally had a light-bulb moment, and she began wailing loudly.

"Eva, stop that right now," Karl commanded. "I can't think when you're making that infernal racket."

Abruptly Eva stopped keening and lapsed into racking sobs, instead.

"Karl, let go of me. You'll be in even more trouble than you already are, if you don't," I said, trying to sound reasonable.

"How can I be in more trouble?" Karl growled. "I killed Victor. That's a murder rap." He paused, sighing. "I did the community a favor. I should be getting a medal for offing Victor, instead of—"

"You haven't been convicted yet," I said desperately.

"Oh, yeah, fat chance I'd get off with that new boyfriend of yours on the case," he scoffed.

"He doesn't know what you did," I said truthfully. "I won't tell him," I lied.

"I'll make sure you don't. It's too bad that the DIY Diva has to take a dive," Swiftly, Karl pushed me toward the gleaming stainless steel kitchen range, pinning me against it with his body while he reached for a large knife that protruded from the butcher block on the mottled black granite counter. In one quick movement, he snatched the knife from the block and brought its edge to my neck with his right hand while he circled my neck with his left arm. I didn't know whether he intended to choke me or slit my throat, but, in either case, it wasn't looking good.

Terrified, I fought back the only way I could. I sank my teeth into Karl's forearm and bit him with all the force I could muster, wishing I had the power of Bear's strong jaws in my own.

"Yeow!" he yelled and promptly ripped the edge of the knife he held along the right side of my neck. I howled in pain as blood trickled from my wound, down my neck, and onto my beautiful blue brushstroke blouse, but there was no time to worry about my ruined handiwork now. He pressed the knife blade to my throat.

Karl had decided to kill me, too.

"Eva, help me!" I pleaded, but she just stared at Karl and me through her tears, a blank look on her face.

"Hey, Karl, you forgot to close your garage door," a masculine voice called as the door between the kitchen and the garage swung open. Karl turned, dragging me with him, the knife still at my throat, to face the intruder.

Cynthia's husband Pete's mouth dropped open as he stopped short in the doorway and took in the scene in the kitchen. Immediately, he held out his arm to prevent Cynthia from entering the house. I could see both Cynthia and Amy right behind Pete at the door. For a second, nobody spoke. We were all frozen in place like a DVD that had been paused.

"What the hell!" Pete exclaimed.

"He killed Victor, and now he wants to kill me," I sobbed.

"Put that knife down, Karl," Pete said.

"No way. Back out of here, Pete. I'll cut her throat if you don't."

His threat was too much for me. My knees buckled, my head spun, and my body went limp. Pete's appearance had surprised Karl enough that he'd loosened his grip on me slightly. I slipped right out of Karl's grasp and landed on the tile floor of the kitchen, cracking my head hard as I landed.

Then darkness engulfed me.

When I woke up, I could see Amy kneeling beside me as a young man in a firefighter's uniform worked to immobilize my head. Light-headed and confused, I couldn't remember immediately where I was. Looking down at me with concern, Pete and Cynthia stood behind Amy. Another firefighter was wheeling a gurney into the kitchen while a couple of uniformed police officers were trying to talk to a weeping Eva. Then it all came back to me.

"Oh," I groaned. "My head hurts!"

"It's okay, Laurel. You're going to be okay," Amy assured me.

"What happened to Karl?" I asked, suddenly afraid that he'd come back to get me.

"When you passed out, he ran out the front door and took off in his car," Pete said. "But don't worry. The cops are after him. He won't get far."

"That's good," I murmured and promptly fainted again.

***

When I woke up the next time, I was lying on a bed in the emergency room of the Center City Regional Hospital, the same hospital where I'd visited Bessie the week before. My head throbbed, the stab wound on my neck hurt, and I felt nauseated. I drifted in and out of consciousness, dimly aware of doctors and nurses milling about. Tracey, Wes, Cynthia, Pete, and Amy all came in and out of the emergency room cubicle, one at a time.

Eventually, I awoke in a different room, and a nurse told me that I'd been admitted to the hospital because I had a mild concussion and that my doctor would be in to see me later. She asked if I wanted some company in the meantime, and I nodded. A few seconds later, Tracey popped in and hugged me tightly.

"Lo-lo, thank goodness, you're going to be all right! Do you remember what happened?"

"Um, hmmm. Karl killed Victor, Trace," I said. "I thought Eva was the killer."

"That was a crazy thing you did, going over to their house to confront Eva. I got worried when you didn't pick up after I tried to call you back. I was having breakfast with that awful client of mine and my team, and I knew it would take me forever to get back to Hawkeye Haven, but I was so worried about you that I called everybody I could think of. I managed to reach Cynthia and Amy, and I tried to reach Wes—I didn't have his number, but Amy still had his card, so she gave me the number—but when I called him, my call went straight to Wes's voice mail."

"You saved my life, Tracey." I said gratefully. "I'd be a goner if you hadn't called the neighbors to come check on me."

"I left the restaurant right after I called them, but—wouldn't you know it?—there'd been an accident on the Interstate, and I was stuck in traffic for an hour. By the time I arrived on my street, they were loading you into an ambulance."

Thinking about my close call made me shudder.

"Wes wants to see you, Laurel. Should I tell him to come in now?"

"I must look awful," I protested. Not only did I look awful, but I was also afraid that Wes would feel compelled to give me a lecture.

"He saw you in the ER, so don't worry about that. I think you should let him come in now. He's really worried about you."

"Well, okay, I'd better put on some make-up and fix my hair."

"You're not going to the prom, girl." Brushing a strand of hair from my forehead, Tracey looked closely at me and relented. "But okay, we can do a little something here. Hold on, Amy has your handbag. I'll go get it."

My reflection in the small mirror that the hospital provided confirmed my fears that I looked frightful. My disheveled hair, my pale-as-a-ghost face, and the large bandage taped to my neck didn't help matters at all. Tracey had to help me put my make-up on because my hands shook when I tried to apply my mascara and eyeliner.

"There, that's better," Tracey declared as she swiped some gloss on my lips. "I'll get Wes."

As the handsome detective entered the drab hospital room, my stomach flip-flopped, whether in happiness to see him or fear that he'd admonish me, I wasn't sure.

Without a word, he lowered the railing on the hospital bed, sat down next to me, and gathered me in his arms. With my head on his chest, I wept, completely ruining the make-up that Tracey had so carefully applied and smearing mascara all over Wes's shirt. I stammered a teary apology as I struggled to pull myself together.

"Shhh, you crazy woman," he said as he rocked me in his arms. "You're safe now."

He ran his fingers through my hair, and I yelped in pain. The tender moment had passed, and I braced myself for the inevitable lecture that would follow.

Chapter 20

But it didn't come.

"I'm sorry," Wes said, as he jerked his hand away. "I didn't mean to hurt you. That's quite a knot you have there."

"Guess I'm not as hard-headed as I thought." I smiled wanly. "Or as smart—I thought Eva was the killer." I glanced at Wes and stammered, "I didn't go over there to confront her; really, I didn't. I was just going to ask her about that brooch of hers, and then Karl showed up, and he admitted that he'd shot Victor, and then he—"

"I get the picture, Laurel. You can fill me in on the details later. Right now, you need to rest and recuperate. I talked to the doc, and she said you'd probably be able to go home in the morning, but you'll need to take it easy for a few days."

"Wes," I whispered. "Thanks for not yelling at me."

Wes shook his head in mock annoyance. "Wouldn't have done a bit of good if I had. You have a mind of your own, Laurel McMillan." He kissed me gently on the forehead and eased off the bed.

"Knock, knock."

The door to my room opened, and Amy stuck her head in.

"You have a special visitor, Laurel," she announced. "Here he comes."

Amy opened the door wider, and Bear bounced in, tugging at his leash so hard that it slipped out of Cynthia's hand. He ran to my bed and jumped up, putting his front paws on the side of the bed, panting excitedly, and wagging his tail.

"We sneaked him up on the back service elevator," Cynthia said, as I hugged my furry pet. By now, Cynthia, Pete, Amy, and Tracey had all crowded into the room, along with Wes and Bear. "I don't think anyone saw us."

"Wrong!" came a strident voice from the hallway. "No dogs allowed in the hospital, except service dogs. You'll have to get him out of here." A shapeless woman, dressed in equally shapeless, pink scrubs stood in the doorway, her hands on her hips. She glared at my friends and Bear as they meekly filed out of the room, but, despite the woman's officiousness, Bear's brief visit had cheered me up, and I couldn't wait to go home.

"Don't worry about Bear, Lo-lo," Tracey said, as she headed for the door. "I'll take good care of him."

"Thanks, Trace. You're the best."

"And I'll bring you some clothes for you to wear when you get out of here tomorrow."

I started to protest that I could wear the clothes I'd donned that morning, but then I remembered that my blouse had blood on it.

"Move it along," the pink-clad pit bull demanded, and Tracey ducked out of my room, closing the door and leaving me alone again with Wes.

"I should get that blouse soaking in cold water right away so that I can remove the stains. I wonder where the rest of my things are." Tracey had left my handbag with me after retrieving it from Amy, but I didn't know what had happened to my clothes.

"They're probably in the closet," Wes said, opening the closet door. "Yes, here's a plastic bag with your shoes and, uh, unmentionables," Wes said uncomfortably.

"Is the blouse there?"

"I'm sorry, Laurel, but it's been bagged for evidence. You'll get it back after the trial."

"Oh, no!" I wailed. "It's my favorite. I designed and made it myself. I even designed and hand-painted the fabric I used. The stain will set for sure if it's not removed right away."

Tears dripped down my face, undoubtedly causing my eye make-up to run even more than it already had. I felt another crying jag coming on. Sure, I was upset about the blouse, but normally that wouldn't be enough to bring me to tears. My emotions were roller-coastering all over the place, and I knew that I needed to get a hold on myself. Wes eyed me in distress.

"I'm sorry, Laurel," he said.

"No, *I'm* sorry. I should have realized that you'd need the blouse for evidence. I guess my nerves are on edge," I sniffed, wiping my face with a tissue I'd plucked from the box beside me on the hospital's nightstand.

"It's no wonder after what you've been through today." Wes's phone buzzed, and he reached into his pocket and looked at the display. "I need to take this," he told me. After he made several short responses, he returned the phone to his pocket and turned to me. "Good news! Karl's been apprehended."

"Oh, that's a relief! What will happen now?"

"I'm going back to the station to question him—that is, if he doesn't ask for a lawyer. In any case, he'll be charged with assault for what he did to you, maybe even attempted murder and kidnapping, but that's up to the district attorney. As for Victor's murder, we'll see. So far, there's no physical evidence tying him to that crime, but we may still be able to develop something."

"He confessed, you know. Eva and I both heard him."

Wes nodded. "We'll see what he has to say for himself now, after his great escape. He was driving his own car when he was taken into custody—not exactly a master criminal. I'm hoping I can get him to repeat his confession."

"Me, too."

"Try to rest now, Laurel."

Wes leaned down and planted a lingering kiss on my lips. I clung to him for a few seconds and then let him go. "No more worrying, okay, Laurel? I've got this. Everything's under control."

***

Three weeks later, a slight nip tinged the early autumn air as we gathered for a harvest moon party at Liz's, and everybody oohed and aahed as the huge orb shone in the gathering dusk. Liz had timed her party perfectly. Cynthia, Amy, and I had all helped to make the decorations. A large wreath of gold, orange, brown, and red lacquered fall leaves hung on Liz's front door while, inside the house, the scent of cinnamon wafted from the potpourri we'd made, and candles twinkling inside hollowed-out pumpkins and gourds reflected the party's theme. A gigantic golden horn of plenty I'd made of paper mâché contained a colorful display of apples, miniature pumpkins, eggplants, and ears of corn with their husks peeled back.

Outside, surrounding the pool, the colonel had set up bales of hay, and we'd arranged straw scarecrows dressed in red gingham shirts, cut-off jeans, and straw hats atop some of the bales. Orange and green floating lights sparkled in the swimming pool, contributing to the festive mood.

Liz had invited her friends and neighbors, not only to party but also so she could introduce Luke as her grandson. She had followed through on her plan to tell him her secret, and although he was surprised at first, he was happy to learn that he had a grandmother he'd never even realized he was missing, one who wanted to have a relationship with him and his family. Luke had been unaware that his father, a man he'd never met, had been adopted as an infant.

Wes and I arrived at the party just as Luke and his wife, a Kate Hudson lookalike wearing a bright red maxi dress and lipstick to match, showed up. Luke introduced us to his wife, and I asked him whether their twin five-year-old daughters had met their great-grandma yet. According to Luke, they'd visited Liz a couple of times, but they were staying with a babysitter during the party so that Luke and his wife could take a rare evening off.

Liz's son Leonard was just as surprised as his nephew, but not nearly as happy. After the four of us entered the house, I spotted Leonard in the crowd, lounging against the wall in the den, holding a martini. Luke offered his hand, and Leonard grudgingly shook it and nodded to Luke's wife, then wandered off into the kitchen. Obviously, he hadn't accepted the new reality yet. I still hoped he'd come around eventually, but I wouldn't want to bet on it.

We made our way out to the patio, where Liz, in one of her bright beaded caftans, and the colonel were talking to another couple who had their backs to us. It wasn't until we approached them that I realized the woman was Bessie. Although at first I didn't recognize the man who accompanied her, he looked familiar. Then it hit me. He was Al, the security guard Bessie had greeted so effusively at her retirement party.

"Great party, Liz," I said as Liz and I air kissed. I didn't want to ruin her make-up, which was perfect, as usual. "Everything looks wonderful."

"Thanks to all the help I had—that includes you and Bobby, too."

I turned to Bessie and gave her a quick hug.

"Did you finally get my dog treat recipe?" she asked.

"Yes, thanks, Bessie. I'm looking forward to including it in my new book. Chloe sent it to me this morning." It had been weeks since Bessie had agreed to give me her recipe for the dog-bone-shaped treats Bear had so looked forward to getting from his favorite security guard every day when we took our morning walk. Bessie didn't use email herself, but her granddaughter did, so she'd asked her to forward the recipe to me. After a few phone calls back and forth, I had realized that the bright, but spelling-challenged, middle-schooler had been sending it to the wrong email address—diydeeva@email.com, instead of diydiva@email.com. No wonder it hadn't shown up in my inbox earlier.

More guests had crowded onto the patio, so Wes and I moved to the far side of the pool where Cynthia, Pete, Amy, Fran, and Brian had gathered.

"Look who's here—our very own Nancy Drew. Laurel, you look great!" Brian said. "Last time we saw you, you were coming home from the hospital," Fran noted.

I felt as though I were back to normal except for the scar on my neck that probably wouldn't ever completely fade away. For the moment, I'd settled on hiding it with my shoulder-length hair, sweeping it forward in loose waves to cover the scar. That wouldn't work, of course, if I wanted to wear a different hairstyle. Eventually, I planned to experiment with heavy-duty make-up to see whether that would hide the scar, but for now, I'd use my hairstyle to disguise the ugly gash that was still red, although the stitches had already been removed. Not overly concerned with the cosmetic problems covering up the scar might present, I just felt lucky to have survived the knife wound, which my doctor had told me had come perilously close to my jugular vein.

"Yes, I hate to even think about it. It's nice to be back to the everyday routine and not to have to worry about a killer in our community," I said.

"Frankly, it's a good thing Karl confessed," Wes said. "We didn't have any physical evidence to support the murder charge."

"We might never have found out it was Karl if he hadn't burst in on Eva and me the way he did. I wasn't expecting him to show up. I was certain that he always played golf on Sunday mornings and went to brunch at the buffet afterwards."

"I know why he went home that day," Pete informed us. "It was his turn to pay for brunch, and he'd forgotten his wallet."

"That explains it. I thought if I could talk to Eva alone, I might come up with some useful information," I explained. "Karl said he'd done the community a favor by shooting Victor. I guess maybe more than a few people would probably agree," I said.

"In a way he did," Pete said. "Evidently, Victor had cooked up quite a scheme. Most residents don't realize it, but there's a yearly independent audit done for the Hawkeye Haven HOA. The accountant who handled it last year was fired from his firm, and another accountant ended up doing this year's audit. That's when it came to light that Victor had been taking kick-backs from some of the contractors he'd hired for HOA business. He wanted to take Karl's landscaping contract away from him and award it to another company that would play ball with him. Of course, the board's tendency would be to accept Victor's recommendations to hire the contractors, but they didn't realize they were helping him to line his own pockets. Victor wasn't a poor man by any means, so he didn't need the money. Just greedy, I guess."

That figures, I thought to myself. Just as Luke had surmised, there was more to Victor's attempts at coercing some of the board members than a mere power play. He'd wanted to secure the votes of a majority so that he could hire only contractors who'd be willing to kick back a substantial portion of their revenue for work at Hawkeye Haven to Victor.

"Guess who else was in on the kick-back scheme with Victor?" Cynthia asked.

"Patty," we residents all chimed in unison.

"Right, and, as of this morning, Patty's company's contract has been cancelled. She's out. We'll never see her around here again," Cynthia informed us. "She could even face charges."

"Woo-hoo! I can't say that I'll miss her," I said. "She's one of the most unpleasant women I've ever met."

"Rachel Caswell told me all about it," Cynthia interjected. "For a while there, I thought for sure that she'd resign from the board, what with all the trouble Rachel's son Kenny has caused, but, now that she's the board president, she's decided to stick it out for the rest of her term."

"You heard what happened to Kenny, didn't you?" Amy asked.

We hadn't; that is, nobody except Wes knew the disposition of Kenny's case.

"His attorney arranged for a plea deal. Kenny's out now on probation and looking at several hundred hours of community service," Wes said.

"That should keep him busy and out of trouble," Amy commented. "He's fortunate that his father could afford a high-powered lawyer like Gerard Foster."

I wondered what kind of a deal Karl's attorney would be able to make with the district attorney. I certainly didn't want to see him again anytime soon. Wes had assured me that he wouldn't get off lightly, though.

As for Eva, her life would be tough without Karl, even tougher than it had already been for a woman who had voluntarily confined herself to her own house. Both Cynthia and Amy had been trying to help her, but I'd steered clear. Although I felt sorry for Eva, I hadn't quite forgiven her yet for ignoring my pleas for help when her husband had held a knife to my throat.

We'd learned that the woman Tracey and I had seen at the strip mall hadn't been Eva at all. Tracey and I had been browsing the racks at Ooh La La, the trendy boutique we'd thought Eva had been entering when we'd spotted her a few weeks earlier, when we'd seen the woman again. Eva's lookalike turned out to be a member of the boutique's sales staff, and she really did look a lot like Eva. Even their hairstyles were similar. Karl had been telling the truth about his wife's agoraphobia: Eva hadn't left the house in over a year.

"Yes, Kenny's fortunate," I agreed. "I hope Karl's not so lucky."

"Surely, he'll be locked up for a long time, won't he, Wes?" Tracey asked, as she joined our group.

"Very likely. The D.A.'s not going to agree to a light sentence."

"Just think, Laurel, he'd still be on the loose if it weren't for you," Amy said.

"We'll have to start calling you the DIY detective," Wes joked.

"Some detective—I thought Eva killed Victor."

"Don't sell yourself short, Laurel. You were on the right track. You picked up on things that nobody else, including this master detective himself, noticed."

"Maybe because I know the community, but I'm glad it's all over, and Hawkeye Haven can get back to normal. I'd much rather be the DIY Diva than the DIY detective. Like you said, murder in a guard-gated community is rare."

"Yep, the odds are against another murder happening in Hawkeye Haven."

I nodded in agreement. The residents of Hawkeye Haven would be safe now that both Bessie's attack and Victor's murder had been solved.

Or would they?

DIY for Dog Lovers – Treats and Projects

Caution: never feed dogs treats with ingredients that they are allergic to!

Laurel's Peanut Butter Dog Treats

Laurel's chocolate Labrador retriever Bear loves these peanut butter dog treats. Although there are only two ingredients, these tasty little morsels must bake for quite a while, so if you're making these peanut butter treats, don't plan on giving one to Fido right away.

Ingredients

4 egg whites

¼ C creamy peanut butter

Note that commercial peanut butter contains not only peanuts but also other ingredients such as molasses, hydrogenated oils, and salt, so if you don't want your dog to eat the other ingredients, use natural peanut butter, instead.

In a mixing bowl, beat the egg whites until they form stiff peaks. Add small amounts of the peanut butter on top of the stiff egg whites, and attempt to fold the peanut butter into the egg whites until mixed. This can be difficult, so the alternative is beat the mixture with the electric mixer until blended, but do not overbeat because some of the volume will be lost if you do. Line a cookie sheet with parchment paper, and drop rounded spoonfuls of the mixture onto the parchment paper about 1 ½ inches apart. Bake at 200 degrees for 1 ½ hours. Before removing the cookie sheet from the oven, test for doneness by removing one treat and letting it cool on a wire rack. If the treat is crisp, remove the cookie sheet from the oven and place the treats on the wire rack to cool. If the treat is not crisp, continue baking the rest of treats for about fifteen minutes. Store the treats in an air-tight container.

Lynn's Pumpkin Doggie Snacks

Laurel's cousin Lynn makes these pumpkin doggie snacks for her beagle Barkley. Barkley's always in the mood to eat a pumpkin snack.

Note: This recipe calls for oat flour. Lynn makes her own oat flour from Quick Quaker Oats cereal. To make your own oat flour, just pulverize the oats in a food processor until they're the consistency of flour.

Ingredients

2 eggs

1 C canned pumpkin

½ t cinnamon

2 C oat flour

Preheat the oven to 400 degrees. Line a baking sheet with parchment paper. Beat the eggs in a large mixing bowl before adding the pumpkin. Mix the eggs and pumpkin until smooth. Sprinkle the cinnamon over the egg and pumpkin mixture and stir well. Add the oat flour ½ cup at a time and mix well. Roll the treat dough between two sheets of parchment paper until the dough is 1/8 inch thick. Use a 2 ¼-inch cookie cutter to cut round snacks from the dough. (Lynn uses the rim of a small juice glass.) Place the round treats on the lined baking sheet. Bake the pumpkin treats at 400 degrees for 10 minutes. The treats can be cooled on the parchment paper (carefully slide it off the baking sheet) or removed and cooled on a wire rack. This recipe makes about 3 dozen pumpkin treats, way more than Barkley or any other dog should have in a few days, so store them in the freezer, layered between sheets of waxed paper or parchment paper in an airtight container.

Bessie's Dog-Bone Treats

Bessie always had one of these dog-bone treats waiting for Bear every morning when Laurel took him for a walk. Now that Bessie's retired from her job as a security guard at Hawkeye Haven, she still makes Bear a care package of treats every once in a while.

Notes: You'll need a cookie cutter in the shape of a dog-bone for these treats. Bessie uses a 3 1/4-inch cookie cutter, but you can use another size, if you prefer. Since these treats contain a lot of fiber, monitor the number of treats your dog consumes!

Ingredients

Two 6 oz. jars sweet potatoes (baby food)

1 T olive oil

½ t cinnamon

¼ C milled flax seed

2 C oat flour

Line a baking sheet with parchment paper. Combine the sweet potatoes and olive oil in a mixing bowl. Sprinkle the cinnamon over the mixture and stir in. Add flax seed and stir. Add oat flour, ½ cup at a time, and mix well. Chill the dough for at least one hour. Preheat the oven to 400 degrees. Roll the dough to 1/8 inch thickness between two pieces of parchment paper. Cut out dog-bone shapes with your cookie cutter and place them on the on the parchment-paper-lined cookie sheet. Bake at 400 degrees for about 12 minutes or until the treats are done. Cool on parchment paper or a wire rack. Store the treats in the freezer. This recipe makes about thirty-two 3 ¼-inch dog-bone treats.

Tracey's Yum-Yum Yam Chips

Bear can't get enough of these tasty chips that Tracey, Laurel's cousin as well as BFF, bakes for him, and they're so simple to make. Laurel likes these treats, too, because they taste just as good to people as they do to dogs. Although Tracey never puts salt or pepper on Bear's yum-yum yam chips, humans might want to add either or both to their own personal taste.

Ingredients

1 raw yam

1 T olive oil

Preheat the oven to 400 degrees. Use 1 teaspoon of the olive oil to apply a thin coat of oil on a metal baking sheet. Thoroughly wash the yam and cut it into 1/8-inch slices. Place the yam slices on the baking sheet. Use a pastry brush to brush the remaining 2 teaspoons of olive oil on the tops of the yam slices. Bake at 400 degrees for 15 minutes. Turn the slices and bake them for an additional 10 minutes. These chips can burn easily so watch them carefully, Tracey warns, and adjust the baking time if necessary. Chips should be browned and crisp. Remove them from the oven, let them cool, and enjoy. Yum! Yum!

Note: Yum-yum yam chips are best eaten soon after they're removed from the oven while they are crisp. Storing the chips may make them a bit soggy, although your dog probably won't mind.

Reversible, Two-Tone, Fringed Dog Scarf

Bear knows he's a handsome boy when he wears the reversible, two-tone, fringed scarf that Laurel made for him. Bear's scarf features a Western print on one side and solid brick red on the other side. The decorative fringe on his scarf is brick red, too.

Note: This project requires sewing two straight stitches on a sewing machine. Beginning sewers can easily make this cute scarf for their favorite furry friend.

Materials Needed
Two 5/8 yd. pieces of suede cloth, each a different color
Thread to match one of the colors in the suede cloth
Large sheet of tissue paper or gift wrapping paper

Instructions
1. Use a yard stick or other straightedge and a pencil to make a pattern on the sheet of paper. First, draw a square, using the measurements below as a guide:
    Small size   16 inches square
    Medium size   21 inches square
    Large size   27 inches square
2. Fold the square of paper diagonally and hold it in place around your dog's neck to check the size. Adjust the size, if necessary. Cut the square diagonally to make the scarf pattern. Add ½ inch to the diagonal edge for a seam allowance.
3. Place the two pieces of suede cloth right rides together and lay flat. Place the pattern on top of the suede cloth. Use pins, tape, or weight with

soup cans to hold the pattern in place while you cut through both layers of fabric to cut out the pieces.

4. Remove the pattern and pin the diagonal edges of the suede cloth, right sides together. Stitch a ½-inch seam. Understitch, turn, and press. Pin unstitched edges to keep them from shifting.

5. For the fringe, cut several 1/8-inch by 5-inch strips of suede cloth. Use all one color for the fringe or alternate both colors. To attach the fringe, start with the bottom point (opposite the stitched seam) and carefully make a ¼-inch slit through both layers of suede cloth ¼ inch from the edge. Laurel uses a seam ripper (very carefully!) to make the slits.

6. Fold a fringe strip in half, wrong sides together. Poke the folded edge through the slits in the fabrics to form a loop. Thread both ends of the fringe strip through the loop and pull them to form a knot to tie it to the edge. Don't pull the knot so tight that the edge curls.

7. Repeat every ½ inch along the scarf edges, stopping to leave the ends that will be tied together around your dog's neck without fringe. (On Bear's large scarf, the fringe stops 7 inches from the ends of the ties.) The ends may be stitched together with a straight stitch ¼ inch from the edge, or they can be left open, whichever you prefer.

Tie the scarf around your dog's neck for doggie dress-up. Don't forget to have your dog pose for a quick pic so you can show the world what a cute furry friend you have.

No-Sew Foam Bed for Pampered Pooches

Laurel made three of these easy, no-sew dog beds for Bear, and the lucky dog has one in the den, one in Laurel's office, and one in the bedroom. Bear loves to flop down on one of his beds and take a snooze in cozy comfort.

Materials Needed
Fleece fabric
Velcro sticky backs for fabrics
4" deep high-density foam

Sizes and Yardage

Dog Size	Foam Size	Yardage
Small	20" X 25"	1 7/8 yd.
Medium	28" x 36"	2 yd.
Large	32" x 44"	2 5/8 yd.
Extra-Large	38" x 55"	3 ½ yd.

Instructions
Determine the correct size for your dog. There is no sewing needed unless you are making size extra-large, which requires two pieces of fabric to be sewn together (just one seam) so that it will be large enough. Prewash the fleece fabric according to the manufacturer's directions so that it won't shrink during future laundering. Wrap the fleece fabric around the foam in the same manner as you would wrap a gift, lapping the lengthwise ends of the fabric. Secure with Velcro in the center. Now fold in both ends, just as you would a gift-wrapped box. Secure with two pieces of Velcro, one on each side of the fold. Flip over, and you're done.

ABOUT THE AUTHOR

An instructor at five colleges over the years, Paula Darnell most often taught the dreaded first-year English composition classes, but she's also been happy to teach some fun classes, such as fashion design, sewing, and jewelry making. Paula has a Bachelor's degree in English from the University of Iowa, Iowa City, and a Master's degree in English from the University of Nevada, Reno.

Like Laurel, the main character in *Death by Association*, Paula enjoys all kinds of arts and crafts. Some of her memorable projects include making a hat and a cape to wear to Royal Ascot, sewing wedding gowns for both her daughters, exhibiting her textile and mixed-media artwork in juried art shows, and having one of her jewelry projects accepted for inclusion in *Leather Jewelry,* published by Lark Books. She sells some of her jewelry and hair accessories in her Etsy shop: www.etsy.com/shop/PaulaDJewelry.

Paula's interest in DIY craft projects and fashion led to her writing hundreds of articles for print and online national publications.

Living in a guard-gated community governed by a homeowners' association gave Paula the idea for the setting of *Death by Association*. She finds that residing in an HOA community can be both a blessing and a curse. A Happy-New-Year greeting from her community association called on residents to "start the new year by reviewing your Rules and Regulations booklet," something unlikely to top anyone's list of New Year's resolutions.

Paula lives in Las Vegas, Nevada, with her husband Gary and their 110-pound dog Rocky, whose favorite pastime is lurking in the kitchen, hoping for a handout.

Printed in Great Britain
by Amazon

42558732R00158